The Other Side of Courage
The Saga of Elizabeth Blackwell

The Other Side of Courage
The Saga of Elizabeth Blackwell

Robert Nordmeyer

Book cover design and layout by
Ellie Bockert Augsburger of Creative Digital Studios.
www.CreativeDigitalStudios.com
using elements provided by the publisher

Inquiries should be addressed to:
CyPress Publications
P.O. Box 2636
Tallahassee, Florida 32316-2636
http://cypresspublications.com
lraymond@nettally.com

ISBN: 978-1-935083-49-8

Dedicated to
Rita, Chris
Christy and Sharon

Acknowledgements

As indicated in the dedication there are four women who helped bring this portrayal of Elizabeth Blackwell's life to fruition. This book would not have been possible without their valuable assistance. My wife, Rita, was chief among those who kept her enthusiasm high, encouraging me to continue pursuing its possibilities and in serving as an invaluable rewrite assistant. Our daughter, Christine Porter provided input as well as helpful advice. My two writing friends, Christy Krueger and Sharon Lashinger, gave not only important support and encouragement but also assisted with suggestions and ideas. Then, of course, there is a fifth woman to acknowledge, Elizabeth herself, without whom there would be no story. Her life was indeed an inspiration that needed to be captured through the reliving of her experiences. Those experiences became the impetus for writing this account of her struggles and triumphs. In addition to these five women, a thank you goes out to Daniel Willis of Bygone Era Books who started Elizabeth on her journey and to Leland F. Raymond of CyPress Publications for helping to continue her on her way. Finally recognition must be given to the "Page-a-Day" calendar people at Workman Publishing for introducing me to Elizabeth in their "On This Day" feature. It was through that little historical note that I first became acquainted with Elizabeth and, as the saying goes, the rest is history.

Prologue

In the early 1800's women had few rights. They could not vote or hold office. Higher education was closed to women. According to American law a wife had no legal standing apart from her husband. In case of a divorce or separation she could not gain custody of her children. She could not sue or be sued nor could she make a contract or even own property. A woman was basically there at the pleasure of her husband or of the male-dominant society. Thus when Elizabeth Blackwell destroyed the taboos against women becoming physicians it was not a single victory but a collective one. Because of that, opportunities soon opened to destroy all other restrictions against women.

As would be expected, Elizabeth's victory was not without consequences. The attitude of society in the early to mid 1800's was to attack any woman who dared to step out of her position. For someone such as Elizabeth Blackwell to attempt challenging the system was tantamount to inviting the wrath of society; to be ostracized through humiliation and degradation. It required unusual courage to confront such opposition as well as stay the course against all odds of failure. In realizing that Elizabeth Blackwell did indeed overcome those many adversities in order to achieve her goal, it has to be inspirational to anyone facing the same insurmountable odds.

While America pays high tribute to those who conquer the impossible, such as Charles Lindbergh, Martin Luther King and Helen Keller, they remain on the visible side of courage. But there are those heroes such as Elizabeth Blackwell who achieve greatness practically unnoticed and she like the others sits on the other side of courage.

Elizabeth Blackwell brought about a major social change in both the United States and Europe. Yet her only goal was to become a physician. And in that pursuit she unwittingly became a pioneer whose legacy can now be seen in the fact that today one third of all physicians in the United States are women. Women are involved in every medical discipline including such specialized fields as Radiation Oncology, Aerospace Medicine and Thoracic Surgery.

Women make up 46.2% of Pediatricians. In medical schools across the country half the students are women. There is a steady growth of women choosing medicine as a career and women are taking leadership roles in all aspects of medicine. Where once there was only one, today there are many.

Elizabeth Blackwell saw her life in a unique perspective. In her writings she often reflected upon the many avenues she had traveled and the experiences gained. Therefore any attempt to summarize her life is best left up to her. She wrote: *"It is not easy to be a pioneer -- but oh, it is fascinating! I would not trade one moment, even the worst moment, for all the riches in the world."*

Chapter One

Elizabeth, at first, had diverted her eyes from the man's genitalia.

Sex, of course, can be perceived in a multitude of ways. It is most provocative, however, when it is considered sinful. Yet who is to judge what is sinful if one is not attuned to the morals dictating the occasion of sin.

Such was the case that afternoon. Certainly there was bound to be a degree of amusement floating around the room as if little boys were learning about sex for the very first time. And perhaps it would be justified. After all they would be viewing the actual male reproductive organs on a cadaver, which typically, under normal circumstances, would not enlist any form of juvenile behavior. However, on this occasion there would be a most unusual peculiarity taking place. A woman would be included in the audience. And that could naturally bring about the capricious tendencies most young men possess thus unraveling the delicacies of a normally solemn activity.

Without a doubt the Victorian norms in 1848 would have absolutely condemned that gathering as not only totally immoral and sinful but also in strict violation of law, both that of God and man. Regardless that it was a class in anatomy at a school of medicine. The simple fact that there was to be a mixture of men and a woman together viewing the most private area of a man was completely against the strict virtuous code of that time. Yet when viewed in its entirety, the fact of a woman attending a school of medicine was as equally sinful in the eyes of many and thus the class in Anatomy at Geneva College in upstate New York was subject to ardent condemnation.

Elizabeth Blackwell was fully aware of these complications. Every day she was being denounced for displaying the audacity of attempting to become the very first woman ever to earn a degree in medicine. And Geneva College was sharing in that same censure for having admitted her. As it would be, the two of them found their scandalous positions to be a mutual comfort of sorts, although there was always a bit of hesitancy on the part of several professors.

On that particular morning, Elizabeth stood but ten inches from the small mirror on the wall of her room at the boarding house staring at her reflection. That day would produce another historic first. In fact, she mused, everything she did at Geneva and professionally would be the very first time in medical history. She knew what to expect in the anatomy amphitheatre later that day and the expression she studied in the mirror showed the hesitant look she wanted to hide. She couldn't practice smiling, that would be totally inappropriate. But then if she wanted to reflect a normal, serious and authoritative persona, the facial features would fall back into the picture of doubt that she wanted to avoid. It appeared that the trepidation Elizabeth held inside was going to dominate her outer countenance and apparently there was nothing she could do to alter that fact.

Knowing that all eyes would be on her that afternoon she decided she would simply go to the demonstration on the male reproductive organs with the same composed attitude she had when viewing the drawings of the male figure in the medical journals. It would be that vision she would carry with her as she approached what she had come to view as another challenge to the male dominance in medicine.

After a quick breakfast, Elizabeth left for her classes. It was a hurried walk and upon entering the School of Medicine she noticed there weren't any unusual glances, chatter or stares. That, she felt, was a good omen. Her fellow classmates were taking this unique moment in the school's history in stride. It would be, as far as she was concerned, just another anatomy lesson yet deep within her convictions she knew it couldn't be.

The morning hours passed rather swiftly and during lunch her mind remained in a self-guidance approach, giving her the kind of confidence she knew was necessary. In mid-afternoon, when it came time for the lesson, Elizabeth began her climb up the wide stairway to the second floor. As she ascended she heard her name being called.

"Elizabeth."

Turning, she saw James Webster, the Professor of Anatomy moving toward her. "Good afternoon Doctor."

"I wanted to talk with you before entering the amphitheater."

"No, I haven't changed my mind."

He gave a nervous laugh. "That wasn't what I wanted to discuss."

"Oh? What then?"

"I wanted to thank you for the revolution you've started."

The word revolution pleased her and she rewarded her favorite professor with a cheerful smile. "Why, thank you Doctor. But you know I couldn't have done anything without the opportunity Geneva College has given me and for the support and encouragement of professors like you."

"Yes, yes, indeed, I do recognize that. But your spirit is very contagious and I'm seeing a vast change in the students' attitude. You have certainly brought our attention to the fact that there is a place for both genders in the medical profession. Unfortunately we here at Geneva stand very much alone and I'm afraid I cannot predict what will possibly happen upon your graduation."

"What I think you're trying to tell me is my degree in medicine may be worthless, is that right?"

"Under the current circumstances, yes, that is a very good possibility. That is why I am allowing you to participate in the dissection we'll be doing this afternoon, to put to rest the misguided notion that women have no place in the medical field."

Elizabeth stared at Webster. "Excuse me, Doctor, but are you saying you want me to actually do some of the dissecting during the demonstration?"

"Yes, exactly. I believe it will make a big difference."

"Doctor Webster, do you truly believe that will change the perception being held by the medical profession or will it simply give rise to more ludicrous stories and jokes?"

He shook his head. "No, I believe it will definitely send a message."

"So you want to use me as the front line soldier to slay the enemy?"

"Not slay the enemy, Elizabeth, but to get them to surrender."

Elizabeth continued moving up the stairs saying nothing further giving Doctor Webster's comments careful thought. Was she, she wondered, truly prepared to do what he was asking? Could she be strong enough to perform without waver or hesitation? Would she be able to remove all other distraction from her mind and focus solely on the task at hand?

Then pondering the possibilities even further she had to seriously question if she could actually take hold of a man's penis or scrotum and perform a dissection in front of a room full of male students?

"No," she told him then realized she had denied his request before she had even answered her own questions. The reaction surprised her and she could see the disappointed look on Webster's face. "While I know your intentions are honorable, Doctor Webster, and you're thinking of aiding this revolution, as you call it, but for me to engage in any kind of dissecting during this particular session would be most harmful, for there would be no end to the stories and innuendos. It's impossible."

"Yes," he said, a frown sprouting on his face. "I...I see your point and I can appreciate your position. No one enjoys being the goat of anyone's unkind remarks." He gave her an understanding smile then turned to continue up the stairs.

No further words were spoken as the two of them entered the anteroom outside the amphitheater where most of the other students had gathered. Upon seeing the professor approaching they began filing into the room. Elizabeth held back, feeling it necessary to spend several minute composing herself and fixing in her mind a positive stance with all other concerns or fears pushed aside. Taking several deep breaths she gripped her writing tablet, tucked it firmly under her arm and walked into the large room.

As Elizabeth entered the amphitheater she could see the cadaver stretched out on the surgical table, a long white sheet was draped over the entire body. It was a scene she had seen before in both previous demonstrations there at the school and in a private laboratory in Philadelphia. The only difference between then and now was the white sheet would not be covering the cadaver's genitalia and the purpose of the demonstration was not on other parts of the body but only on the pelvic region.

The mood was quite somber. Elizabeth could not help but feel the seriousness that had swallowed up the room. She got the sense the class behaved as if attending a funeral, as if they had assembled there to bury this poor man rather than cut apart sections of his body for the purpose of learning. The composure of each student brought immediate relief, for there would be no undue pressure placed on her or the class. It was to be all business.

"Mr. Gibbson, Mr. Browning," summoned Webster. "I will ask that you assist Doctor La Ford and me during this demonstration. You'll find your aprons in the closet." Even the strict formality in Webster's voice was quite foreign to Elizabeth. But it was as she had hoped and prayed it would remain as such.

Moving to the table the two students stood to one side. Doctor La Ford took the end of the white sheet at the head of the cadaver and lifted it carefully over the face then continued removing it from the entire body. The subject of their examination was a man in his mid-forties, of a slim built who appeared to have spent much time outdoors. Elizabeth, at first, had diverted her eyes from the man's genitalia. Eventually, regaining her sense of propriety, she forced herself to view what they would be studying and despite all the talking she had done to herself in preparing for that moment it nevertheless came as a definite shock. The sight caused her to clasp her hands together to create some form of emotional self-control. She caught herself starting to react, something she had worked hard to avoid.

As she viewed that cold, still body of what once was a living human being and began to concentrate on the man's complete nakedness, the throbbing of uneasiness increased bringing on a flash of mild perspiration as her heart pounded painfully. She knew she had to calm herself, shift her mind back to the purpose for being there and focus on the task at hand. Still, as much as she struggled to neutralize her feelings, she couldn't divorce herself from the assault being waged on all that she had held as decent, moral and proper.

She began to recognize she must have been showing some signs of discomfort, for she could hear a few snickers coming from the back of the room. Turning around to look she saw several faces flushed with embarrassment. There obviously was a silent wave of awkwardness now sweeping through the room. Glancing around to some of her most ardent supporters she could see them sitting quite still with their heads bent down attempting to block out any sign of disrespect for her. Others in the room were either grinning or working hard to stifle a smile. She caught herself starting to react to her classmates unnerving behavior, something she had wanted to escape. For an alarming moment she wanted to smile. Shocked at what was racing through her mind she quickly squeezed her eyes shut knowing full well that to smile would destroy everything, sending out false signals and there would be no serious application to the lesson. The whole purpose would be lost and perhaps never regained. Squirming to restore an emotional balance, her hands squeezed harder. Everyone in that room was obviously feeling the tension. For her part, Elizabeth considered their behavior as something rather ludicrous, unnecessary and not called for. Yet she had to admit to herself she too was feeling most ill at ease.

"Are you ready gentlemen?" asked Webster moving toward the two students, scalpel in his hand. He turned to address the rest of the students. "We will want to examine the scrotum first, as that is the main organ where the reproductive process in the male takes place." Looking over to the student assistants he gave instructions. "The dissection must be straight down the middle. Avoid if at all possible cutting any part of the testes."

Remarkably, a great transformation suddenly engulfed the room and every student became a serious observer. It was as if the assembly had completely forgotten there was a woman present. Elizabeth had become a non-entity, as she had prayed she would. The amphitheater was no longer an arena for spectacle but rather a forum for intellectual pursuit.

During the scheduled two hour demonstration the class closely examined the complete reproductive system of the male. Elizabeth took exacting notes, trying as best she could to sketch some of the components to better explain the information. At one point she had become confused and sought to have a clarification but hesitated for fear she may state her question incorrectly thus causing a possible double entendre. She needed to have a description of a complex system explained more fully.

Raising her hand as others had been doing she attempted to catch Doctor Webster's eye. It took several seconds but eventually she was successful.

"Yes, Miss Blackwell?"

Taking a deep breath she spoke slowly. "Doctor Webster, I am not quite sure I clearly understand the function of the epididymis. You covered that section rather quickly and I was not able to understand everything you said."

The room grew amazingly still. All eyes immediately focused on Elizabeth. It was a new chapter in the rarity of the moment that caused her fellow classmates to suddenly become petrified. Having a woman ask a question during an anatomy class on the male reproductive system was absolutely foreign to those sitting there although her presence had been fully accepted. It was just the fact of hearing a female voice ask such a question that made everything quite startling and, of course, quite unexpected thus causing the moment to freeze for several long seconds.

Finally Doctor Webster gave an answer. "Yes, well, the epididymis is this whitish mass of these tightly coiled tubes that are cupped against the testicles" he said pointing to the section he was describing. "Can you see that?"

"Yes, Doctor," she answered keeping her voice calm, wanting to greatly mitigate the awkwardness of the moment.

"The epididymis acts as a maturation and collection depot for the sperm," Webster continued, "before the sperm passes into the vas deferens that will then flow the sperm to the ampullary gland and prostatic ducts." He stopped and looked up at Elizabeth. "Does that clear up the matter for you, Miss Blackwell?"

"Yes, I believe so, Doctor, but I may need you to check my spelling when the class is over."

"What words, Miss Blackwell?" His tone seemed to be taking on a touch of irritation.

"I won't take up any more time here, Doctor. I'll check with you afterwards."

"Very fine." He said the irritation seemingly removed.

Elizabeth looked at her notes to be sure she could pronounce the words she believed she had misspelled by repeating the phonetic sounds she had written. But unknown to her she was repeating the sounds softly out loud.

"Was there something else, Miss Blackwell," added Webster the irritation returning.

Recognizing once again she had disrupted the procedure she gave him a weak grin then shook her head thinking it best not to speak any further.

Nodding in acknowledgement he continued with his presentation. Elizabeth could feel her face flush from the rudeness she had displayed and immediately bit her lip hoping that it would quell the blushing.

The session ended much too soon for Elizabeth, for the information imparted was not only highly informative, but the finite inner-workings of the body and it's multiple intricate functions were most intriguing to Elizabeth. And while short, it was without doubt a most rewarding afternoon. Remaining seated as the others began filing out she realized that while there were many victories won that day, of greater importance, because of her presence, she had gained much more knowledge than if she were relegated to the private session that had been suggested by Doctor Webster the day before as a way of mitigating a perceived catastrophe. There was absolutely no substitute for the many questions, comments and answers that came out of that gathering. No private lesson could have produced such an exchange nor would she have learned as much if only she were asking the questions. As she exited the room she could tell the entire experience had been strongly imprinted on her fellow classmates, for the talk was only on the medical aspects of the demonstration and not one disparaging word did she hear regarding the presence of a female in the room.

She waited for Doctor Webster to leave, wanting to pay him a well-deserved compliment for an excellent anatomy session. As the last of the students left and there seemed to be no one remaining, she wondered if perchance she had missed the Professor. Reentering the room she saw him sitting in his chair off to the corner, his body slumped and hands to his face.

"Doctor Webster," she said softly trying not to startle him.

His head jerked up and for a second he only stared at Elizabeth. Then regaining his composure he quickly stood to greet her. "Elizabeth. I thought everyone had gone."

"Are you all right, sir?"

"Oh yes, just a bit tired. Well, to be truthful, exhausted. That demonstration, I must confess, took everything out of me."

"You were stressed?"

"Oh, yes, quite stressed."

"Because of me?"

James Webster looked at Elizabeth with an apologetic expression. "Yes," he said firmly. "But you must realize, Elizabeth, this kind of thing has never happened before. I know for a fact all my fellow professors here had their eyes on me. Great pressure there, I tell you, great pressure. If I had destroyed this opportunity, Geneva's reputation would have been seriously damaged. It had to be done just right."

"But you did marvelously well, Doctor Webster."

A weak smile emerged from his doleful face. "So I've been told. It seems others felt they had achieved much today as well." His head nodded in recognition of that fact. "Yes, achieved much."

"As I did."

"Especially you, Elizabeth. Just by virtue of you being in this room during this particular dissection was an advancement for the medical profession. Your presence here has changed medicine for centuries to come."

Picking up his suit coat off the arm of the chair and putting it on, he leaned down to retrieve a wide, black satchel. He looked at Elizabeth. "Well, young lady, shall we move along. You have another lecture to attend and I must go transcribe my notes on what points need to be in the examination at the end of the term."

"You don't have a set examination?" she asked.

"I use to. After today, though, I feel my exams have been too lenient."

Elizabeth laughed as she followed him out of the room. "It looks like I'm going to have to apply myself more."

"Good."

Elizabeth stayed on the second floor as Webster started down the stairs. After several steps he turned around, looked up and smiled. "Thank you Elizabeth" he said. "Thank you very much."

Hesitating before moving on to her next class Elizabeth couldn't help but think of this moment in the sense of her father's life, especially his resolve. It was perhaps his tenacity and persistence she inherited and that energy alone had propelled her to this moment in history. Indeed, Samuel Blackwell was standing there next to her and the flow of his qualities and character had definitely infused her with the power to push forward.

Chapter Two

At one point Samuel watched the entire fire rapidly transform from an orange hue the likes of which he had never seen before to a blue-green brilliance capturing that of a perfect turquoise stone.

It wasn't so much the ferocity of the pounding as it was the rapidness that caused Samuel Blackwell to charge nervously down the hallway toward the front door while harboring thoughts of ill doings. The family had just begun an extended summer holiday in a home in Olveston, a rental property about nine miles from their home in Bristol. As he moved he was engulfed in darkness unable to determine the time. He could only surmise he had been awakened in the very early hours of the new day. Stumbling closer to the door, he could hear his name being called in frightened tones and immediately Samuel

Blackwell sensed that some horrendous tragedy had befallen him and his family.

"Mr. Blackwell! Mr. Blackwell!"

With the door swung open the man stood but inches from Samuel Blackwell's face.

"Yes, yes, what is it? What is the matter?"

"Your refinery, sir, it's…it's on fire, sir, an explosion. The buildings are in flames."

Samuel gave a quick glance in the direction of his sugar refinery, and over the rooftops of the neighboring buildings caught sight of a faint orange glow dominating the distant sky, a glow that could only foretell the disaster he would witness once he had reached his business.

"Yes," Samuel whispered, the effects of shock penetrating his mind. "Yes, I see. Yes, I'll get dressed. Do you have a buggy?"

"I do sir."

"Then I will beg a ride from you. Wait here. I'll be with you momentarily."

As Samuel rushed to the bedroom to don his clothes he staggered back, stopping quickly to avoid colliding with Hannah who had followed him to the door and whose face now reflected the horror of what she had heard.

"The refinery, in flames?" she asked her voice trembling.

"Yes. Now please excuse me Hannah, let me pass I must get dressed. The man is waiting for me with his buggy."

Hanna pushed her back against the hallway wall and watched as Samuel made a dash to the bedroom. The fright of knowing the consequences of what was happening spun through her mind in that darkened hallway. She could hear Samuel crying as he dressed. It was a saddened sound, the same as when she had revealed to him the death of their last child who had died at childbirth. Samuel Blackwell was normally a strong man, able to withstand emotional strains, but these unnecessary losses were so devastating he was not afraid to cry.

Samuel returned to the front door rushing past Hanna speaking not a word, carrying his suit coat with only one of his braces attached to his trousers and the laces untied on his boots. He called to the man as he sped through the door. "Has the fire brigade been alerted?"

Hanna could not hear the response and now watched as her husband climbed into the buggy wanting to be there with Samuel to give him comfort and strength. But that was not her place, although she knew Samuel would not think anything against a wife being of equal position with her husband. Still, she stood in the door and watched the buggy race down the road, finally losing sight of it as it made the turn at the corner.

"What is it, mother." It was Anna, the eldest. She stood halfway on the stairs looking down upon an anguished woman clutching the edge of the door. It startled Hannah.

"The refinery," she answered without turning around. "It has caught fire. An explosion I believe the man had said."

"The refinery? Father's business?"

"Yes, your father's business." And only in that moment in answering her daughter's question did Hannah Blackwell come to realize exactly what the explosion and fire truly meant. Their livelihood was being destroyed. The very source of their income, the earnings that paid for the house in which they lived, the servants, the good meals, the comfort of being warm and the joy of visiting new places, this summer home; all now burning in the heart of Bristol and she could only stand there feeling absolutely drained.

"But," the girl questioned. "It is the only business father owns. That means..."

"Yes, it means everything is being destroyed." She turned to face her daughter. "It also means he will have to rebuild the refinery and start anew. His patrons will return, perhaps, depending upon how long it will take father to put together another plant."

"And," Anna continued her inquiry, "won't that take all of father's savings?"

Hannah Blackwell's eyes first looked up and then they gently closed as her head moved ever so slowly back and forth. "What savings?" she said, her voice trembling. "There is no extra money. We use all the earnings from the refinery. We will have to borrow from the banks and place everything we own as collateral."

The young girl sat on the steps and gazed pitifully at her mother. She was old enough to fully grasp what her mother was saying; had advanced sufficiently in her studies to understand how the financial system worked and was able to draw several conclusions including the prospect that her father may not be able to raise adequate funds in order to carry out the construction of a new facility. The shuffling of feet brought Anna out of her muse and she watched her mother move slowly down the hall back to the bedroom leaving Anna with nothing further to say that could relieve the pall of gloom now filling the home during those early morning hours.

The buggy bounced unmercifully as it made its way over the rough road. The country roadways required Samuel to hold tightly to the side bars. His mind could only envision a ruinous future, a true devastation for his young family.

Keeping his gaze on the glow in the distant sky he attempted to sort through what lie ahead. And now with Hannah's latest health development and the destruction of his refinery, uncertainty poured upon his troubled mind.

It was only last week when everything seemed ideal as he stood in the shadows of the plump squatty trees in the small park near their home in Bristol observing his three daughters at play. The few moments were allowed as part of what Samuel Blackwell considered to be a recess, a temporary and brief hiatus from their studies. It gave both the three older girls and the governess, who was their tutor, a respite and a brief reprieve from the rigors of being educated at home. The girls' situation was vastly different from two of their brothers who were able to be sent to any regular institutions of learning they chose. Girls, on the other hand, were not allowed in schools and therefore home study was required if an education was to be gained. It was Samuel's decision to have such an arrangement, for he strongly believed in the advancement of women despite the customs in 1831 of women serving in a more subservient role. Men like Samuel Blackwell were rare in those early years of the nineteenth century and in most cases people of Blackwell's nature, who seemed bent on changes, were both despised and suspect.

"Come along now girls," he called, seeing that the thirty minutes he had allowed had expired.

"But Father," one of them protested, swinging her long curls to the side of her face as she twirled around to face him. "We've just begun to play our game."

"Elizabeth, you need to resume your studies so that Mrs. Justin can return to her other duties."

"But father," she continued then stopped abruptly upon seeing her father raise his hand for silence. Elizabeth Blackwell knew a raised hand was the final word and there was never any argument with Samuel Blackwell. "Yes, father," she said demurely following her two older sisters, Anna and Marian, along the path that exited the park. Still there was reluctance in her steps and a silent insistence that the day was too glorious for her to be kept inside learning things that would probably never be used when she became an adult. Yet no matter how much Elizabeth might have secretly protested she was not to escape a well-rounded education.

"Hurry along, Elizabeth," came her father's voice, a bit more firm as they moved away from the park which sat a short distance from their home.

"I can't wait for the end of this week," Elizabeth quietly mumbled to herself, "when all of this silly education nonsense will be over and we go to Olveston and I can enjoy the beautiful warm days of summer." It was a typical attitude of a ten year old. The older girls at thirteen and sixteen seemed to have wholeheartedly embraced the teachings. Elizabeth's younger sisters, Emily and Ellen, were not yet enrolled in their father's plan for education since they were toddlers. Their exemption became a source of envy on the part of Elizabeth each time she saw them lulling away their time with fun make-believe adventures.

The quartet continued their fast pace toward the large home on Nelson Street. It was their second residence in Bristol, a most unique structure. Two homes had actually been joined to provide sufficient room for the growing Blackwells. A large walled-in courtyard gave the family an attractive space for relaxation among the many trees and the large flower garden that graced the area. It also provided the passageway to Samuel's sugar refinery adjacent to the property, a convenient arrangement and thus one of the reasons for moving to Nelson Street when Elizabeth was but two years old.

Samuel Blackwell was losing important time away from his refinery. He only assumed the role of recess chaperone because the girls' mother, Hannah, had an appointment with her doctor; one she couldn't forestall, and thus the supervisory duty fell to Samuel. Ironically, he assumed the obligation with the same type of reluctance that Elizabeth now harbored as she trudged behind, periodically receiving irritating glances from her father. Hannah was due home shortly and Samuel was getting nervous.

It wasn't but a few minutes after they arrived home that he heard his name called. He was in the back bedroom getting ready to return to the refinery.

"Samuel."

He beamed at the sound of her voice. "Back here, Hannah."

"I'm home."

"Yes, dear," he called back, chuckling at his wife propensity for stating the obvious.

"The doctor," she began as she approached him moving down the hall, "said..."

"Wait," he half whispered moving toward the door to close it. "This is not something for the children to hear."

Hannah frowned. "It's not all that serious, Samuel."

"Still, it is a matter between you and me and not for others to hear."

"Very well, then," she said taking a seat in a large comfortable chair positioned by the bay window. "Doctor Melville said I am not pregnant and the problems I've been having has to do with my cycle changing."

"Changing?"

"Yes, dear, I'm getting older; I'm thirty-seven, no longer a fair maiden."

"Thirty-seven does not seem all that old to me. You shouldn't be experiencing any alterations in your body's functions."

Hanna Blackwell's lips drew tightly together; her eyes squinted as she stared at her husband. "A woman of thirty-seven is old, Samuel, and the body is not afraid to reveal that little fact to the woman who must suffer the consequences of aging. We have a different system than you men and age is the dictator of how that system functions."

Samuel donned his coat and gathered his papers. "Yes, I do realize that. I was directing my comments to you, my dear, and not to your systems. You are still the most beautiful woman in all of Bristol if not the world whose youth has never changed and who remains to be the most ravishing female there ever was."

Hanna shook her head and provided him with a large smile. "Are you feeling unusually solicitous because I'm not pregnant or because I am the most beautiful woman you have ever seen?"

In a gentle, intentional bow he leaned over and kissed her on her cheek. "Because you are the most beautiful woman I have ever seen."

"But," she added," Doctor Melville did caution me about having more children. I am prone, as you well know, Samuel, to miscarriages and complications with pregnancies." Hanna Blackwell was reminding her husband they had lost eight of their children and that she wasn't as consistently stable as perhaps other women of her age. "Doctor Melville said further children could result in new problems and we should think carefully about not expanding our family."

"I was not thinking at this very moment of having more children."

"Oh?" she responded, providing him with a joking laugh. "And what is on your mind at this very moment?"

"My need to return to the refinery before they forget who I am and shut the doors.

By the time Samuel Blackwell arrived at his refinery the entire structure was engulfed in flames. The fire brigade, made up of volunteers, had arrived entirely too late, having been summoned long after the explosion had occurred. And with the hour being so early in the morning the rousting of the fire fighters took more time than usual. Consequently the possibility of saving the structure was doomed from the very beginning and all this assembly of volunteer men could do was try to keep themselves from harm by staying clear of the still-exploding piles of raw sugar.

An eerie crackling was heard as the flames consumed the sugar and the large vats used in the refining process. The color of the fire would change from a brilliant white to the deepest of reds and all spectrums in between. At one point Samuel watched the entire fire rapidly transform from an orange hue the likes of which he had never seen before to a blue-green brilliance capturing that of a perfect turquoise stone. The type of dance the flames performed cast ominous shadows in all directions as the wooden boards disintegrated and portions plummeted to the ground. The force of their violent landing spewed sparks in all directions, threatening to shower small burning embers upon any individual foolish enough to be standing within close range of this intense exhibition.

"Sugar dust," he was told by the fire warden in charge of the brigade.

"But," Samuel began then hesitated knowing that the proposed argument he was about to deliver in his defense was not, indeed, a very good defense, for his assertion that he did not allow sugar dust to accumulate in his refinery could not be substantiated. There had been an explosion and indeed that was too obvious. The warden was in a better position to suspect the cause of the explosion based on his knowledge of fire origins. Samuel Blackwell was in no position to defend and it was more prudent at that very moment to remain silent, for to do otherwise could provoke a deeper investigation that could jeopardize his ability to rebuild by reducing his power to borrow.

"Yes?" the warden asked.

"Nothing," Samuel responded. "It was nothing, just a moment of shock overtaking my thoughts and I can't even now remember what it might have been that I wanted to say."

"You realize, sir," the man said. "There will be a cost involved in our efforts to bring this fire to a conclusion."

Samuel paused as he stared at the brigade leader. "I have not ventured that far in my assessment of this tragedy. All I know at this moment is that I am ruined, good sir, and that is all a man in my position can think of at a time like this."

There was no reply. For certain the fire warden knew exactly what Samuel Blackwell was saying. There have been many others before him who had lost everything as a result of a fire. He had seen the destructive powers of fire and could empathize with this tall, broad shouldered man standing there beside him and actually feel the pain and sorrow Samuel Blackwell was suffering. If through no other form of determination one only had to look upon the tormented face to see the imprint of total hopelessness and gloom etched deeply in the eyes and mouth and the slump in the body that echoed that pain.

Just then a large orb of fire erupted sending flaming ash in all directions. The sound of the explosion startled Samuel and he quickly cowered behind the fire marshal grabbing the man's jacket. It might have been somewhat symbolic in his seeking protection, for it was possible, at that very moment that Samuel Blackwell was also seeking, in some form of subconscious manner, protection from ruination.

It would take until early afternoon before Samuel could return to the summer home. The family was waiting in the parlor where they had been sitting since mid-morning, engaged in trivial activities in an attempt to divert their thoughts from the disastrous fire and their fate. Elizabeth was the first to jump up and greet her father with a compassionate hug.

"Father," she said, "You look tired. We've made your favorite soup and some warm bread. You must be hungry. We can go to the dining room table to have lunch if you prefer"

Samuel Blackwell, his clothes smelling of burnt sugar and smoke, his face haggard, looked affectionately upon her. She seemed at the moment to be much older than her age, so much more mature and changed. Or was it he and the circumstances that had changed? His hand softly patted her shoulder as he went with her into the parlor as the others stood, all but Hannah who by now was looking as weary and drawn as her husband. As he caught sight of Hannah, Elizabeth could feel his hand tighten within hers. But she said nothing and continued to lead him to the chair.

"I don't need the soup, Elizabeth," he said sitting down. "But thank you just the same for offering it. It was most kind of you children and you Hannah to prepare this for me but at the moment I am neither hungry nor in the proper mood to eat."

Hannah spoke. "Did we..."

"Yes, my dear Hannah. We lost everything," he told her. "But," he added in the best reassuring voice he could muster. "We are not down. We shall build a new refinery and resume our lives where we were before this tragedy occurred."

The room remained silent until Anna, never one to mince feelings, asked, "And the banks, have they already guaranteed that, father?"

Samuel's face went pale; his eyes sprung open. "I beg your pardon, young lady!"

"She is concerned, Samuel," Hanna said trying to defuse the tension, "that you may not be able to raise the capital you need from the banks to rebuild the refinery and thereby leave us in..." She didn't finish the sentence. "She's frightened, Samuel. We all are. What is to become of us?"

For a brief moment he didn't answer staring off in the distance apparently retracing his morning or perhaps wondering indeed if he was going to be able to raise the necessary funds. Then quickly regrouping his thoughts he spoke in a reassuring tone. "We will survive this, my dear Hannah." he said. "I will build a new refinery and you and the children will not have to worry."

"Then we can be assured all is well."

"All is well," he said. "Now," he continued, rising out of the chair, "you will have to excuse me, for I am tired and in need of some rest before I do anything else, including," he said pausing in his walk and turning to face the family, "securing the capitol we'll need for our new tomorrow. That will be done later."

Continuing down the hall toward the bedroom he quickened his pace and upon reaching the room closed the door with a gentle surrender.

Hanna looked around at the sullen faces. What to do next, she wondered. Then rising out of her chair she headed toward the kitchen. "I believe," she said in a tone of indifference, "there is nothing left to do but simply enjoy the soup and bread ourselves.

Chapter Three

August, 1832
United States of America

Eventually, though, as with all matters, the climate of change disappeared and familiarity overtook fears, hesitations and doubts and the ten members of the Blackwell family slowly ushered in their new roles as Americans.

Elizabeth leaned far over the railing of the small cabin's cot spewing out that which remained in her stomach that hadn't already been regurgitated. "I'm going to die," she moaned, "surely I'm going to die."

"Elizabeth," Emily shouted jumping out of the way. "Not again. Can't you go out on deck to do that?" Elizabeth's younger sister looked down at the putrid sight, her face grimacing. "So now I'm supposed to clean up again, right? I'm telling you, Elizabeth, I'm getting very, very tired of all this"

"Go away. Leave me alone. Let me die without you making me feel guilty about it."

The room was beginning to smell as perspiration rolled slowly off Elizabeth's face and onto the pillow. She cringed at the thought of continuing what would undoubtedly be a long and arduous voyage across the Atlantic. There was, of course, no choice for her. The Blackwell family was emigrating to the United States of America; a plan she at first had resisted then one to which she subscribed then resented and finally embraced. However, as she now lay on her bed, her grip on the rail tightening with each rolling wave that tossed the sailing vessel about, there were no emotional feelings concerning this venture except for the solitary wish she would die and put an end to this misery of all miseries.

The impetus for the venture began on the night of the refinery fire. As Samuel Blackwell watched the flames taunt and tease him he determinedly made up his mind that the refinery in Bristol would not be rebuilt. He would, however, be back in the sugar refining business again, but not in Bristol or England or Europe or any where else in the Old World. It was to rise again in the New World. With each bump of the jostling buggy on his return trip home the plans he fashioned and the new life he envisioned began to materialize. By the time he had reached his house he knew exactly what he had to do. In drawing together his affairs the most critical would be raising needed cash, a task that included selling their home and the property where the refinery once sat. He would be required to round up the debts owed him by his customers, firms he had allowed to defer payments, but who now would be required to pay for the goods he had delivered. It was a determined exit he had made from the buggy that fateful day, prepared to step away from the ruins of his life and make the Blackwells of Bristol the Blackwells of New York City in the United States of America.

It would be a long journey across the ocean, fifty-four days on the swirling seas. Samuel Blackwell had booked passage on a merchant ship, the Cosmo. 1832 saw a limited number of large sailing vessels and to get bookings as quickly as he did was most fortunate if not a bit more costly than he had anticipated. Nevertheless his eagerness to begin their new life in New York compelled him to pay the higher price and in doing so divorced himself as quickly as possible from Bristol and England.

"You will have to get out of that bed," Emily chided.

"To do what? Stand on deck to vomit and view a vista of nothingness except raging waves that are bent on destroying not only my spirit but my life as well?"

"Being theatrical is not going to sway me to feel sorry for you, Elizabeth."

Elizabeth slowly raised her head and stared at this sister five years her junior. "This is not being theatrical," she argued. "This despair I will carry with me for the rest of my life, as short as it is destined to be at this moment."

Yet Elizabeth survived the fifty-four days at sea and her new life in America began. For close to a year the family struggled to acclimate to this new world in which they had settled. Eventually, though, as with all matters, the climate of change disappeared and familiarity overtook fears, hesitations and doubts and the ten members of the Blackwell family slowly ushered in their new roles as Americans. During that time Samuel began the tedious task of planning and building his new sugar refinery, a task unlike doing business in Bristol. His education, as he preferred to call it, into the life and practices of this American city was swift and revealing. Despite facing new conditions and some obstacles, Samuel was able to get his business established and quickly garnered a reasonable number of clients. However, life in America was not as satisfying as he would have liked it to be.

"I just can't get over the practice of slavery being allowed in this country," he told Hannah one morning over breakfast. "It is worse here in this country than in Europe."

The matter of slavery in the United States was becoming a source of irritation for Samuel. He had fought hard to end slavery in the English territories when he lived there and now he found himself confronted with the disease, as he termed it, in his new chosen land. "I am learning that the whole of the southern states in this country not only foster it but the cruel, inhumane treatment of the slaves is actually condoned and in many cases being justified by the authorities. And I find that absolutely deplorable."

"Well, thank heavens New York does not allow slavery," Hanna reassured him.

"That doesn't matter in my case, Hannah. I still remain deeply entwined in that dastardly practice."

"You mean the supplies of the raw cane."

"Yes, unfortunately. They use slave labor to harvest and haul the cane to the storage houses in the south and then I purchase it from suppliers here in New York. So you see, Hannah, my hands are automatically dirtied by accepting the cane."

"Well, not really my dear. I believe you're punishing yourself more than you deserve. But if you feel that way why then don't you just change suppliers?"

"I can't. That is totally impossible. There are no others. And to make matters worse all the suppliers here in New York have no shame accepting that cane. So therefore, you see Hannah, I have no choice. I am forced to use them."

He grew silent, his hands fumbling with the spoon as Hannah cleared the table leaving her husband to his contemplation, which didn't last all that long.

"That's it," he exclaimed startling Hannah.

"What is...it," she asked.

"Our solution," he said adding nothing further. Pushing back his chair he stood. Then with a slight smile on his face he moved quickly down the long hall to his study. There he would begin to formulate a plan that would allow him to escape the bindings he so strongly detested. The door closed and Hannah would not see him for the rest of the day.

The streets of Cincinnati in 1838 were vastly different from those of New York City. People who drove their buggies and rode horses were a bit more polite. The little town on the western frontier reflected a more genteel approach to all that mattered and that quality had great appeal to Samuel Blackwell.

Cincinnati was perched on a pleasant plateau alongside the vast Ohio River surrounded by undulating green hills. As they traveled down the river from Pittsburg, Elizabeth marveled at the width and length of this great waterway. The scenery was exceptional and vastly different from her native homeland. Perhaps, she thought, she was about to enjoy yet a third different world.

Closing down the New York refinery, the Blackwell family moved to the town of forty thousand inhabitants to rectify the slave issues involved in the procurement of sugar cane. And although Samuel attempted to find other sources, the price, so he was informed, would have been prohibitive. It was only after searching for a better option that he learned of the sugar beet fields in Ohio with paid farm labor. These fields produced an excellent quality of the raw material he needed. Plus Ohio was a state that had outlawed slavery. The decision to relocate was not a difficult one and upon informing the family of his resolve he found no resistance to the prospect, for slavery was as abhorrent to his family as it was to Samuel Blackwell.

Of some irony the discovery of the opportunity in Ohio came at a most convenient time, or so it would seem. The New York refinery was beginning to suffer from the country's economic failures, undergoing loss of revenues in what was being referred to as the Panic of 1837. As a result of this financial crisis his business was swept up in the depression that followed the Panic and subsequently the refinery became more of a liability rather than an asset. The move to Ohio wouldn't have necessarily allowed him to escape the nation's economic woes, but the cost of operating his sugar refinery would be much lower. And being in the western region of the United States he had a newer and perhaps more receptive consumer base. From his viewpoint the financial outlook would vastly improve with this new venture.

43

However, it was not a perfect exchange and the move to Ohio was a bit tenuous. Because of the refinery suffering economically, the financial position of Samuel Blackwell was quite unstable. There was very little money and most of what he did have was to be invested in the establishment of a new refinery outside Cincinnati. The quality of life would be quite different from what it had been in Bristol and even New York. Still, life in Ohio would provide a certain degree of comfort and satisfaction and meet the needs of the large family. Of higher importance was the political and moral environment of the region, which was quite attuned to that of the Blackwells. Ohio matched their adamant position on the matter of slavery and the state fostered an ambitious quest to achieve equal rights for women.

For Elizabeth, the time in Ohio became one of new discoveries, of her self and of the world in which she was emerging. As a young lady, now seventeen, her focus was no longer on her environment but rather on her destiny.

That realization became apparent one morning while she and Hannah did the laundry in the basement. Elizabeth's focus capriciously surfaced when she quite unexpectedly asked, "What are your thoughts on women attending college, Mother?"

It was silent for a moment then Hannah slowly turned to look at her daughter. "I am not quite sure I understand the purpose of your question."

"Well, I am simply curious...perhaps more interested than curious, or maybe I should say it's a matter that has entered my mind and..."

"You want to attend a school?"

"A college."

Hannah's hands hung suspended gripping the wet bed linen she had been washing. Water ran down her arms but she seemed to be oblivious to that fact. "College?" She asked then repeated her question only in a bit more curious tone. "College? What on earth for?"

"To advance my education and gain advantages, Mother. Education is the key to success. That is something you have always believed."

"Yes, I know, but there are no schools that admit women," she said lowering the linen back into the large tub of water. "I'm afraid you're a little too ahead of your time, my dear, and dreaming the impossible."

"Oberlin College admits women," Elizabeth said. "An Ohio school."

"Oberlin College? Never heard of it."

"It's new, five years old, up north by the lake and they admit both men and women."

Hannah shook her head. "You must have read that wrong, Elizabeth. Women are not being admitted to any schools. That is why we're fighting now to change all that."

"I saw it in the newspaper, an advertisement seeking students."

"Here," Hannah said handing the dripping wet linen to Elizabeth. "Take this outside and hang it up when you've finished wringing it out. And you can dream your dream out there. Besides, Elizabeth, who is to pay for this magical education of yours?"

Elizabeth chose to ignore the negative inferences and hurried up the stairs to exit the cellar. Her mood was that of stubborn disgruntlement as she went about her assignment. Yet her mind was far from the rigors of laundry. The advertisement by Oberlin College, which she had clipped from the newspaper and placed in her small cache of important treasures, remained a clear vision in her mind. Elizabeth's desire to attend a college, as far as she was concerned, was not a dream. Educational opportunities now existed for women and despite the limited finances of her family she felt she could find sufficient work that could afford her that opportunity.

Despite serious planning, Elizabeth's opportunity suddenly became the victim of her mother's prophecy. Elizabeth's path shifted toward stagnation rather than the course of transformation ordained to be.

Chapter Four

Hannah Blackwell did not want to cry, did not want to become angry or demanding. She simply, at that point, wanted to take her husband home and tend to him for as long as she could.

For some time now Elizabeth had been noticing a change in her father's demeanor and it wasn't just her, others noticed it as well. Where once there was a robust step to his walk, it was now somewhat difficult for him to move about. His features had taken on a slightly dour expression and the absence of a lively conversation was certainly not indicative of the man they all knew. And although those conditions were quite obvious to everyone, no questions were ever raised. However, once Samuel's decline became too upsetting for the children they finally confronted their mother. That was when Hannah resorted to making feeble excuses. But those excuses worked only a short while. When the complications grew to such a degree that the matter could no longer be ignored Hannah crumbled under the weight of the truth.

The morning was chilly the day Samuel and Hannah went to the physician's office. Clouds blocked the sun adding to the ominous anxiety felt by Hannah. It was difficult getting Samuel in and out of the carriage. The walk up the stairs to the doctor's office was arduous and the energy needed to make the climb exhausted Samuel requiring long periods of rest every few steps.

Hannah was told to remain in the waiting room while Samuel was being seen by the doctor. It was an awkward condition for which Hannah could only wish that Samuel's visit would be quick. A short visit would mean there was nothing seriously wrong with her husband and it would also relieve the edginess she was feeling being confined in that room.

Much to Hannah's chagrin the visit lasted much too long. She took to fiddling with her fingers while glancing at the scant objects scattered about the waiting room. A smile to others sitting there did nothing to ease her restlessness and finally, unable to contain herself, she hastily rose out of her chair and took to pacing. With each creak in the floor boards she would whirl around to stare at the examining room door in great anticipation of seeing her husband.

Instead, when the door did open she faced the doctor who, upon seeing her, waved his hand and summoned her to join him in the examining room.

"I want to discuss your husband's condition with you, Mrs. Blackwell," he said directing her into the room where Samuel sat slumped-shouldered in a corner chair, an expression of forlorn doom on his face. "I'm afraid I don't have any positive news."

Hannah stopped abruptly, gripping the door handle, feeling a sudden flush of heat swirl through her body. A tingling sensation stung her hands. "Samuel," she cried out. "What is the doctor saying?"

"Please, Mrs. Blackwell, take a seat over here and I'll explain everything."

"What is it?" she practically screamed. "I want to know."

The doctor nodded, taking her arm to escort her to a chair. He could feel the resistance. "Yes, of course," he assured her. "Please sit down."

"Samuel?" she cried out. "Samuel..." but didn't finish, for slowly, almost gracefully, she fell to the floor having fainted from the shock of facing the inevitable.

Dropping quickly to one knee beside Hannah, the doctor lifted her head and began gently patting her cheek. Samuel Blackwell couldn't move, couldn't assist, didn't have the strength to get up out of the chair and tend to his wife. He could only sit there and look on as Hannah laid on the floor the color absent from her face. A new kind of terror tore at his emotions knowing the agony to which he was about to subject his wife and children. There was nothing he could do at that point to alter what was happening. The fate confronting him and his family was sealed.

"She's coming around," Samuel was told.

"Thank you doctor," he said his voice weak and shaking.

The doctor placed a hand under Hannah's arm and advised her to sit and not to talk. Hannah remained silent until she was able to stand then was guided to a chair.

"He's dying, isn't he?" she asked.

A quick nod was the ominous answer. There was no need for words.

"And I assume there is no cure?"

Again came the slight nod. Then the doctor spoke. "I feel your husband has developed a biliary condition that has been eating away at his body far too long. Your assumption is correct, madam. There is no cure at this stage."

Lifting her head she looked at the shallow face of Samuel with a deep feeling of sadness, not for her but for him and the suffering he was undergoing. Hannah Blackwell did not want to cry, did not want to become angry or demanding.

She simply, at that point, wanted to take her husband home and tend to him for as long as she could.

With a renewed sense of resolve she stood. "Thank you doctor. Please send us your bill and I will see to it that it is promptly paid."

"Very well, Madam."

Aiding the doctor in assisting Samuel out of the chair, Hannah took the arm of her husband and together they exited from the examining room, through the waiting area, out the main door and down the squeaky steps to the waiting carriage. The doctor would not see Samuel again.

It was in late spring in 1838, three months after the visit with the doctor, when Samuel Blackwell died. He achieved his wish, dying at home, in his sleep. The funeral was brief and the burial proper. Outside of the family, not many were in attendance being that the family had not made many acquaintances. His refinery workers, what remained of them, paid their respects. The ceremony brought to a close the life of a man who strove to provide a good, productive and fulfilling life for his family yet, through the irony of times and circumstances, Samuel Blackwell ended up providing them with nothing but debt.

For several weeks the family did little to determine their future. It was as if the state of shock was destroying all incentives. Of course the sheer fact of survival eventually confronted them and reality began to set in. Anna, the eldest of the eight children, took it upon herself to assess their financial position.

"Father owed much at the refinery," she told her mother as the two sat at the dining room table, papers and records spread out before them. "Selling the business could provide the money to pay off those debts. But there wouldn't be, I believe, anything left for us. Father left barely enough for us to live on for the next month. After that the money will be gone."

"But...but I always thought Samuel had set aside sufficient funds to prevent this very situation," Hannah told her.

"Apparently, from what I can determine from these papers, the business here and when he operated the refinery in New York kept eating away at what funds he had. We are, in essence, Mother, destitute."

Hannah cast her eyes down, her hand clutched into a fist. "We are not destitute, Anna. I detest that word. We are all healthy and strong and educated. We can work."

"Work?" Anna asked in a skeptical tone. "In case you've forgotten, Mother, women are not that easily employed. Also Samuel and Henry's business ventures have only just begun and they too are in debt to the banks. The rest of the family is too young to work."

"Then we shall employ ourselves," Hanna said.

It took several seconds before Anna could grasp exactly what her mother had suggested. "Employ ourselves? You mean open a business of our own?"

"In a manner of speaking, yes."

"But we have no money to do that."

Hanna shook her head. "We don't need money to open our business."

Anna stared at her mother fearful that the death of her father had affected Hannah's ability to use rational judgment. "I'm afraid I don't understand your point, Mother. What are you trying to say? What are you thinking?"

Hannah looked down at her hands clutched together in apprehension, waiting, contemplating what she was about to suggest. Finally she spoke. "I am thinking of a school for girls, Anna, here in this house. I have had this concept in mind when I first learned of your father's fate, not ever thinking of doing it because we needed to but to have something to do to take my mind off of this...this...isolation of mine. The four of us can do it, you, Marian, Elizabeth and me. We're capable."

Again the room went silent. Anna needed time to comprehend the concept. Then with doubt on her mind she questioned the proposal. "A school? You're thinking of running a...private school? Mother, none of us knows anything about teaching. I...I don't really think that is a very viable idea."

53

"But you girls were taught in our home" Hannah argued. "You received a very good education. We can do exactly the same. We will work from textbooks and follow an established routine. I am sure we can find many willing families who would welcome this opportunity to have their daughters educated."

Anna was troubled. This was not exactly a workable concept in her estimation; not exactly the form of rescue she had envisioned. However, Hannah's concept did have some merit. Yet realistically it presented many obstacles. Still, when all evaluations were exhausted, in all truth, it was the only idea they had.

"All right, perhaps," Anna said cautiously. "But I think the four of us need to sit down and thoroughly discuss this idea, Mother.

Hanna laughed. "Anna, you have just told me we have no funds. We cannot take our time deciding what we're going to do. Obviously we need to do something to earn a living and apparently we need to do it rather quickly."

Anna drew back her head, her mouth puckered. "Yes, I see your point," she said. "Well, then, perhaps we need to get Marian and Elizabeth in here and start discussing this right now. If they feel they can do it then we can try and put this idea together."

"It's somewhat together already," Hannah said a slight hesitation to her words.

"What do you mean?"

54

"Well, I explored the idea with some mothers at the mercantile while shopping the other day and they seemed interested. I did not say I was thinking of opening a home school for girls but just asked what they thought of the idea."

"How many?" Anna asked.

Hannah shrugged. "Two, maybe three. But they might know of others."

Anna paused, then nodding she stood "Good. Then I'll go find Marian and Elizabeth."

Chapter Five

June, 1843
Cincinnati, Ohio

You should become a physician. I truly believe that if a lady doctor had been attending to me I would have been spared my worse sufferings.

It was a frustrating shake given to the towel as Hannah turned and looked at her relaxed daughter. Elizabeth was sitting comfortably across the window ledge seat, legs pulled up to serve as an easel for the book she was reading. "Good lord, Elizabeth," Hannah said, "you need to get yourself busy doing something constructive. No woman of twenty-two should be sitting around like what you've been doing reading all the time. You need to get out, get active. Come over here and be useful. Help me fold these towels."

Chiding Elizabeth was not something Hannah Blackwell did on a regular basis, but this studious daughter of hers was beginning to stir up a minor degree of irritation. Elizabeth's disengagement from any worthwhile activity, as far as Hannah was concerned, was treading on the cardinal sin of sloth.

With a deep sigh, Elizabeth let the book rest on her lap and glanced over to where Hannah stood. "If you remember, Mother, I have just come from being very constructive, and you know what happened. It nearly drove me crazy."

"You mean that school in Kentucky? That teaching job of yours?"

"Yes."

Hannah's head wagged slowly in mocked skepticism. "Oh, yes, of course, the teaching nearly drove you crazy. That is not the way I remember you saying it. I thought it was the horrid conditions of the slaves and the way they were being treated that compelled you to leave."

With a look of exasperation on her face, Elizabeth slipped down off her window seat to assist in folding the towels. "I am afraid the people in Henderson would disagree with you, Mother. They do not consider their treatment of their slaves to be horrid conditions."

"But that's what drove you out of there."

"Yes and the fact that the elders of the town didn't have the faintest idea of how an education system should be operated"

"It's a small town, Elizabeth, a hamlet, and no small town has a system, as you call it."

"Just the same the whole year was very upsetting. I should have stayed here and continued teaching music after you closed our school. And I'm sorry we did close it. We were doing quite well for the four years we ran it."

Hannah picked up the basket of towels and headed for the door to leave the room. "The boys were doing very well with their businesses…didn't need to keep the school open." She stopped at the door and turned around. "Oh, by the way, I saw Grace Donaldson at the grocery store today. Mary has taken a turn for the worse."

Elizabeth winced. "Oh, no, I'm so sorry to hear that."

"Grace said Mary was asking about you. Wanted to know how you were doing."

Elizabeth could feel a mild blush fill her face. "Yes, I supposed she would, seeing that it's been a while since I've visited with her. I really need to get over there to see her again. It's just that I…"

"Yes, you should go see her soon," Hannah said interrupting Elizabeth. "Grace said you could come anytime during the morning hours. Those were best for Mary."

Heading out the door Hannah left Elizabeth with her mouth open. "It's just that I haven't been…"

"I don't believe you have any excuses, Elizabeth," Hannah said and was gone.

Feeling unjustly reprimanded Elizabeth turned to stare out the window to pout, watching the slight breeze ruffle the leaves on the neighbor's large sycamore tree. It was a futile attempt at erasing the guilt she felt. Mary Donaldson was a dear friend, dying of cancer and Elizabeth had only gone to visit her twice in the month and a half since she had returned to Cincinnati from Kentucky.

"I'll go see her this morning," Elizabeth called out peeved at being shamed into doing something she should have done long before.

"Yes, do that," Hanna answered from the end of the hall with almost a smile to her voice.

Elizabeth left for the Donaldson house an hour later. The home was within walking distance, close to a half mile away. It was a most pleasant day, a day conducive for a leisurely stroll through the neighborhood. But the burden of guilt remained with her casting a pall over the true reason for the visit. She had been derelict in not visiting her friend more often, especially since Mary Donaldson was suffering from an incurable cancer. But Elizabeth returned from the teaching position in Kentucky and fell into deep depression, choosing to avoid contact with people and skipping many activities and functions. It was the type of behavior that naturally prompted the concern of her mother.

Upon reaching the Donaldson home, Elizabeth took a few seconds to reinforce her spirits. The thought of seeing her friend suffering gave her grave reservations. After taking a deep breath she ascended the few steps, her feet moving in a hesitating fashion as she approached the front door. A gentle knock was given.

"Oh, Elizabeth," Grace Donaldson said, pushing open the screen door. "How nice to see you. Please come in."

"Mrs. Donaldson, how are you?"

"Oh, I guess all right...doing as well as can be expected. It's been a bit difficult these past few weeks."

Elizabeth cleared the doors and stepped into the small foyer. "I can imagine."

"I suppose your mother told you that Mary has had a relapse."

"Yes, she did and I am very sorry to hear that. The last time I saw Mary she seemed in relatively good spirits."

"Oh, her spirits are still amazingly high. It's just the body is slowly giving away." She pointed to the hallway. "Shall we go see if she's ready for visitors?"

"Yes, I would like that. Thank you."

"You might have to limit your time, Elizabeth," Grace Donaldson whispered as they moved down a darkened corridor. "I'm not too sure how strong Mary might be this morning."

"Of course," Elizabeth nodded. "I simply wish to say hello."

Halfway down, they approached a door slightly ajar. Elizabeth could tell the room was purposely being kept dark. The shades had been drawn and no lanterns were turned on. The room was small, void of much furniture. Mary lay

61

silently in the bed and it pained Elizabeth to see her so inert and thin. There was a time when Mary Donaldson was robust and full of energy. Their friendship was a relationship Elizabeth deeply cherished. Now that Mary lay dying of cancer Elizabeth found it difficult accepting the fate of her friend, part of the reason for hesitating to go visit.

As the door opened, rusty hinges caused an unexpected squeaking. "Who's there?" Mary asked, her voice feeble and quivering.

"Elizabeth Blackwell, Mary. May I come in?"

"Elizabeth," she said after several moments of silence. "Yes, my dear Elizabeth, please do come in."

"I will stay for only a few minutes. I suspect you could use all the rest you can get."

Apparently the comment seemed paradoxical to Mary, for she gave a short laugh. "Rest? My dear Elizabeth that is all I can do these days. Waiting for death has allowed me that luxury."

"Luxury?" quizzed Elizabeth moving further into the room and taking a seat close to the bed. "I don't look upon your condition as a luxury."

"The rest I am being afforded is the luxury, not the dying. Dying," she added, "is the price one pays for living. And since we all cannot escape death's beckoning it is senseless to even try. Therefore, I simply lay here waiting and while waiting I rest. And it is indeed a luxury."

"And your pain, if I may inquire. Have they been able to ease that for you?"

The room became silent. Mary shook her head. "The pain has not subsided, Elizabeth. As you know, and I have spoken to you about this before, I am not being seen on a regular basis or being given sufficient attention." Pausing, she struggled to catch her breath with heavy gulps of air. Continuing she added, "Male physicians appear to be totally unsympathetic to the needs of women." Again she waited, then turned on her side to face Elizabeth more directly. "I have been thinking, Elizabeth. You like to study and your health is good and you have leisure time, you're a perfect candidate for studying medicine. You should become a physician. I truly believe that if a lady doctor had been attending to me I would have been spared my worse sufferings."

The idea proposed by Mary caught Elizabeth completely by surprise. She didn't immediately know how to respond. The idea was preposterous. But that sentiment, of course, could not be expressed to this dying woman. Finally, after several seconds of giving thought to what to say Elizabeth responded. "I'm afraid I am not that candidate, Mary, far from it. And besides, as you know, women are prohibited from practicing medicine. There would not have been any opportunity for you to have been seen by a woman."

"Still, a woman would have given me better attention because we are sisters," she said then closed her eyes attempting as before to catch her breath. After several difficult moments her eyes gradually opened and she stared at Elizabeth. "I have often thought that you would make a wonderful physician. You are a caring woman and the giving of yourself that you do so well is such a beautiful gift. That intellect of yours absolutely lends itself to the field of medicine. And so many women would benefit from your skills."

Elizabeth laughed. "That is a very nice compliment, Mary, but if the truth be known the very thought of working with the human body is repugnant to me. No, I'm afraid I am not the rescuer you envision."

"Repugnant is a very strong sentiment, Elizabeth. Surely you don't mean that."

"I do. The field of medicine is of no interest to me."

"But don't you see. You have the qualities to be a perfect physician, someone I could…" Her voice cracked. She tried to talk but the voice became shallow and her face grew pale. Words had been cut short. Mary was struggling to breathe and a violent hacking erupted. The fuss startled Elizabeth causing her to spring quickly from the chair, confused as to what she should do.

Within seconds Grace Donaldson was in the room pulling covers off her daughter. "I was afraid of this. She overexerted herself."

Elizabeth stepped back and watched as Mary was raised into a sitting position, her mother pushing on the chest in rhythmic motions. Slowly the coughing ended with Mary regaining her breath even though a heavy wheezing could be heard as the lungs fought to gather in air.

"I'm afraid you'll have to leave, Elizabeth."

"Of course, yes, I understand. I'm so sorry this happened. I didn't realize…"

"It's not your fault, Elizabeth. Mary so wishes to talk with friends she forgets her limitation."

Moving toward the door Elizabeth called out, "I'll come back later, Mary."

It was a hasty retreat from the room. The sight of Mary's struggle to breathe greatly distressed Elizabeth and she moved swiftly down the hall. Disease and death had become abhorrent to Elizabeth. An inner conflict with the disparity of illness confused her; why some are chosen to suffer and others are not. Why she wondered, as she let herself out, did Mary become the victim and not her? Is life all that complex and unfair?

Mary Donaldson died shortly after Elizabeth's visit. There was no other chance to sit and converse with attempts to comfort the dying woman. Elizabeth attended the funeral and burial, gave her condolences to the mother and quickly departed the cemetery. Earlier in life, as a young woman, Elizabeth had found funerals to be an assault on the sensibilities of those who were left behind to grieve. Funerals to Elizabeth were overdone, over extended with too much emphasis placed on the ceremony rather than the matter of closure. And because of this way of thinking she spent as little time as possible at the funeral without being disrespectful

Elizabeth preferred once again being by herself during the days following Mary's death. She would take walks in the small park several blocks from where they lived often finding much comfort resting under a large tree, allowing her mind to contemplate all that was transpiring around her.

Yet with each meditation she could sense a strange taunting bothering her, a jabbing caused by the last urging of her friend. Despite Elizabeth's attempts to ignore Mary's words, the voice of Mary Donaldson dying in that darkened room with words being forced out between struggles for air began to unwittingly ensnare Elizabeth in their demanding grip leaving no simple escape possible. It was indeed an uncanny position in which Elizabeth found herself. Despite the ceaseless echoes of Mary's voice, the brutal facts of reality were still all too evident and could not be ignored. Becoming a physician for a woman was a complete impossibility. It was a field totally dominated and controlled by men and that alone had proven to be a most impenetrable barrier. Mary Donaldson's plea, unfortunately, could only remain to be nothing more than a shallow hope.

Still, reality or not, Elizabeth could not escape the lingering words of her dying friend. And even though there were continued efforts to distract herself from the memory of that conversation she found herself forced to acknowledge that no impossibility was impossible until proven with absolute proof that it was impossible. Realizing she would never be at rest with Mary Donaldson's plea until all obstructions had been challenged Elizabeth became surrounded by the obvious paths. All pointed to insubordination.

"Mother," she said to Hannah one morning. "I'm in a bit of a quandary"

"Quandary?"

"A troublesome nagging that has me being torn in two directions."

Hannah gave an understanding smile. "Mary Donaldson again, right?"

"Yes, Mary Donaldson's last words to me. I can't rid them from my mind and I have been struggling with ways to even begin...or...even more importantly circumvent the prohibition that the medical profession has of barring women from entering the field."

"So you are actually giving this whole thing serious thought, this idea of becoming a doctor?" It was asked with a touch of skepticism.

"Well, yes, I suppose I am and I know it's an improbable idea. But I'll never know unless I thoroughly explore my chances. And worse of all I still am not absolutely convinced that I truly want to pursue this dream or how to go about doing something like this. I'm in a...."

"Quandary, yes I know." Hannah said lifting the lid on the pot of stew to catch a whiff of its progress. Waving her hand over the pot she told Elizabeth, "Then I suggest you write to some of our doctor friends and ask their opinion."

"Ask doctors?" she reacted stressing her words in a sarcastic manner. "Oh, yes, of course, right, certainly. They'll just simply dismiss the idea as idiotic and most likely have a good laugh at my expense."

"I don't believe so, Elizabeth. These are dear friends of ours and they will be very honest with you. If they see any possible way you might approach this idea of becoming a physician they will tell you and be kind and encouraging. These men are of a liberal mind such as we. They won't dismiss the concept too lightly."

Elizabeth watched her mother give the stew a gentle stirring and allowed the words of encouragement from Hannah to filter through her qualms and doubts. Much of Elizabeth's thinking had been on a rather narrow path of simply charging the barriers with full force. But her mother's suggestion was providing a side door or at least a possible approach for determining the chances of even exploring the concept.

"Well, I suppose it wouldn't hurt to try," she said turning to leave the kitchen. Yet in trying she would be required to solicit those gentlemen's advice with a carefully worded approach in order to convince them the concept had perhaps reached its time. Words, specifically chosen words, became her objective. Moving inattentively down the hallway Elizabeth began composing her letter; a unique challenge to say the least. And as she strode the few feet to her bedroom, words began whirling in and out of her mind and all the while her earlier doubts followed closely behind.

Chapter Six

May, 1845
Philadelphia, Pennsylvania

And yet there remained a determination in her, a force that some of her siblings and friends felt was bordering on insanity.

Eyes glared at Elizabeth; the face reddened flushed with anger. "Goddamn female," he said pounding his fist on the wide mahogany desk. "Women like you are desecrating the purity and honor of womanhood. How dare you come here and ask me to be a part of this outrage...to disgrace this institution in granting your request. Have you no shame?"

"To correct you, sir," she snapped back, "I am not attempting to destroy womanhood.

Further more my request to be admitted to your medical school is not an act of disrespect."

"Unheard of, absolute utter hogwash. Medicine is no place for a woman let alone an insolent wench such as you."

Elizabeth's eyes closed as she hesitated before speaking. It was the fourth university hospital in the past six weeks that had granted her an interview with the Dean of Admissions only to result in abject humiliation. Even though she had suffered various degrees of verbal abuse and callous treatment, she had not been sullied in the manner to which she was now being subjected.

"This is 1845, sir. I find it absolutely unbelievable that a man in your position of responsibility has not awakened to the fact that women are as competent and capable as any man. Are you blind to this obvious fact?"

Eyes bulged as he bounded out of his chair, a long bony finger shaking, pointing to the door. "I will hear no more of this audacious rubbish. Leave now. Get out of my office this moment. I can assure you Miss Blackwell the likes of you will never enter a medical school."

It took every degree of constraint to control her anger. She could feel her hands close in tight fists. Then surprisingly Elizabeth found herself laughing, a definite mocking laugh. And for some unexplained reason, instead of displaying more anger the Dean could only stare in disbelief and watch as Elizabeth rose from her chair and ambled jauntily out of his office disappearing into the wide ornate hall.

Quickened steps along the walkway matched the rapid flow of thoughts as she moved in the direction of the cabstand. Interestingly, with each step she took she counted; each step synchronized with the number of vulgar terms used by the various deans of admission in describing her lineage. Then the steps slowed. Her mind began to reverse itself and the reoccurring clouds of doubt settled in debating the wisdom or folly of it all. Occasionally she would pause to reflect on the appointment just completed. And all the while, as she walked, she mumbled her vile displeasures with the entire world of academia.

It was the summer of 1846, a time of much discontent for Elizabeth. She had exhausted most of her financial resources, had reached the end of her list of medical schools and saw her determinate quest begin to wither and rot away. Where once there were encouraging words from those physicians who were friends of the family now there was only a reiteration of earlier cautions that the medical profession was wholly resistant to admitting women into their sacred ranks.

Yet there remained a determination in her, a force that some of her siblings and friends felt was bordering on insanity. The impenetrable wall Elizabeth encountered appeared to grow as word filtered among those in the medical field of this impudent young woman who was bringing chaos and trouble to their domain. Still she persisted, at times having no directions to follow. She walked a blind path with only imperfect grit guiding the way.

There was, however, some semblance of hope that existed in the person of Doctor Joseph Warrington, a man in private practice and a lecturer at one of the larger medical schools in Philadelphia. Elizabeth had come to know him through references provided by one of her physician friends. Warrington, she was told, was of a liberal nature and was intrigued by Elizabeth's concept that a woman could be as qualified a doctor as any man. It was to Warrington she went seeking guidance when first moving to Philadelphia. References and entrees to the Dean's offices were provided by him. But when learning of the rude and offensive treatment Elizabeth had received from these men Warrington became furious and spoke harshly to those he had considered his friends.

Ever the creative mentor, Warrington had conjured up many unique routes for Elizabeth to follow to gain access to a medical school. There were, however, some of his inspirations that were totally unacceptable to Elizabeth.

"I took the liberty of consulting with a friend of mine," Warrington told her during a meeting in his office to review various options, "mentioning to him your desire to be admitted to a medical school. While he shared my conviction that you are facing an impossible goal he was most adamant that you not follow my suggestion of going to Paris."

For a moment it appeared to Elizabeth she had been sharing the room with a complete stranger. Had he not come to understand her goal and mission? Never once did she have any desire to give up her quest for a medical education in America or travel to Paris in carrying out what Doctor Warrington considered to be a viable option. He had suggested she pretend to be a male student, dress as one, style her hair as a man and speak in low tones. In that manner, he said, she would gain admission into a medical institution. Interestingly though, his suggestion was not the first she had received. She had heard the identical idea from a medical instructor who, upon presenting his idea, offered to have several of his students attending courses in Paris keep an eye on her while she was in her disguise to alert her if the professors at the institution suspected the ruse. These suggestions were revolting to Elizabeth who found the concept quite insulting and definitely degrading.

She shook her head. "No need to worry, Doctor Warrington. As I have mentioned before I have no intention of going to Paris. I intend on being a student in an American university and not demean myself by fakery and deceit."

"Indeed," Warrington said, a capricious grin forming on his face. Then laughing he told her, "You do have spunk Elizabeth that I will give you. And perhaps that will be the key that eventually gets you into a school. Being the old Quaker that I am I firmly believe that if it is to be the will of Providence that you become a doctor then it will so be ordained. But in the meantime, as Providence debates the issue I believe we should be looking into other possibilities as well."

"Other possibilities?" she asked. "I'm not sure there are any left."

"Writing letters and having personal interviews would be fine if…"

"If I were a man, yes, I understand that. But…"

"But those methods are not necessarily ineffective in your case. They just need to be refined and perhaps redirected. And that is what I intend to do. I believe we have many more options to explore and hopefully in a few days my search and inquiries will produce fruitful results."

As she left his office that afternoon she harbored grave doubts, feeling Joseph Warrington could not devise any different concept that would increase the likelihood of her being accepted into a school of medicine. Waiting for a cab she grew leery of his optimism. A new approach would not change the mindset of the medical profession. If there were alternatives to the regular methods they would have to be extreme. Doctor Joseph Warrington, she feared, was beginning to become slightly irrational.

However, by the time a note had arrived several days later suggesting a time and date for their meeting her opinion had changed. She had come to realize her dismissal of his continuing hunt for innovative concepts was placing a screen between her and sound reasoning. An open mind was needed. Obviously his strategy had not been given the proper consideration.

The morning ride to his office brought about the vacillation Elizabeth had come to despise. It had been tormenting her for the past several months, tearing her from joy to despair. The forces of hope and doubt battled once again for her attention that morning and the conflict at one point brought her close to instructing the driver to turn the carriage around and return to her rooming house. Eventually, though, hope became the victor and she arrived at Warrington's office filled with much anticipation.

"Good morning Doctor."

"I have been eagerly awaiting your arrival. I've discovered an interesting idea I wish to review with you." As he stepped aside she moved into his office.

"That is wonderful because you have raised my curiosity."

"I believe there is one element we've been overlooking."

"Oh? And what might that be?"

Warrington opened a drawer in the desk and retrieved a sheet of paper. "You've been concentrating on the larger, better known schools of medicine."

"Yes, because I don't believe I would obtain a worthy education with anything less."

"Ah, but I've discovered you may be mistaken with that kind of thinking."

"Mistaken?"

"I believe so. You see there are many excellent smaller colleges with schools of medicine as part of their curriculum that have produced many fine doctors, some of whom have gone on to excel in their specialties. I believe you might wish to shift your focus and begin contacting some of them."

"But wouldn't I have to continue in one of the major schools to earn my degree once I have completed my studies with a smaller one?"

"No, not at all. You would earn a degree in medicine absolutely similar to that obtained from a major school. Their degrees are recognized and accredited by all governing boards"

Elizabeth leaned back in her chair, a finger toying with her lower lip. "And where might these school be?" she asked.

"Primarily in the Northern states...country schools they're called."

"Country schools?" Elizabeth exclaimed becoming more erect in her chair. "The sound of that is not all that encouraging, Doctor. I would say that puts a questionable level of quality on their curriculum."

"No, that is not the case, Elizabeth. It is not quality that differentiates between the two. It's quantity. I've learned that the main difference between the larger schools and these smaller ones is just the size of their student bodies. It's that simple. The curriculum and quality of instruction are similar. I've come to believe the mindset of the smaller school would be more liberal and more open minded; more advanced thinking. Therefore based on those assumptions I would encourage you to explore these schools as an alternative choice."

Saying nothing, Elizabeth stared at the sheet of paper sitting on Warrington's desk. In a decisive move her hand reached out. "May I?" With his approval she lifted it off the desk and scanned the names of the schools. There were none she recognized. Obviously Doctor Warrington had taken the time to assure the institutions he was recommending were of high quality and fine reputation. Bringing the page closer, her eyes slowly scanned the listings once again.

"I've located twenty-five," he said. "They I believe might be receptive to your request for admission. You will need to seek their prospectuses, read them carefully and then determine which of those you feel confident in contacting."

"Do you know anything about them?"

He shook his head. "No only what I've told you, very little else."

Elizabeth could see the paper trembling slightly as she continued to read. Lowering the page to her lap she glanced at the names once again wondering if contacting those schools would be of any value. "Thank you Doctor," she said standing, gathering up the page and her purse. "I'll begin my research immediately and let you know what I've found."

"Excellent and please do keep me informed."

As she reluctantly exited his office she lacked her usual enthusiasm. The concept of a smaller school was so foreign to what she had been envisioning since she made the commitment to pursue Mary Donaldson's dying wish. Despite what Warrington affirmed, Elizabeth was skeptical of his claim that the smaller schools were equal to providing her the same education as that of the larger institutions. The whole proposal rested uneasily on her mind. The new path introduced by Warrington raised the indecisiveness to once again probe her thoughts. Much to her chagrin the debate raged until she reached the cabstand. And now feeling the brunt of all that had burdened her she found herself tiring of it all.

Chapter Seven

Then the hush was broken as a whisper quietly speculated that the old man was trying to josh with the class and that they should go along with the teasing and reciprocate by agreeing.

Doctor Charles Lee sat pensively in his office staring at the letter in his hand even though the hour was getting late. Classes had concluded at Geneva College and the building was vacant except for a few lingering professors. The fall term had just begun and the new crop of students was raising questions in the mind of this aging gentleman. He found himself the victim of a growing generation gap and on occasion he had expressed that sentiment.

However, the Dean of the Faculty of the medical school at this small college in upstate New York now faced an even more complex conundrum. It concerned a brief but compelling letter he held in his hand. After several passes over the text he decided the writer of the letter deserved some kind of consideration even though it was completely out of the ordinary. But how? With eyes fixed deeply on the sheet of paper he was unaware of a rather rotund, slumped-shouldered middle-aged man enter his office.

"You awake, Charles," Doctor James Webster asked in his typical taunting fashion.

Dean Lee raised his eyes scoffing at Webster's lame attempt at humor. "James, I am glad you stopped in."

"Oh, and why is that?"

"I need your help," he answered reaching over his desk to hand the letter to Webster. "Read this and tell me what you think of it."

"What is it?"

"Just read it and then tell me what you think."

Seating himself, the Professor of Anatomy glanced at the letter his eyebrows furrowing and he fell into the chair completely engrossed in what he was reading. When finished he looked up and smiled. "Well, now, this is novel," he said. "I have not ever seen one of these before. A rather brave and bold young woman wouldn't you say?"

"It was inevitable, James."

"You think so? I would not have thought any women brazen enough to suppose she could enter the field of medicine." He looked at the letter again. "So what are you going to do with it? Show it to the President of the College?"

"I don't really know. I believe it should not to be dismissed lightly. I think we need to be fair and considerate. The woman does deserve some form of hearing, if that is what we can call it."

"By whom," Webster asked.

"Well, I suppose by the faculty members and then let the majority rule."

"Charles, you know what their answer is going to be. You might as well write the young woman back and tell her the school is not interested in her request for admission."

"No, I believe she at least deserves a hearing."

"Fine, suit yourself. But it will be an exercise in futility."

"Maybe so, but at least I would feel that we were being honest with Miss...her name again?"

Webster glanced at the letter. "Blackwell. Elizabeth Blackwell."

"Yes, Blackwell. I'll request a gathering of the faculty for tomorrow afternoon."

James Webster smiled, rose from the chair, returned the letter and left the room laughing. The Dean thought he heard Webster mumbling to himself but couldn't determine exactly what he was saying.

Later the next afternoon, members of the faculty of the College of Medicine gathered in the assembly room, many complaining at having to stay on. Lee positioned himself in front of the group, the letter from Elizabeth in hand. After calling for quiet he wasted no time addressing the issue at hand.

"I've asked you to be here this afternoon, gentlemen, to perform a rather unusual function and I want you to please do it with stringent diligence. I have here a letter from a young woman who is requesting admission to the School of Medicine. And before any of you automatically dismiss it as frivolous I want a serious, open minded discussion conducted on this matter."

"Impossible," a voice shouted with several others agreeing giving a resounding, "Hear, hear!"

"There is no reason for us to debate this matter," added another. "Women have no place in medicine you know that. No need to debate this issue Charles. This is a waste of our time."

The frustrated Dean held up his hand. "Gentlemen, please keep an open mind on this matter. The young lady deserves an unbiased consideration."

"Why?"

"Simply because it is the first such request we have received and we have no precedence to go by. Plus she has been given some serious preliminary instructions on medicine under the tutoring of both Doctor John Dickson and his brother Samuel and private lessons in anatomy under Doctor Albert Allen.

Therefore with those credentials I believe we definitely owe it to this young woman to give it solemn thought."

Silence filled the room. Then, clearing his throat, James Webster stood and spoke to the matter. "I have been giving this letter some deep thought ever since Charles brought it to my attention yesterday afternoon. And I've drawn a single conclusion."

"And what might that be James?" Lee asked.

Looking around at the curious faces he smiled. "This truly is not a matter that should be in our hands. I believe it should be placed before the student body, for they will be the ones who will be required to share the classrooms and laboratories with this young woman and spend time with her in their studies. I say we simply assign the responsibility of deciding this matter to the students."

For several seconds a pall of silence swept over those gathered. However, it wasn't long until a soft murmuring was heard, one that quickly grew into louder conversations among the men. Then, as if on cue, one by one their voices began affirming their agreement with Webster's suggestion until it was obvious Charles Lee did not need to take a vote.

"It appears all of you are in agreement with James am I correct?"

Affirmation was swift.

"Fine, I shall then present this young lady's request to the full student body tomorrow morning. I am sure we will have a swift answer.

Thanking the men for their attendance, Lee ended the meeting and stood watching as the room emptied. One stood at the door hesitating. James Webster turned to face Lee. He sported a most mischievous grin.

"Now tell me Charles, was that a stroke of genius or not?"

Lee shook his head. "More like desperation rather than genius, James."

"But you wanted an impartial discussion and you were not about to get it. So as I sat there listening I felt there were many in the room, including myself, surprisingly so, who would favor admitting the woman to the school."

"Oh, why?"

"Just think, Charles, what it would do for Geneva College. It would certainly bring much attention to the school and we would be given credit for being innovators and far-thinkers."

"Or condemned as idiots and troublemakers."

"Charles," Webster scolded, "you must not harbor negative thoughts. Besides, the student body will most likely vote not to admit her so you don't have anything of which to be concerned."

The Dean gave a short grunt and folded the letter placing it in his vest pocket. "We shall see, James. We shall see."

It was well known that the students at Geneva College were a rather rowdy bunch. Thus it was of no surprise that the entire group, assembled in the large room, carried on with much frivolity and mischievous nonsense. Several reasons for the meeting were being advanced followed by ludicrous laughter. The suggestions were heard far down the hallway as Lee and Webster approached the room.

"The boys are in a typical juvenile mood today, Dean Lee."

"Wonderful, just what I need."

"Did you expect anything different?"

"No, but that will change when I present them with the challenge."

"Don't be too sure."

The men approached the room with some trepidation although James Webster was actually looking forward to the session. As they entered the large assembly arena some semblance of order altered the mood. Finally there was a call for silence by Charles Lee. But it took a while to calm the young men down. Eventually a stern expression by Dean Lee achieved the result he was seeking.

"Gentlemen" he began. "I have asked to meet with you this morning so that you may assist your faculty in making a rather delicate decision." Reaching into his suit coat pocket he withdrew the letter and opened it in a formal manner taking his time before reading.

"I have received a unique letter, and after presenting it to the faculty members it was their decision that we should involve you gentlemen in making the final resolution." Holding the letter higher he proceeded to read the contents in a slow and deliberate voice. When finished he lowered the letter and looked about the room. There were expressions of stunned disbelief. "So what say you, gentlemen? Would you be in favor of admitting Miss Blackwell or not?"

For a moment it appeared Doctor Charles Lee had totally mesmerized the entire group of students, for no sound was heard. Then the hush was broken as a whisper quietly speculated that the old man was trying to josh with the class and that they should go along with the teasing and reciprocate by agreeing. From another corner came the speculation that the Dean had nothing better to do but to fantasize. That comment produced hearty laughter that soon erupted into a complete babble of voices.

The exasperated Dean raised his hand and called for silence, an effort that had very little effect. Looking at Webster he shrugged, prompting Webster to jump to his feet to shout a command.

"Silence!" he roared achieving the results Lee wanted and with a few dribbling comments remaining Charles Lee expressed his surprise at the group's reaction.

"But Doctor Lee," came a response from the back row. "Your little attempt at comedy was done so perfectly, so seriously and straight-faced that we couldn't help but express our amusement."

"But I was serious," Lee argued.

Again the room filled with laughter. "Well, of course you were," someone teased. "So then you deserve to have our vote." Turning to look at the rest of the group he asked, "So, how many of you are in favor of admitting a woman to this school?"

Every hand rose bringing the class into another uproarious chorus.

"No, no," Lee shouted, "you don't seem to understand. I am not trying to be comical here." He waved the letter around as the laughing subsided. "I'm very serious. This is a genuine letter from Miss Blackwell asking to be admitted to our school of medicine. The faculty felt you gentlemen should be the ones to make this decision since you will be the ones having to associate and share your classrooms with a woman. So we are leaving it up to you to decide. And I need a unanimous decision one way or the other. It must be unanimous."

"Doctor Lee" someone from the group called out. "Are you trying to tell us that this is actually a legitimate request?"

"Indeed I am."

"Seriously?" another asked. "You mean to tell us you have actually received a letter from a woman wanting to become a doctor, wanting to be admitted to our college and that the faculty didn't want to make the decision?"

"That is exactly what I am saying, young man. And I want you gentlemen to deliberate on this and give me your answer. And I repeat it must be unanimous"

The tenor of the room suddenly changed. Disbelief showed on several faces as others began a whispered discussion. The din resembled that of a busy beehive.

From the middle of the group a young man stood. "Professor Lee."

"Yes, Mister Smith."

"This woman. How old is she?"

Lee shrugged. "I have no idea of knowing that. I can only surmise she is young, perhaps your age or a bit older. I would guess she would be in the group of today's young women who want to change the world. But that is immaterial."

"To you, perhaps," Stephen Smith replied resurrecting the laughter. "And the letter said she had done some preliminary studying?"

"Yes, quite a bit. She appears to be very serious about becoming a doctor."

The debate among the group resumed and after several minutes Smith once again stood. "Well, sir, we all agree that it might be quite novel and interesting having a young woman among us. Certainly would be different and therefore we have no problem admitting this woman to the school."

"I object," cried out a voice from the far end of the first row. "I am not in favor."

An immediate display of displeasure arose with shouting and booing. Crumpled up papers became the weapons of choice thrown at what was conceived to be, for the moment, the enemy. Those around him pounded on his shoulders. The subtle attack began to concern Dean Lee.

"Gentlemen, gentlemen please stop this rowdiness. You need to calm down, behave yourselves. Let the man speak his mind."

With all eyes focused on the victim of this frenzy, fear gripped the beleaguered student's face as he scanned the room searching for any sign of appeasement. "I...I have nothing to say," came the whispered response.

"How about saying aye, Millard?" a voice called out.

There was hesitation then the young man nodded. "Aye," he mumbled, barely audible.

As the room erupted in a chorus of cheers two bewildered professors looked at each other, Webster sprouting a large smile; Lee having the look of a condemned man.

"Amazing," Webster said. "Absolutely amazing. I would not have given this request a ghost of a chance."

Charles Lee stood dumbfounded. "Never in my years would I believe I'd be seeing a woman enter a school of medicine."

"It's a new generation, Charles. The young people are taking over. You might as well get use to it."

Lee gave a faint smile, nodded and turned to leave. "I suppose, then, I should go prepare a letter of response to Miss Blackwell. I'll need a formal resolution from the student body, James. Would you see to it that they produce one?"

"It'll be my pleasure," Webster told him and watched as a slumped-shoulder Dean of the Faculty left the room. Webster turned to observe the excited students and wondered aloud what Geneva College was going to be like having one young woman studying among all of these rowdy young men. "Amazing. Simply amazing."

Chapter Eight

November, 1847
Geneva, New York

The familiar scratching of the pen on the paper
heightened her senses as she watched with great
joy Charles Lee methodically write her name on
that exceptional page.

Unmistakably the mood was hostile. She
watched as eyes followed her. The path from the
boarding house to the campus of Geneva College
was usually empty in the early morning. But
today, her first day, several women of the town
stood along the way, some blocking the path
forcing Elizabeth to step off on to the lawn to
continue her journey. There was whispering but
indiscernible. Displeasure showed on their faces.
In their eyes Elizabeth Blackwell was a jezebel
taking womanhood onto the path of the devil and
stepping outside of the boundaries of propriety.

Ignoring the snubs of the local women,
Elizabeth kept her focus on a large brick building

that loomed ahead, appearing to her as the formidable fortress she had come to conquer. Representative of her moment of triumph, was the manner in which she grasped the oversize handle and pulled open the heavy door with a vigor far beyond the strength she knew she had.

Entering the building she examined her surroundings, giving close scrutiny to the vastness of it all. Her destination was a small office at the end of the wide, three-story marbled corridor. There, as instructed earlier, she would find Doctor Charles Lee's office. After several minutes of waiting in the anteroom and seeing no receptionist she felt it necessary to call his name. Waiting, she then heard, "In here, Miss Blackwell."

Hearing her name came as somewhat of a surprise. Consequently Elizabeth's curiosity caused a breach of proper protocol. Bypassing any form of greeting she stepped into his office and asked, "And how did you know it was me?"

There she found Charles Lee standing, a large grin on his face. "Good Morning, Miss Blackwell,"

Stunned for a moment Elizabeth felt her face warming. "Oh my goodness, Doctor Lee, I am so sorry for my rudeness and not offering you a proper greeting."

"No need to apologize, Miss Blackwell. I can understand your confusion. News travels fast in a small town such as Geneva and I was alerted to your approach well in advance of your arrival. But be that as it may be, welcome. I've been looking forward to having you here."

"Thank you Doctor Lee. I too have been eagerly anticipating this moment and I am most grateful to you and the College for taking this bold move of admitting me."

"In all actuality, Miss Blackwell," he said directing her to a chair, "it should be your fellow students whom you should thank. It was they who are allowing you to join them." Moving to his chair he began to sit. "Please be seated," he instructed.

"Thank you. Yes, I suppose I should thank the students, as I read in your letter and in their resolution. I must say I was quite intrigued by that procedure. You are, to say the least, quite innovative here."

The comment gave him cause to laugh. "Our faculty members would still be in debate if it were not suggested that the students make the final decision since it would be they who would be sharing classes with you."

"Well, regardless of that action I do believe it was you who initiated an open forum on the subject and therefore began this courageous course of action."

Producing a sly smile he replied, "As it shall be."

Rising from his chair he moved in the direction of a tall file cabinet that sat inconspicuously in the corner of his office. Pulling open a drawer he retrieved a large journal. It was carried to his desk in some sort of ceremonial manner, so Elizabeth thought, and upon laying it down his finger gave the cover several quick taps. To Elizabeth the old velvet-covered tome reminded her of a sorcerer's handbook of magical spells.

"This is our registry of students," he told her. "Each year we start a new page. Your name will be inscribed on the list here as the latest entry."

Without any ceremony he lifted the heavy cover and opened the book. Wetting his middle finger he began turning the pages until he reached the one for which he was searching. "Ah, here we are. We will assign you number one hundred and thirty." Sitting down he moved a small ink container closer and dipped his pen in it and began writing. The familiar scratching of the pen on the paper heightened her senses as she watched with great joy Charles Lee methodically write her name on that exceptional page.

And then she waited.

She waited to hear the sounds of rejoicing, the shouts of liberation; the festive celebration of enlightenment. Yet there was no magic, despite her powerful surge of adrenalin, no row of cannons firing a salute and tribute. Ironically, it all seemed so uneventful; so ordinary. And although she had not given any thought to what this moment might be, it would seem at least there should have been more to it then this. But there wasn't. Instead, a few strokes of a pen into the school's registry had unceremoniously converted her from ordinary citizen to a medical student, the very first woman in the world to ever do so. She so wanted to stand and applaud vigorously to the point her hands would blister; to release a thunderous roaring of approval. But proper decorum forbade it and she remained seated, a pensive expression hiding her emotions with eyes staring at the book as if any moment it would release all she had wanted it to be. And as much as it was difficult to admit, this simple deed would be her only fond recollection of a most precious historical moment and soon this moment would be just another unembellished chapter.

The Dean, blotted the entry, closed the journal and upon standing extended his hand. "Welcome to Geneva Medical College," he said the wide smile returning. "You, of course, will be entering the classes several months behind the others, but I am confident you will not have any trouble catching up."

She shook the man's hand and looked deeply into his eyes. "You have no idea what a significant move you have made today, Doctor Lee."

"Oh, but I do and I have great faith you will bring much honor to this school."

The ceremony, as Elizabeth preferred to look upon it, had concluded and she turned to leave. Looking back she said, "Thank you, Doctor Lee. Thank you so very much." She saw him nod then she quickly turned and hurried from the office before he had a chance to see tears rolling slowly down her cheeks.

Elizabeth's first entry into this new venture came about in the study of Kinesiology -- a two hour lecture. It was the inaugural fusion of the female element into what used to be an all-male sanctuary, an element for which many were not prepared. Yet, in holding to their pledge to be gentlemen when she began her studies, the silence in the room spoke of that honor and Elizabeth was stunned by the almost austere reception.

While exiting from the classroom upon conclusion of the lecture, a young man walking beside Elizabeth said in a whispered tone, "well done."

"Thank you," she responded, pleased at the gentlemanly manner in which this new classmate presented himself.

He turned to look at her and grinned. "I'm sorry, Miss Blackwell, but I have this bad habit of speaking my thoughts aloud. I was actually directing my comment to my colleagues. It was an absolute dramatic change from our usual classroom behavior and I thought we all acted quite admirably."

"Oh yes, yes indeed it was a most rewarding and productive experience. By the way, I'm at a disadvantage. You know my name but I don't know yours."

"Oh, I'm sorry, forgive me. I'm Stephen Smith."

"Mister Smith, it's nice meeting you."

"You seem to be quite at ease, given the magnitude of what you're attempting here."

"I was reassured by all of you that my attendance here would be met with true gentlemanly politeness and courtesies. With that assurance what is there to fear?"

Smith nodded and laughed. "That is true and that was certainly demonstrated at this morning's lecture. It was absolutely amazing. Your presence in that lecture hall created an incredible revolution, and for the better I might add. I believe your attendance at this school is going to bring about a whole new dimension in conduct."

"How nice of you to say so, Mister Smith, how ever so nice," she said as he began to move on.

"Good-day Miss Blackwell."

"Good-day Mister Smith."

Elizabeth stood in the vast hallway suddenly realizing she had no idea as to where she should go next. She had no class schedule, no knowledge of where the different rooms might be or to what direction she should turn. Hurrying after Smith she called out to him.

"Mister Smith. Mister Smith, please wait."

He turned and saw her approaching. "Yes, Miss Blackwell? What is it?"

"I...I feel quite embarrassed. But I have no idea where I am to be or how to get there. I have not been issued a class schedule or the names of the rooms in which my classes are to be held."

Smith nodded and smiled. "None of us have a schedule. The order of study is fixed, each day being the same as the day before. The lectures and demonstrations are limited in scope, for there are only a few elements in medicine that we study this first term: Kinesiology, Biology, Pharmaceutical, Epidemiology, and of course the most entertaining of all, Anatomy."

"Entertaining?"

"With Professor Webster it is."

"Sounds intriguing."

"Indeed."

"And so how do I learn this schedule?"

"By just following us."

"We all attend the same classes?"

"Small college, Miss Blackwell, yes."

Elizabeth glanced around and discovered what Stephen Smith was saying. Indeed every student was heading in the same direction, funneling into the same hallway and disappearing into the same room. It was a routine they all knew and, of course, after the first day she, too, would have her schedule well mapped out and have the fundamentals of attending Geneva College effectively captured.

"Mind if I walk with you to...our next..."

"Lecture, Miss Blackwell. All of our classes are lectures except Anatomy, which in addition to the lectures we participate in the dissecting and surgical practices on cadavers." He hesitated before continuing. "Have you...been exposed to the study of Anatomy?"

"Yes, in Philadelphia."

"Ah, so you are then quite aware of all parts of the human body?"

Elizabeth could feel a slight blush rushing to her face. "Yes," she answered as demurely as she could. "I am not a novice."

Her response caused Stephen Smith to laugh. "Good." He turned and began walking. "Come, Professor Lambert awaits us."

"And he teaches...?"

"Epidemiology, the study of..."

"The causes, distribution and control of diseases," she quickly inserted, making her point she was not, as she had declared, a novice.

Elizabeth avoided Smith for the rest of the morning not wanting to bring about a dependent relationship with the young man. And he, too, seemed satisfied leaving Elizabeth to fend for herself. They were both polite to each other, smiling and nodding in acknowledgement.

Elizabeth preferred it that way. She preferred being by herself so as to maintain her focus on her studies. She diligently took as many notes as possible, writing fast enough to capture every word spoken but slow enough to make it legible for transferring to a more permanent journal.

Prior to dismissal for the day the final class was to be that of Anatomy. Elizabeth had heard from several students that Professor Webster would not be present for the day's lecture or demonstration. The class would only be guided by the demonstrator, Doctor Corydon La Ford, and would primarily be taking turns practicing their skills in the surgical dissecting of a cadaver. The students, of course, had had their preliminary introductions to the study of Anatomy the month before. Elizabeth would be entering the class for the first time and theoretically working from a disadvantaged position. Nevertheless, because of her studies with Doctor Allen, a physician in Philadelphia, she was perhaps more advanced than the other students and therefore she felt no hesitation in performing the same procedures as they.

Yet once the class was underway and the moment for the dissection arrived Doctor Le Ford had reservations regarding Elizabeth's involvement.

"Perhaps you would simply wish to observe, Miss Blackwell," he suggested.

"No, not really, sir. I am rather well versed in Anatomy and am quite prepared to conduct this procedure according to your instructions."

Eyes squinted. Beginning to speak, he quickly hesitated. "Yes, I...I see. Very well then," he told her, "please join me here at the table."

She chose to face away from her classmates. She did not need or want to observe any impolite reactions that might be prompted by her dissection of a half-naked man. She would assure all proprieties would be in their proper order.

Picking up the scalpel, Elizabeth could feel every eye focused directly on her. She once again realized the historical implications of her actions. With the first penetration of that scalpel blade into the skin, she thought, the separation of the sexes would be eradicated simply because it mattered not the gender of the person performing the dissection but rather the preciseness and accuracy.

The area of practice in which she would participate was the lower left leg from the knee to the ankle. Those who had gone earlier had already performed their work on the opposite leg. With careful precision Elizabeth drew the scalpel down along the thin blue line that had been drawn by Doctor Le Ford. Her hand trembled slightly. It had to be clean; had to be a stellar incision; had to be better than the group before. That one long cut, running the blade swiftly through the cadaver's skin avoiding any mistakes would destroy any preconceived notions the male practitioners might ever have had. A woman could, indeed, perform as good as or better than a man.

She looked at her partner. He was to expand her incision to open the muscle. But he hesitated and was told by La Ford to complete his assignment. As the student's hand lowered Elizabeth could see it begin to shake.

"I can't...not with her standing here," he told Le Ford.

"Mr. Caldwell, we are not here to dissect the propriety of a woman being present among us for the purpose of studying medicine but to dissect a cadaver for the purpose of learning about medicine. Either you perform your task or leave the class and forfeit your degree in medicine."

The admonishment shocked Elizabeth, for it seemed quite harsh, more severe than necessary and she began to correct Doctor La Ford then hesitated. Instead she gave reassurance to the student.

"If you wish, Mr. Caldwell," she said, "I can stand aside and be replaced by someone else. It may make matters more comfortable for you."

Catching the look of irritation on Le Ford's face the student shook his head and placed the scalpel on the muscle and with a vicious stroke slashed the leg with what could only be considered an act of spite.

"Excellent," Elizabeth cried out, knowing that Mr. Caldwell needed some critical moral support in order to avoid the wrath of Le Ford.

The class broke out with a loud round of applause.

Doctor Corydon Le Ford glared at Elizabeth. "Perhaps, Miss Blackwell, you would like to continue leading this session. You seem to be a perfect judge of a student's ability to hack away at a body."

"I apologize, Doctor Le Ford," she said, realizing she had overstepped her bounds. "I shall restrain myself from now on." She looked over at her Anatomy cohort noticing a slight grin forming on his face. He then caught her eye and winked.

By four that afternoon the rain had stopped, or at least it had taken a hiatus and upon the conclusion of her last class for the day Elizabeth decided to stroll casually on the high crest alongside Seneca lake. She wanted the opportunity of reviewing what she had just accomplished. Wishing not to focus on the historic significance, she gave thought to the uniqueness of her experiences; the various lessons she had been provided, the new information gained and her participation as one with the other students.

Before finishing her walk to Arlene Waller's boarding house where she had taken up her residency, she decided to stop and watch the artful ripples being formed on the lake as the wind swept across the water. Standing there enjoying the restful sight she could hear voices off.

in the distance. Glancing over she saw the same women she had seen that morning huddled together staring in her direction. When they spotted Elizabeth looking their way they quickly turned their heads, the talking stopped, and within seconds each of the women had departed in opposite directions leaving Elizabeth to ponder the acrimony she had created in this small town. It pained her to know she had now become an object of scorn.

That evening's meal was a most welcomed one. Those at the table were proving to be very enjoyable companions with the exception of a doctor's wife, having recently taken up residency at the boarding house with her husband. Doctor Harnet seldom ate at the table, apparently keeping long hours tending to his patients. But it was not an impolite shun from the wife, just simply a shun.

"And how did your day go my dear Elizabeth?" inquired Eleanor Wilson, one of the long-time residents at Arleen Waller's boarding house and an immediate advocate for Elizabeth's mission.

"Excellent, Mrs. Wilson. It was a red-letter day."

"Oh, I am so glad to hear that, aren't you Mrs. Hartnet?"

The doctor's wife glared at the little slump-shouldered lady whose silver hair always gave the appearance of a shiny halo surrounding her head. There was no reply.

"I knew you'd agree," Eleanor Wilson said. "I believe it's about time we had a woman in the medical field. I certainly would allow being seen by a woman physician."

"Why, thank you, Mrs. Wilson. That is quite refreshing to hear," said Elizabeth.

"And what do you intend doing after you get your degree?" Wilson asked

Elizabeth folded her hands under her chin letting her eyes roam off into space. She waited before answering. "I want to serve the poor," she slowly said, "mainly women and children. There is such a need for this segment of our society. I'm afraid they've become the forgotten ones."

"Commendable," the older lady told her. "Not out for just the money and fame like a few of our doctors?" She turned her head to smile at the doctor's wife.

"It's quite difficult knowing what lies ahead for me, Mrs. Wilson. I have to make it through medical school first then I can plot out my course."

"You'll make it through medical school my dear Elizabeth. You don't have to worry about that."

As she sat stirring her coffee Elizabeth could feel the cold stare of the doctor's wife fixed upon her. How unfortunate Elizabeth thought that this woman's cultural bindings as those from the morning walk forbad them to share in the joy of women being freed from their bonds. How very unfortunate indeed.

Chapter Nine

February, 1848
Geneva, New York

If the matter is viewed as one from impure and unchaste sentiments then, yes, one could find my presence embarrassing. However, I cannot envision a man of medicine whose mind was not so lifted by the study of Anatomy that such sentiments would have an influence over him.

The long days of winter grew more intense forcing Elizabeth to spend more time indoors, a condition that presented little concern to her. The spellbinding aura of college life had begun to transform Elizabeth into a changed person: more resolved and fixated on her studies. Her participation in the various classroom assignments was now all that mattered and she soon discovered that if permitted she would immerse herself into the study of medicine twenty four hours a day. It quickly became obvious this driving desire to learn and to advance as quickly as possible would be advantageous, for she was rapidly acquiring a level of knowledge far superior to many of her classmates.

James Webster immediately saw in Elizabeth the great potential that previously only she had recognized. In return Elizabeth formed an immediate liking for the professor and considered him to be her most venerated mentor. It was a strange association; two completely different personalities, but one, nonetheless, that benefited Elizabeth greatly.

Yet as the school term progressed, James Webster quickly learned that the integration of Elizabeth Blackwell into the fold of Geneva College would present unique challenges bordering on serious complications. Until the middle of February his complete series of anatomical lectures and demonstrations had gone very well and had posed few problems. But now one such scheduled session — one on the reproductive system of the human male — confronted him with a most troublesome challenge.

The dilemma rested not in the restraint he must continue to carry out but whether to allow Elizabeth Blackwell to attend that particular lecture and demonstration. It meant that a completely undraped body of a male cadaver would be exposed before both male and female and the strict morals of the day absolutely prohibited such an occurrence to be rendered before women. To compound the situation, attendance at every Anatomy session was mandatory and was a critical part of the medical curriculum. Basically that translated into the fact that if she were to acquire the complete education necessary for graduation she would have to participate in that class. And that rather convoluted paradox was what presented James Webster with his predicament. Fortunately, with sufficient thought on the matter, a simple remedy came to him. He would offer her a private session.

Webster concluded that a discussion with Elizabeth, explaining the delicate predicament facing both of them, and his resolution to that quandary, would erase his concerns, for surely she would see the wisdom in his proposal.

On the selected morning he had Elizabeth summoned to his office.

"You wanted to see me, Doctor Webster?"

"Oh, Elizabeth, yes, yes, please come in and take a seat."

"There was no explanation in the note as to why you wanted to see me," she said sitting down.

"No, I thought it best we...we talk it out." His voice had a constraint to it.

"Something wrong?"

James Webster shifted his body awkwardly in his chair and avoided eye contact with Elizabeth. "No, no, nothing is wrong. It's just that something has come up, well, it didn't just come up, it's been there all this time, but it has now developed…"

"Doctor Webster you seem to be struggling with what you want to tell me."

"Yes, I suppose it does appear that way doesn't it."

"Then what is it you wish to say."

There was a noticeable pause before he spoke. He flashed a quick smile. "Well, I've debated on how best to handle this and I am going to present you with this note of explanation." His hand reached out holding a sealed envelope. There was a minor shake to his hand.

Taking the envelope Elizabeth began to open it when Webster stopped her.

"No, no need to read it now. Do so at your leisure."

"But…" she said then quickly stopped, recognizing the professor was behaving rather oddly and for her to protest or to read the note in front of him would only cause her favorite professor further anxieties. Instead she simply smiled, nodded and placed the envelope in her reticule. "Is that all, Doctor?"

"Yes, yes, Elizabeth, thank you…thank you for coming." He stood wishing to expedite her departure; perspiration dotted his brow but went unnoticed by Elizabeth. It was difficult forcing a smile but he managed then nodded and smiled again.

The whole affair was quite foreign to Elizabeth. In the short time she had known the professor he had never behaved in such a strange manner. She was most eager to read his note to learn the reason for all of the mysterious behavior.

The moment she reached the hallway she moved to a bench that lined the wall and hurriedly sat to retrieve the envelope. Unfolding the note inside she began reading only to stop, her eyes closing tight in a pose of anger then slowly the note was lowered to her lap. Lips tightened and a deep breath was slowly inhaled. It was difficult believing what he had written. Sitting there with her hands clinched she began to give her favorite professor a verbal scolding for what he had proposed.

"How dare he exclude me from that demonstration," she whispered. "I am just as much a part of this class as any man sitting there. How dare he!"

Elizabeth remained seated for several long minutes attempting to generate needed calm and not let the emotions of the moment dictate her thinking. Rising slowly off the bench she headed for the massive doors to merge with the brisk winter air, refreshing the mind, giving the whole matter further thought. With her hands jammed deeply into her coat pockets, her hair cuffed gently by the breeze, she let words flow in and out of her mind as a response formed. She began composing a reply she would write that evening establishing what she believed were her rights to participate fully in the same offerings provided to all the other male students at Geneva. Exclusion was unacceptable.

Elizabeth suffered through a restless sleep that night. Her mind played out a multitude of scenarios envisioning James Webster's reaction to what she had written. Was her wording strong enough? Would he understand the inferences she had included? Was this the proper method of demanding her rights?

On arriving at the medical building the next morning she went directly to Doctor Webster's office. And while his door was open he was not there, a stroke of good fortune. She was hoping not to see the man thus keeping the impact of the note unspoiled. Dropping the small envelope on his desk she hurried from the room and moved quickly to her first lecture.

It was approaching eleven o'clock when Elizabeth was handed a note while attending a lecture summoning her to Doctor Webster's office after the class had concluded.

Standing in his office doorway apparently waiting for her Webster appeared nervous. Watching her approach he stepped forward greeting her with a sheepish grin.

"You have thrust a commendable sword into my apparent pompous..." he caught himself from becoming vulgar. "Self," he continued.

114

"Please step inside, Elizabeth and let us discuss your note."

"I am pleased you read it, Doctor."

"Not only read it but I have digested it many times over. It is beautifully written and your points of debate are most elegant and have put me to shame for not recognizing the issues and positions you have raised. I feel I've acted irresponsibly in requesting you be absent during a demonstration. I see now where I was wrong and I believe your fellow students will feel the same. I would like your permission to read your note to the students at this afternoon's lecture to receive their acclamation, which I am certain it will be."

She hesitated then answered. "Of course, Doctor Webster, I have no objection."

"Good. I believe it best that you wait in the anteroom while I read it to the group and in that way you would not be subjected to any undue attention."

"If you think that's best, sir."

"Yes, I do, for everyone's sake."

"Then," she said rising out of her chair, "I shall see you at the lecture."

"Fine. By the way, Elizabeth, the day after tomorrow is the scheduled dissection of the male reproductive organs. I thought you would want to prepare yourself."

Elizabeth smiled. "Doctor I need no preparation. I know what I will be viewing."

His face flushed. "Yes, yes, of course, a fact you carefully spelled out in your note. I must learn to accept you as a bona fide student of medicine sans gender."

"Thank you again, sir," she said moving quickly to leave the office.

Impatience was not one of Elizabeth's character flaws. However, under the circumstances she now stood in a most impatient manner: hands folded, then unfolded, short steps in both directions, a toss of her head to shake away the restlessness.

"Why are you waiting out here, Elizabeth?"

Startled on hearing a voice she turned to see Stephen Smith standing off to the side. Taking a few seconds to catch her breath she told him, "Doctor Webster requested it."

"Why?"

"He's going to read a note of mine."

"A note?"

"Yes, an affirmation regarding my participation in his Anatomy class."

"But," Smith said, "you already have been participating. "Why an affirmation?"

"It has to do with me being a woman."

"Oh?"

"Doctor Webster feels there are certain lectures and dissections at which I should not be present."

'Oh, yes, of course...the reproductive systems, right?"

"As if that was a mystery." Elizabeth was beginning to tire of his questioning.

"And therefore he's going to read a note you wrote protesting his decision?"

"No, I didn't protest. I simply explained why I should not be excluded."

"Well, I'll be most interested in hearing what you have to say."

"Then you'd best be getting in there, Stephen. I see Doctor Webster entering."

Inside the large chamber James Webster prepared himself for the task facing him. He was neither anxious nor eager but rather resolute that he would carry out this self-imposed assignment with proper aplomb knowing the consequences of faltering and making the situation worse for both Elizabeth and him.

"Gentlemen, as you know, Wednesday we will begin our study and the dissection of the male reproductive organs closely examining the reproductive system. After giving this much thought I initially felt that it would not be proper for Miss Blackwell to be present during these sessions. I had written her requesting that she absent herself from those proceedings, as you know it would cause great conflict with both social and religious morals and ethics thus embarrassing the school. I told her that by having her present during that session it would bring about an injustice to the class by the

117

unsatisfactory manner in which I would feel required to demonstrate. I did offer Miss Blackwell an ample opportunity for a private study."

He paused and took a drink of water empting half the glass. Patting his mouth with his handkerchief he then picked up a sheet of paper and stared at it for several seconds.

"Miss Blackwell," he continued, "addressed my request with a response in writing, which I shall now read. When concluded I will ask for a group decision." He cleared his throat, looked up and smiled. "Dear Doctor Webster. I have carefully reviewed your written correspondence to me in which you respectfully requested that I absent myself from certain lectures and dissections, primarily the study of the male and female reproductive systems. And while I can certainly appreciate the large degree of embarrassment it would cause you and perhaps the class, I believe that such embarrassment can only result from the approach and attitude that you and the others might adopt. If the matter is viewed as one from impure and unchaste sentiments then, yes, one could find my presence embarrassing. However, I cannot envision a man of medicine whose mind was not so lifted by the study of Anatomy that such sentiments would have an influence over him. Of a practical nature, if you, dear sir, would be so embarrassed by me being there during these sessions then I would be more than happy to abandon my seat in the first tier and remove myself to the very last tier thus with your sincere interest in the subject you would be allowed to proceed and be totally unaware of the presence of student number 130 in the gathering. I respectfully request that you rescind your desire for me to absent myself from these proceedings and allow me to take my rightful place among my fellow classmates. Gratefully yours: Elizabeth Blackwell."

The room grew silent as Webster placed the note on his desk. Then looking up he addressed the class once again. "I have been justly rebuked for the position I had taken and I now believe that a woman so animated by such views of her profession as Miss Blackwell that truly she deserves to receive every possible encouragement the class and faculty could give her."

Satisfied he had made his point he walked to the door and signaled for Elizabeth to enter. No sooner had she stepped into the room than everyone in that assembly immediately rose giving a thundering ovation the likes of which Elizabeth had never heard. The sound of the overwhelming affirmation ran through every nerve and tissue of her body and she could feel herself shaking from the immense joy and excitement she felt. Tears formed and quickly she shook her head to rid herself of the tell-tale emotions.

Another test of an archaic system was weathered by Elizabeth; another affirmation of the rightful role of women in medicine. It was not perceived as a victory but rather the widening of the pathway so that others could eventually follow.

That evening Elizabeth slept well.

Chapter Ten

March, 1848
Philadelphia Pennsylvania

Human waste and vomit and the smell of rotting flesh and unclean bodies made it practically impossible to escape the foul conditions so common in a place such as Blockley.

The drab walls most certainly spoke of the somber profile of the building. The room was bare of any decorations; not a framed still life or painting of a landscape anywhere. Nothing. Even the drapes on the one tall, narrow window were colorless, institutional grey. The single worn wooden desk, a rather uncomfortable looking swivel chair behind the desk, a tall corner file cabinet and the lone visitor chair was all that adorned the room. The wooden floor was bare and showing extreme wear. It could have done with a bit of sweeping not to mention the odor of the place was most unpleasant.

Elizabeth observed all of this as she sat waiting for Walter Glipin to return to his office. The first term at Geneva had come to an end and continuing education in a hospital setting was now the requirement for the next seven months. Her presence in that cramped room came about after a week of effort trying to secure a position with one of the major hospitals had concluded in absolute frustration. Harsh rejection had not evaporated despite the fact she was now a student of medicine. Consequently, Elizabeth had only one remaining contact, one secured by Joseph Warrington, a hospital that would provide experience, but perhaps not in the ways she had envisioned. Now, for Elizabeth, desperation had become a strange and cherished mentor.

The Blockley Almshouse in Philadelphia was an immense facility serving the poor and indigent. It had a horrible reputation. As a charity institution the patients were more like inmates doomed to live a life in filth and desolation. Hospital personnel had to endure the daily exposure to the wretched odors that permeated every corner. Human waste and vomit and the smell of rotting flesh and unclean bodies made it practically impossible to escape the foul conditions so common in a place such as Blockley.

"Ah, here it is," Glipin said moving hurriedly through the door. "It had been moved from my files to the outside office." Taking his seat behind the desk he tossed open the file. "Now, let's see. Geneva Medical School began fourteen years ago in 1834." He looked up at Elizabeth. "Not all that old." He continued reading from the file. "Well, this is good. It has an excellent rating."

"Yes," Elizabeth concurred. "The faculty is outstanding, maintaining a high level of instruction."

He closed the folder and leaned back in his chair. "We've never had a student from Geneva intern here."

"I believe you are correct," she said. "Most of those with whom I spoke are being accepted at the private hospitals."

"Yes," he mused, "of course they would be. And you, Miss Blackwell, why have you selected Blockley?"

She was expecting the question -- had prepared an answer, but it was certainly not that Blockley was her last desperate hope. Accordingly she answered him with what she thought he would want to hear or perhaps needed to hear. "I assumed Blockley offered more opportunities to learn about a variety of ailments and infirmities, something the other hospitals could not provide."

He laughed. "I see, meaning, you would be learning how the dregs of society were treated on the meager budgets our city government provides."

"Not in the least, Mr. Glipin," she responded. "I'm most empathetic with the plight and conditions of the poor. By observing their health problems and troubles first hand I'll receive a far greater range of education for treating the human body and spirit, especially the spirit, than my contemporaries will be getting in their respective hospitals."

Walter Glipin was unprepared for what he heard and could only stare at Elizabeth with curious eyes. Then squinting as if to defuse the appearance of confusion he practically whispered, "I see." It was the only response he was able to give. A moment later he added, "Yes, indeed you would receive such an education." Sitting up straight in his chair he shifted his body and shoved the file folder aside. After rereading the letter of introduction Elizabeth had provided he told her, "Blockley is controlled by politics Miss Blackwell, as you might imagine, being a government entity. If I were to bring your petition before the board it will surely be denied by the opposition parties simply because I, a Whig, had brought it forth. Therefore if you wish to be admitted here under the category of staff you will need to convince those of the opposite parties of the worthiness of your credentials."

His comment stunned Elizabeth. He was raising the issue of politics a matter quite foreign to her. Was she expected to become involved in the sordid practices of demagoguery in order to observe hospital operations? Nothing in her background trained her for something such as this. But then if she was capable of challenging the system perhaps politics in this instance was similar.

Desperation eventually intervened. Quickly reshaping her line of reasoning, logic began to dominate. Blockley was her final hope to acquire the continuing education she so vitally needed and therefore if it required the efforts of political persuasion to achieve that end then certainly she could muster up both the courage and skills required to carry it out. A faint smile formed on her face and she nodded. "May I have their names and where I might contact them so I may personally make my petition," she said without a waver in her voice.

It would take another 2 weeks before Elizabeth was accepted into Blockley. Having convinced the governing board of her worthiness, a start date was established and from that moment on she was to be confined to that disreputable facility for the next seven months

Now she stood in the office of the hospital's Matron, Martha Alexander, preparing herself to be introduced to the surroundings to which she would invest her time.

The voice had a stern tone to it. Martha Alexander did not possess a delicate personality but rather brimmed with a robust energy: loud, domineering and at times crass. She was the picture-perfect image of a head matron of a charity hospital: a rather large-framed woman, starched white cap, white stiff uniform, black high-button shoes and a blue and white striped apron. To say she dressed to fit the role would be an understatement. If one were to judge her from a simple, first-opinion stance the woman would come across as someone to fear, as someone who could easily intimidate even the most grisly of bears. But upon deeper examination, the soft doe-like eyes would dispel that first opinion until she opened her mouth to bark out an order or to discipline one of the workers. "We've never had the likes of you here before, Miss."

"Yes, so I've been told," said Elizabeth keeping her voice in a subordinate tone.

"And you're going to be a doctor?" The question had an incredulous lift to it.

"Yes, next January."

The starched Matron scoffed. "Nothing's normal these days." She moved to her desk and lifted up several sheets of papers. "So, let's see where the hospital wants to put you." She mulled over the papers for several seconds then looked up; a slight hint of a smile had formed. "Third floor."

"Third floor?"

"The syphilitic ward."

Elizabeth felt her breath give way as she took in two heavy gulps of air. "I assume you mean the ward with the patients with syphilis."

"Yes, all women. A private large room has been set up for your residence there."

"All women? Does that mean that is to be the only area for my observations while I am here?"

"I can't answer that," Alexander said moving away from the desk. "Shall we go see your new accommodations? We'll bring up your trunk later."

There was a natural hesitance, almost reluctance. Then realizing what appearance she might be giving she straightened her back and smiled. "That would be fine," she said.

"The stairs are this way," Alexander said pointing. "I assume you're healthy enough to ascend three flights without dawdling."

"Quite."

The two moved down the hall toward the staircase. As they began their climb to the third floor, Alexander outlined what Elizabeth could expect. "The third floor is the most boisterous area in the hospital. Most of these women have gone slightly insane with the disease and while harmless they nonetheless do display odd behavior at times and may seem to be a threat but they are not."

"The insanity you speak of," said Elizabeth, "is not true insanity is it? Or is it more the effects of neurosyphilis?"

Martha Alexander turned to look at Elizabeth. "You can be the judge when you see these women. I say insanity because they act like the inmates of our asylum. But the medical term is as you suspect. Our hospital director, Doctor Benedict, can most likely tell you more of their condition."

As they moved to the final landing of the stairs Elizabeth was told, "Of the forty women in the ward I would say about ten of them are somewhat well behaved. It's the rest that give us the most trouble. They are lewd and at times uncontrollable. Their behavior is disgusting and their mouths filthy. That, perhaps, is the reason why they are here at Blockley."

"Does anyone try to rehabilitate them?"

Alexander laughed. "Miss, this is an almshouse, the last refuge of the poor. It's a charity hospital not a holiday retreat. There is no rehabilitation attempted here. We're lucky if we can just placate these people. You're dealing with the scum of society, the lowest of the low, the wretched and downtrodden. These people are halfway to death's door by the time we see them."

"So no one tries to work with these women?"

The impertinent smile on the Matron's face gave Elizabeth the answer to what must have appeared to be an innocence unbecoming of a charity institution. "You've been captured too long in those hallowed halls of academia my dear. If you last out your seven months here you'll find the answer to that question."

It was not appropriate to dispute the Matron's attitude about the patients. It was not the time to engage in any discussion regarding the word charity or in the Latin sense, *caritas*, meaning love. Instead it was simply the time to gain critical knowledge of medicine's failures in the real world.

Dearest Mother,

You jest, of course, in suggesting that I seek rest and the avoidance of any further occasions wherein my nerves are stretched to their limits. That is impossible in this place. Blockley Almshouse is not the institution in which peace and serenity abound. In fact they are conspicuously absent along with all normal functions usually found in a regular hospital.

I am still in shock from the incident of which I spoke in my last letter. I cannot shed the horrible image of that dangling ripped bed sheet hanging from the third floor window. My heart races with every recall of that moment.

As I had explained, this miserable victim of syphilis, her body saturated with those ugly skin ulcerations and that horrible rash, screaming vulgar epithets as she clung to that old soiled bed sheet, kept demanding to be left alone, to allow her to continue her escape. Regrettably her insanity prevented her from recognizing what a horrible mistake she had made in tying only two sheets together in order to lower herself some forty feet to the ground. She had also misjudged the condition of those old worn and soiled sheets, some quite threadbare and capable of ripping with the slightest tug.

Why none of the other women in that syphilitic ward tried to stop her from tying those sheets to the window frame and climbing out I'll never know. I learned later that several of her fellow patients mocked her, perhaps in their own crude way of trying to talk her out of her foolish attempt. Certainly any number of them together could have prevented her from her folly. Yet they just stood there, so I was told, perhaps calculating, watching as if one less of them might provide more for the others. I don't know the answer to that puzzle and it saddens me.

When I had arrived after hearing the screams I tried my best to persuade her to return to the room. Yet, she was determined to escape the hospital claiming her life would be better off back on the streets of Philadelphia. Her rationale was similar to so many others here at Blockley. Their street life, so they claim, was much better than the restraints and deprivation and crude treatments they had to endure here. Pathetic as that might be, I often find myself agreeing with them and yet I can do nothing, for I am not a true part of the facility but only here as a student to observe.

When the bed sheets finally ripped, as they were certainly destined to do, and the poor soul fell to her death, it was as if I had made the same plunge. As I looked down at the horrible sight I could see her head was twisted sideways, folded in a contortioned manner and her limbs twisted

130

*in gruesome ways. Blood covered the green grass
compounding the ghastly vision of an attempt to
live gone pitifully wrong. Pain stabbed at my
stomach and I could not prevent retching up its
full contents. I became faint and needed to seek
refuge from the horror of it all. I still find it
difficult sleeping a full night. I doubt if I ever
will. Such is the reward for having been assigned
to Blockley.*

*I am sorry, Mother, for continuing to
dredge up these many travails of mine. I do
appreciate your understanding and tolerance and
I should accept your advice to simply concentrate
only on the mission. What is is and cannot be
changed therefore let it be buried.*

*Please continue to stay in touch. I need
your reassurance and excellent advice. I cherish
each piece of communication which I receive from
you.*

*Your loving daughter,
Elizabeth*

The talks Elizabeth had with Matron Alexander
provided insight not possible through ordinary
observations. When time and circumstances
allowed, Elizabeth would visit the Matron's large
room located in the central section of the
sprawling hospital. There she would often find
Alexander comfortably situated in an ornate
armchair her feet propped up on a velvet
footstool, a pad of paper in her lap on which was
written the staff's duties and chores for the day.

Catching her alone was practically impossible since the staff members were required to come to her room to receive their orders and often they would be required to make more than one trip. Elizabeth always marveled at the endurance of the hospital staff, for they had to suffer the Matron's demanding nature when issuing the various tasks. But the tasks always were done and always in a timely fashion.

One late afternoon Elizabeth peered around the open door to see if Alexander was busy and found her to be alone. Elizabeth wanted to discuss a matter of protocol, the proper method for disciplining a rowdy patient.

"Matron," she called out.

Alexander's head jerked up as if she had fallen asleep. "Miss Blackwell," she said clearing her throat. "Yes, what can I do for you?"

"Do you have a few moments?

"Yes, I'm not busy right now. Come in, take a chair."

As Elizabeth moved into the room she was not certain just how she was going to approach the subject, for Martha Alexander was not above harsh treatment of the patients. But Elizabeth felt the episode she had witnessed was beyond the usual disciplinary practices of the hospital.

"I wanted to know the hospital's policy for disciplining a patient."

Alexander smiled broadly then grunted out a slight chuckle. "Policy? There is no policy."

"Nothing written regarding ethics?"

132

That question elicited even a louder grunt and a longer chuckle. "Ethics?" she asked. "Miss Blackwell this is not the new Saint Joseph's Hospital. We're running a charity here, a place where the slop of this city gets discarded; wretched paupers who have had no proper upbringing and have never followed any rules. With an ugly horde like that you don't have ethics."

The comment surprised Elizabeth. Nowhere in the tone of voice or the words chosen were there any feelings for the people themselves, a commentary on how the hospital staff viewed those who had come to the almshouse to receive needed help. "Surely you're not suggesting that anything is appropriate in disciplining these people?"

"No, I'm not suggesting that. I'm saying that each situation is unique and there can't be any protocol or standard procedures. It's up to the staff to deal with the problems in the best and most expedient method possible. We don't have time or sufficient staff to be gentle with these people. You take appropriate action and no one asks any questions. Why do you ask?"

Elizabeth shook her head. "I suppose it would be futile mentioning an incident that bothers me."

"Yes, it would be," came the frank and stern reply. "No matter what you saw, Miss Blackwell, it's not the first time nor will it be the last. I'm surprised you have just now witnessed our disciplinary methods."

"Oh, I have been aware all along, but the other incidences were not as severe as this action."

"Is that a fact? So what was it?"

"The poor woman was being kicked and cursed. I tried to intervene but was told to leave, and told in no polite manner I might add."

Martha Alexander stared at Elizabeth. "Welcome to the reality of Blockley," she said in a cold steely voice.

"But surely there are better ways of handling difficult people."

"I don't think you're grasping what I am saying, Miss Blackwell. These people are unmanageable. They would rather die on the streets than die here."

"Yes, I've seen their desperation."

"The sheet lady?"

"Yes." Elizabeth paused wondering if she should continue the conversation. Then asked, "why does the city even bother running an institution like this if the patients don't want to be here?"

"Because politicians can't let people die on the streets. Too much public outcry. So they bring them here and we're supposed to heal these half-dead laggards and when we don't the politicians clamor and accuse us of all sorts of ills."

"But the city officials condone the beatings?"

"Those are very rare...and I know about the incident you're mentioning. Rest assured appropriate action has been taken against the orderly responsible."

"So the hospital doesn't condone that kind of behavior."

"Not if it isn't warranted. In that case it wasn't," she said, paused, fixed her eyes on Elizabeth once again and added, "in most cases it isn't."

The room grew silent. Elizabeth studied the woman sitting opposite her. "How do you live with this job?"

"I do it the same way you're living with your problems, Miss Blackwell. It's not the best situation but it is the situation I'm in and I have no choice. I don't have to stay here and some days I want to walk out and never come back. But believe it or not I wouldn't know where to go or what to do. I've been here too long and have grown entirely too hard and probably wouldn't fit in anywhere else."

"So you're saying you don't have a choice?"

"Just like the paupers that come here."

Before Elizabeth could pose another question they were interrupted by a nurse knocking on the door. "Matron Alexander, are you busy?"

"What's it look like?" she barked out. "What do you want?"

"I can come back."

"Then do that."

Elizabeth interceded. "I can leave now, Miss Alexander. I believe you've answered my question."

"Questions, Miss Blackwell" she corrected. "You had more than one question. Did you get all the answers?"

"I did, thank you."

"Fine. You come back and we can talk some more."

"Yes, I'll do that," Elizabeth told her and stood to leave.

But Elizabeth left the room doubting she would ever come again seeking answers. The substance of Martha Alexander's beliefs lacked, so it seemed, any empathy toward the poor. There was a hardness that repulsed Elizabeth, distancing the two women. To Elizabeth, Martha Alexander displayed a type of loathing so uncharitable that, as far as she was concerned, disqualified her to be associated with the care and treatment of those unfortunates in that hospital. But perhaps it was good that Elizabeth did have the conversations with the Matron. The talks opened Elizabeth's eyes and mind to the many realities which she had not seen before. The education she was receiving at the hospital was proving to be more than medical; the true essence of a deprecating approach to life was being exposed to her as well.

Chapter Eleven

July, 1848
Philadelphia, Pennsylvania

Elizabeth's heart pounded. Certainly the mother was deceased and the young girl was rushing into an unprepared confrontation with death, destroying the optimism Elizabeth now knew she had falsely instilled.

Water droplets clung to the old rust-stained gutters of Blockley like their frozen counterparts had in the winter. The poor souls confined inside tried not to hide their perspiration-soaked shirts and blouses. It was useless. Many patients simply shed their gowns and preferred nakedness to the sweltering heat. No one seemed to care.

The weather had become unbearable in the summer of 1848. Temperatures were in the mid nineties and the humidity had been hovering around eighty five percent for days as the oppressive heat consumed everyone. What Blockley did not need now was more problems and aggravation. Yet it was unavoidable.

That summer Blockley Almshouse became snarled in a condition that originated some three thousand miles away. The devastating potato famine in Ireland had all but destroyed that country. Many of its citizens were dying. Those who were fortunate enough to escape emigrated to the United States bringing with them diseases caused by the fever that gripped their nation. With Blockley being one of the larger charity hospitals in the country, it was chosen to receive the bulk of these ailing transplants. Most of them suffered from Typhus, a disease transmitted by lice and pests that were onboard the filthy ships that brought the emigrants to the United States. The sickness was marked by high fever and delirium along with painful headaches and an agonizing rash. It often ended in death. And now Blockley had the challenge of caring for them.

The Hospital was already filled to capacity. There was no additional space in which to house these new arrivals. To the medical staff it was impossible to fathom the depth of this new influx of horror. Yet for Elizabeth Blackwell the situation was to be a front line observation post. She would become a privileged witness in a real-life laboratory.

Within weeks the foreign horde began arriving. Wagon after wagon transported the infirmed to the doors of the hospital and stretcher upon stretcher brought them to any open space. Some of the lucky ones were issued mattresses or pads of some type. The vast majority, however, were provided only dirty blankets on the floor.

As the wards began filling the grumbling of the regular patients picked up, fearful of the rumors of a devastating disease invading the hospital. Some of the regulars loathed the Irish while others felt the stench of the dirty travelers would bring about a new kind of sickness. Not one patient, though, complained of over crowding except to say there was no room for them to move about. Ambulation, surprisingly, was not an overt concern.

But it was treacherous attempting to maneuver in those crowded quarters. After a bit, the patients who could move simply upped and left despite having no permission to do so because the suffering of those on the floor became unbearable. In some cases bedlam would erupt between the indigents and the Irish only to be quelled by weary orderlies whose tolerance was thinning and whose tempers grew dangerously short.

Several weeks after the foreign patients had arrived Elizabeth was drawn into the tragedy of it all, a situation that would strain her emotionally. It began as a normal morning. The sky was filled with bright sunshine and a soft northerly breeze rendered the day slightly cooler than during the past several days. It was a day that beckoned Elizabeth to seek time in the large courtyard where she would often observe the patients who were allowed free time in that area. As she stood under one of the few trees in the large yard a soft voice interrupted her thoughts.

"You work here?"

Elizabeth turned to see a young pitiful child, perhaps thirteen years of age. Her clothes were covered in the soil of the city and in need of repair. She spoke with a definite Irish accent but the English was surprisingly good. Elizabeth stared at the doleful figure in front of her. "No," she answered. "I'm a student learning about medicine. Why?"

"My mother is dying. I want to find someone who can help her," the young girl said her voice drained of any emotion.

"Is your mother here at the hospital?" Elizabeth asked turning to face the child.

"Yes."

"And you, are you sick with the fever too?"

"No, I came to see my mother."

"Are you living with relatives here in Philadelphia?"

"No," was the only answer. She started to leave.

"Wait," Elizabeth told her. "Where are you going?"

"To finds someone who can help my mother."

Elizabeth knew about Typhus having spent much time reading about it ever since the Irish were brought in. She could help. After all she was as well versed in the disease, as were many of the young interns. What Elizabeth knew of the illness it was very likely the child's mother was beyond help. Undoubtedly her condition had already been diagnosed and treatment started. Yet the young face of struggling hope stirred a strong feeling of compassion in Elizabeth and she nodded. "Take me to your mother."

With renewed enthusiasm the girl bolted toward the main building. But Elizabeth now found herself hesitating; reality trumping the compassion of just moments before. The conflict in which she had allowed herself to become entrapped could very well jeopardize her involvement with the hospital. But at that moment Elizabeth concluded that nothing was sacred at Blockley and violations of rules, ethics and morals were committed daily. What harm, then, would one more do to the system?

Meeting up with the girl at the door to the building Elizabeth asked, "Where is your mother?" The commitment had now been made.

A shaking finger pointed to the second floor windows. "Up there," she said quickly opening the door and standing aside to let Elizabeth pass.

"And what is your name?"

"They call me Molly."

With the echoes of their quickened steps filling the corridor, the two moved toward the stairs. Elizabeth knew she couldn't help the child's mother if death had already visited yet she continued moving forward. Waiting at the top, Molly pointed in the direction of her mother's location and then pleaded for Elizabeth to hurry. Losing sight of the child Elizabeth continued her climb knowing approximately where the mother might be. It was a ward for the critically ill. Concerned she might have given Molly false hope, Elizabeth began searching the hall for a resident physician yet no medical personnel could be seen. The pressure to abandon her unwise decision now prompted her to slow the pace.

"Hurry, hurry," she heard Molly's voice call.

Looking ahead Elizabeth spotted the girl standing in front of the area where those who were near death were housed. Elizabeth's heart pounded. Certainly the mother was deceased and the young girl was rushing into an unprepared confrontation with death, destroying the optimism Elizabeth now knew she had falsely instilled.

Approaching the area, Elizabeth was jolted upon hearing a piercing scream coming from the room. The voice was definitely that of Molly. Rushing in she saw a delirious Molly screaming and crying hysterically, standing over a sheet-draped body the corner of which had been pulled back to reveal the cold stare of yet another victim of the Typhus.

"Molly," Elizabeth said hurrying to the girl's side. "Molly, I'm so sorry."

The child turned to glare at Elizabeth, anger filled her face. Sobbing she screamed, "You killed her. You didn't hurry...you didn't run. You killed her."

"Molly, Molly" Elizabeth called. "You've got to stop this...stop it now."

Uncontrollable sobbing echoed in the vast death-filled room as the young girl was pulled away from the corpse of her mother. Struggling to free herself from Elizabeth's grip Molly turned and stared at Elizabeth. Then slowly the struggling stopped and young hands reached out to draw Elizabeth closer. Within seconds Molly's arms were tightly wrapped around Elizabeth's body as the hysterical crying slowed.

"What's going on here?"

Elizabeth turned to see an orderly heading in their direction. "It's all right now," Elizabeth answered. "Everything's under control."

"We heard screaming."

"Yes, this young girl's mother has died. She found her on the floor covered with a sheet. It was a horrible shock."

Dropping down on one knee next to the body he pulled the sheet further away. Elizabeth grimaced at the contorted expression on the face as if the poor woman had to die alone with no one there to ease her pain. The orderly felt the neck then glanced up at Elizabeth. "Body's quite cold. Must have been dead for about an hour or so." Elizabeth could feel Molly tighten her arms as she buried her face deeper into Elizabeth's chest.

"Then why wasn't she removed from here?' Elizabeth asked, an irritated tone to her voice. "Someone covered her. Why didn't they take her away?"

Moving his lumbering body up the orderly stared at Elizabeth. "We don't have time for that. We'll get around to it when we can. There's too many of these Micks dying here so we haul them out when we get to it. This is none of your business anyway."

"For the love of God, man," Elizabeth yelled. "Watch your mouth. This poor young child has just lost her mother. Where's your decency?"

The man laughed. "Decency in this place? If you find it you can bring it to me." He turned and headed for the door. Looking back he added, "And you better get that filthy waif out of here or you both will get into trouble."

Elizabeth's eyes glared pure anger at the man then watched with disgust as he hurried from the room. "Molly, we have to go now, okay?" Elizabeth said gradually pulling herself away from the girl. "There's no need for you to get into any trouble."

After several long moments the girl's arms relaxed and began to loosen their grip around Elizabeth. Then with swollen red eyes

Molly glanced up at Elizabeth, blinked twice to clear remaining tears and before Elizabeth could realize what was happening her temporary ward had darted for the door and disappeared.

"Molly, wait, please wait, where are you going?" Elizabeth's plea went unanswered as she moved quickly into the hall. "Molly wait." But her shouts were too late. Molly Flynn, age thirteen, a native of Dublin, Ireland, now orphaned and destitute was gone, merged into the ruthless underbelly of Philadelphia's sordid population.

Elizabeth could only stare after her. Her vision now blurred by all the suffering masses lying there, some writhing with pain, other cursing their God for the unjust punishment being inflicted upon them. It was a shocking sight although not new. However, in this context it was representative of all that had gone wrong with society and what was wrong with Blockley.

Moving away and descending the stairs Elizabeth felt relief knowing she had but two months left of her assignment. Yet despite all efforts to divorce herself from the seven month experience, Blockley would forever be embedded in her soul.

Chapter Twelve

October, 1848
Geneva, New York

For a brief moment Elizabeth wanted to scream out in pure ecstasy. The very quintessence of her pursuit to be a physician was sitting there in that chair terrified by the very system that was supposed to help her.

The return to Geneva had a poetic twist to it. It wasn't exactly a reunion with what was familiar but rather a sense of freedom. Geneva took on the profile of the rescuer; no longer the formidable fortress as first perceived but more like an Eden of sheer sanity and intelligence. Blockley had provoked that transformation. From the day Elizabeth stepped away from the Philadelphia Almshouse everything evolved into a secure sense of well being. And yet at times she would wake in early morning with a feeling of trepidation wondering if she was still adrift in a sea of ignorance.

147

It was early October when she arrived back at Geneva. The welcome was unusual. Two weeks after classes began the beauty of fall had suddenly evaporated. An early, unexpected snowfall had hit the northeast part of the country. While the town slept the blizzard left its mark then moved rapidly along. Upon awakening, residents had the feeling they had slept through several weeks of autumn and into mid winter.

Indeed it was a deep snow. Elizabeth, as with all the others, was very much mystified as to how a storm could be so quiet and yet deposit an over abundance of snow. Could it be she slept so soundly, that nothing would have disturbed her, a feat impossible at Blockley? Or, as she gazed out her window, was she witnessing a true anomaly of nature. Regardless, the issue of snow was beside the point. Her studies had resumed, several were quite challenging, and it was these new ventures that dominated her attention.

The path she selected to the college was packed with snow but in some rare sections the walkway had been cleared. Her travel required caution nonetheless, for the snow had turned to ice in several spots and with the cinders yet to be spread the conditions remained perilous.

Once inside, the comfort of the large medical building erased all the misery of the outdoors. With her coat hung on the hook in the cloak room and the rubber shoe coverings stowed, she retrieved the lecture notebook from her satchel and moved out into the hall. She was looking forward to an ordinary day, one that would be refreshing in the knowledge she would gain. Unfortunately, at the Geneva School of Medicine not all things were consistently ordinary or routine.

"Elizabeth."

"Oh, good morning, Anthony."

"Good morning. Doctor Webster wants to see you."

"See me? For what reason?"

"He didn't say."

"Does he want to see me now?"

"I suppose. He just told me as he hurried out of his office to send you to him."

"Send? Where?"

"To his examining room at the school's clinic."

"The clinic? Where's that? I've never been there."

Anthony Karsmatten shrugged. "Don't know. I haven't been there myself."

"What's the room number?"

Again Anthony raised his shoulders, his hands held out in an empty gesture.

Elizabeth's mouth puckered in exasperation. Giving a faint smile she gathered up her notebook. "Thank you Anthony. I'll find him."

Ignoring strange looks, Elizabeth began searching along a long, seemingly endless corridor attempting to locate the entrance to the clinic. Eventually she succumbed to frustration and asked a passing custodian for directions. To her surprise she was standing beside the clinic door.

The clinic's interior struck Elizabeth as a remarkable maze of tributaries sprouting off the main corridor. Rooms lined each branch and at the end of the main passage there appeared to be a ward of some sort. To locate the vague Doctor Webster in this confusing pattern was impossible. Fortunately she spied an intern heading in her direction.

"Excuse me," she called out. "Doctor Webster, his room? Where may I find it?"

Waving his hand as if conducting an orchestra the young man continued moving down the corridor answering her, "Two doors down on the left, number 26B."

"26B, fine, I have it. Thank you."

Arriving at 26B she found it closed. "Doctor Webster," she inquired knocking gently.

"Yes."

"Elizabeth Blackwell, Doctor."

The door swung open. "Elizabeth, oh, thank heavens you're here. I need your help." Grabbing her arm in apparent desperation he pulled her into the room.

In the corner sat an elderly lady, perhaps in her early seventies. Her grey hair was tousled, shoulders hunched and her sad eyes showed obvious fright. Her mouth quivered. She was dressed in shabby clothes and one hand held a rosary.

"Elizabeth, this woman came to us complaining of severe pains in her abdomen. It could be a variety of afflictions, but she needs to be checked quite thoroughly, which will require examining her for any unusual swelling or pain. I've been trying to convince the woman she needs to undress so that I can examine her. But she refuses to do so. She speaks no English and I'm afraid my gestures have perhaps been quite inappropriate. I fear she is very frightened. I thought she might respond to a woman's examination."

For a brief moment Elizabeth wanted to scream out in pure ecstasy. The very quintessence of her pursuit to be a physician was sitting there in that chair terrified by the very system that was supposed to help her. The doctor's routine instruction to the patient was obviously a complete violation of all she held sacred and pure in both her religious beliefs and for her privacy. Unwittingly, Webster had effectively destroyed the great fallacy in the medical profession that the field of medicine was no place for a woman.

Stifling her feelings Elizabeth drew closer to the woman, realizing there was going to be a communications problem. She began with a smile as gentle as she could muster, then nodded and finally attempted to reach for the woman's hand. It was quickly withdrawn. Perhaps, Elizabeth thought, a soothing, compassionate tone to her voice might erase the fear even though the woman wouldn't understand.

"I'm here to help," she began, speaking in a slow, soft voice. "I," pointing to herself, "can help you," pointing to the woman. She repeated the smile, nodded and then waited. Old, tired eyes stared at Elizabeth but the quivering of the mouth had stopped. Elizabeth could see the woman's fingers rapidly thumbing through the beads of the rosary but no prayers were being recited, there was no movement of lips. Once again Elizabeth tried to take the woman's hand and this time succeeded. Holding it gently she stroked it, slowly, evenly, attempting to impart compassion. "It's going to be all right," she practically whispered and smiled again.

"Can you examine her," Webster asked.

Without looking at him and keeping her eyes on the woman's face she slowly shook her head back and forth to signify her answer.

"Then how are we going to treat this woman?"

Elizabeth released the woman's hand and turned to face Webster. "I've been in this medical school for just one semester, Doctor. I am basically a novice, in no position to conduct an examination of anyone. I do not know what I am searching for, what to feel or see or touch. It is neither prudent nor ethical for me to attempt such an examination."

Webster frowned then took in a deep breath. "All right then. There's nothing we can do for this woman."

"Nothing, Doctor? Is that your best answer to a problem like this?"

"Elizabeth, I'm not to be scolded because this woman does not trust a professional doctor to examine her. It's not that I refuse to do anything."

"I realize that, Doctor and I can empathize with your dilemma, but I am not in any position to do an examination and you know that."

The room went silent. The two stared at each other. Finally Webster spoke. "If I stood behind a screen and told you step by step what to do and you related to me what you see or feel or recognize as a problem do you believe you could do that?"

"That is very risky, Doctor. I am not trained to recognize malformed organs or swellings or even discolorations that might appear."

"Yes, I realize that, but if you don't conduct this examination with my guidance then we have to send this woman home without any treatment."

"You don't have to tell me the obvious, Doctor Webster. I realize what the choices are here. But I don't believe your option is a practical or moral one."

"And ignoring her is?"

Elizabeth glared at the man. His tactics angered her. James Webster was transferring the onus of this woman's condition directly on to her. He was abdicating his own responsibility and in turn creating a paradox for Elizabeth. No matter what she decided she would be wrong. "Doctor Watson," Elizabeth said in an agitated voice, "You make my decision most painful. You've trapped me into an impossible position. Whether I do or don't do as you request I'm doing wrong. You have not left me with a way out of this."

"Indeed," he said. "Well, then, welcome to the medical profession, Elizabeth Blackwell. Doctors must make decisions that deeply hurt at times or are not morally correct and we can stand a chance of being absolutely wrong. Medicine is not a perfect science. You are now learning that there comes a time when desperation requires determinate action. So do I get the screen or not?"

Puffing her cheeks out she nodded, "Get it." But it was a reluctant submission.

Within seconds Webster returned pulling behind him a white screen on a frame that sat on a wheel base so it could be moved about easily. The wheels squeaked as he positioned it to block the doorway. Then quickly he took up his stance behind it in the hall.

"Proceed," he told her. "Tell me everything you see as she disrobes, her movements, the color of the skin, any abnormal looking protrusions, the amount of fatty tissues gathered in any one place and anything else you might glean as an indication of the woman's problem."

"I'm not even sure, Doctor, I can get this woman to disrobe. She can still hear your voice and that, I'm sure, will be a deterrent. This is not going to work."

There was no immediate response. Then without any indication of what he was about to do a nearby sheet came flying over on top of the screen. "Here, have her put this on as she disrobes. You can then do most of the examination without revealing any part of her body."

"Then why have her disrobe in the first place?"

"You can't adequately feel or see or even smell with her clothes on. You need complete access and visualization to do the examination correctly."

Elizabeth turned to look at the woman. Taking in a deep breath she slowly exhaled, shaking her hands to help relieve the tension. Studying the old, craggily, weathered face she gave a reassuring smile. But before Elizabeth could attempt anything further the woman reached out and took Elizabeth's hand in hers. Elizabeth felt she had seen a slight smile being returned by the old lady. It was going well, but how to get her to disrobe?

Speaking as casual and unobtrusive as possible she told Watson, "I'm going to try to get her ready now, Doctor. Do not reply, and when you begin giving me instructions do so in a very soft voice."

Elizabeth motioned for the woman to stand, lifting her hands as if pulling the woman from the chair. The troubled eyes blinked several times; then to Elizabeth's surprise the woman mumbled, soft stumbling sounds. Amazed at what she had heard Elizabeth tried to repeat the words and as she did they sounded French. That, of course, would be logical being that Geneva was relatively close to the Canadian border. Having studied French, Elizabeth felt she could communicate in the language well enough to be understood if indeed the woman was French. She decided to investigate.

"Parlez vous français?"

The old lady's eyes widened and the smile deepened. She nodded enthusiastically. "Oui!"

"Très bon," Elizabeth answered and broke out into a large smile of relief. They had a common language. Elizabeth considered it a small miracle. "Je vais vous aider," she told the woman then spoke to Doctor Webster. "We have a major break through, Doctor. The woman speaks French."

"So I..."

"Shhhh," she quickly responded. "No talking unless absolutely needed."

Gesturing and speaking her basic French, Elizabeth told the woman she would have to disrobe in order for her to make a proper examination. She waited then took both of the woman's hands to assist her in standing. "Vous aurez besoin de vous tenir debout," she instructed pulling slightly on the hands that by now were gripping Elizabeth's hands even more tightly.

Elizabeth kept her eyes on the old woman and with careful movements she started to rise from the chair. Then in a sudden burst of screaming the woman's face cringe in agonizing pain, and her body began shaking.

"What was that?" Webster yelled out.

"I'm trying to get her to stand and obviously it causes her great pain. She's now shaking and crying as she stands before me. I don't think I'm going to be able to examine her."

"I want you to place your hand over the location of the appendix and push rather hard."

"Do you suspect appendicitis?"

"Push and let's find out. Warn her about what you're going to do."

Elizabeth smiled once again and speaking in a subdued tone she told the woman, "Je vais persévérer votre corps et il peut faire mal mais nous devons apprendre qu'est-ce qui ne va pas."

"What did you tell her?"

"That I was going to push on her body and that it may hurt but that we need to find out what is wrong."

"And?"

"And what?"

"Did she recoil or shake her head or want to sit down?"

"No, she's just staring at me and holding my hands very tightly and crying."

"Then free your left hand and do the examination."

"She won't let loose."

"Tell her you need that hand to check her pain."

"J'ai besoin de cette main pour vous vérifier, madame."

"And," Webster wanted to know.

"I'm trying. She is slowly loosening her grip. All right, my hand is free."

"You know, of course, where the vermiform appendix is located?"

"Yes, Doctor."

"Then press."

Elizabeth looked directly into the woman's eyes and moved her hand slowly down to where she was to press and inched closer to the woman's body. "Je vais appuyer sur votre corps maintenant et il pourrait blesser mais nous devons le faire."

The woman's face winced and she closed her eyes. Elizabeth placed her hand over the appendix and with a deep breath pushed.

The woman's scream was heard throughout the clinic as she reeled backwards collapsing in the chair clutching the area of her pain, her head swinging back an forth. Tears spilled down her cheeks.

"Arrêtez, arrêtez, il est trop douloureux," she cried, screeching out the words.

"What'd she say," asked Webster.

"She asked that we stop the pain to please stop the pain."

"Acute appendicitis," he answered. "It has to come out."

"You're not going to be able to administer ether to her let alone get her on a gurney to be wheeled into the operating room."

"She came in here didn't she so she must want us to help her."

"But now she's in extreme pain and she's frightened."

"Tell her what needs to be done."

Elizabeth lowered her body until she was face to face with the woman and then reached for the hands once again. "Nous avons besoin de l'appendicite et vous aurez besoin d'être mis en sommeil en premier. Nous devons le faire maintenant."

"Non, non, non," the woman screamed shaking her head again.

"We have no choice. You have to administer the ether to her in there so we can get her into the operating room," Webster told her.

"But, Doctor..."

"Or she will die, Elizabeth. Do you understand? Or she will die. Now do as you're being told. I'll be right back with gauze soaked in ether. Try not to breathe it in, keep your distance or you may have a struggle. It's the only way."

159

"But," she protested yet knew her objection was futile.

When Webster returned the distinctive odor of the anesthetic was overpowering. Elizabeth took quick short breaths to avoid inhaling the substance. The patient was still withering in pain but the screaming had stopped. Elizabeth looked at the pathetic sight before her and felt extreme pity for the old lady.

"Here," Webster said, his hand reaching around the screen. "When you get it in your hand do not hesitate. Immediately place it over the woman's nose, forcibly if necessary. Do not hesitate or you will have a royal battle on your hands."

The smell was causing Elizabeth to become a bit light headed herself and she glanced quickly at the woman who by now had stopped her writhing and was staring at Elizabeth with wide curious eyes obviously questioning the odor. Elizabeth feared the panic may have already begun.

Snatching the gauze from Webster's hand Elizabeth swung around and aimed it directly at the woman's nose. Within seconds, before the woman could realize what was happening, Elizabeth had pushed the gauze tightly against the woman's face and felt the struggle. It lasted but seconds. In a peaceful gesture the woman's body slowly sunk down into the chair.

Elizabeth immediately searched the room for a container in which to dispose of the gauze.

But by now the room reeked of ether and her lightheadedness was increasing to the point where she felt she too would be joining the old lady in deep slumber.

Dropping the gauze on the floor she turned and bolted for the door, pushing the screen aside, slamming into Doctor Webster and two interns who had joined him. Then moving rapidly into the hallway she began running from the tang that now permeated the whole area.

She moved half way down the hall before she was no longer bothered by the ether. Inhaling deeply several times to rid her lungs of the anesthetic she found it necessary to lean against the wall to steady herself. Disregarding all else she began hearing a commotion in the hall and in looking up she could see the interns wheeling the woman out on a gurney heading in the opposite direction, obviously in the direction of the operating room. Doctor Webster followed behind.

At that moment Elizabeth determined she was no longer needed. Yet she was most pleased and satisfied with the whole experience. Another mark had been notched in the stodgy old system and Elizabeth began her retreat from the clinic with a broad smile as she headed to the lecture of which she had already missed thirty minutes.

The winter sky had begun to darken when her day concluded. Clouds were forming as she headed back to the boarding house. It might have been the heavy grayness that hung over the small town or simply being tired after a trying day, but Elizabeth carried with her a deepened mood of melancholy, a sense of being totally isolated. It was a frame of mind she couldn't explain, not knowing if the experience with the old woman that morning had affected her spirits. She felt she should have been elated with what had transpired, that she was helpful in possibly saving the woman's life. But the trip home carried a curious burden of gloom as she wondered if her involvement in medicine would affect her moods for the rest of her life. Will the practice of medicine carry with it a curse of separation and loneliness?

Snowflakes began drifting down. A new snowfall was underway. Tomorrow would be whiter than this day. But Elizabeth Blackwell was totally oblivious.

Chapter Thirteen

January 1849
Geneva, New York

"I thank you Sir. With the assistance of the Most High, it will be my lifelong effort to bring honor on this diploma."

Much to his disgust the mirror did not fully reflect the stocky body of five foot-six inch James Webster. It was impossible for him to get a close, head-to-toe image of himself in his ceremonial gown. Fortunately, his disgruntlement would only last a brief moment. It would be the image of Dean Charles Lee struggling with the hood to his gown that would cause Webster to forget about himself and to become amused. What silliness, he thought, that this learned man of academia was certainly not displaying the behavior of an intellectual wherein all it took was a little common sense to simply don the ceremonial hood for the occasion.

"Do you need some help with that, Charles?" he asked turning around.

"This darn fool thing. I don't know why we must wear all this garb anyway."

"Tradition, my dear man. Tradition."

"Tradition be hanged," Lee snorted.

Webster laughed. "Indeed it will be today, Charles. And not only tradition but customs, protocol, standards and norms, all being swept out the window with the conferring of the medical degree upon Elizabeth Blackwell this morning."

"It staggers my mind, James, that this graduation has attracted so much attention. Why, I've been told people from all over the countryside and even some newspaper people have converged upon our fair little village to witness this moment."

"History is being made, Charles. They want to be a part of it. And Geneva College can be justly proud to be the center of attention."

Charles Lee gave a brief harrumph. "There have been moments, James, when I wondered if we did the right thing."

"Of course we did," Webster argued. "It is time these archaic barriers be brought down. We will stand as forerunners in this cause and will definitely take our place in the journals of history."

"A bit of an exaggeration don't you think, James?"

"Not in the least. You and I will be written up in the historical accounts.

Doctor Lee gave another disapproving grunt and pulled the hood around attempting to straighten and arrange it in the correct position. "My tam?" he asked. "Have you seen the fool thing?"

"On the shelf by the door, Charles. Right where you placed it a few minutes ago."

"Oh yes, of course." He paused then shook his head. "I'll be quite happy when all of this is over. Too much fuss, entirely too much fuss."

But to James Webster the fuss, as Lee preferred to call it, carried a more significant meaning. He saw a noteworthy allegory being fused into the day's commotion. The structures of antiquity were crumbling and James Webster relished the role of Joshua helping to make the walls of Jericho come tumbling down. Contrary to Lee's dislike for pomp and ceremony, Webster always found the ritual of graduation to be one of a metamorphosis. And, he believed, that transformation deserved all the fuss and attention due it, especially the one on this particular morning..

"When you're ready Dean Lee," Webster said in a slightly mocking tone, "we can head to the faculty breakfast and listen to the astute words of our dear Bishop DeLancey."

For Elizabeth Blackwell the fuss to which Dean Lee alluded brought great excitement and joy. Yet the day would also propel her into the

165

limelight, a position she knew was inevitable but one she wished to avoid. That, of course, was impossible.

It was to be noted, however, that not all, perhaps a large majority, would share in the elation Elizabeth was experiencing. Having trampled on sacred taboos, the medical degree she was about to receive was not welcomed by everyone. Barriers may have been broken, but strong opposition to women in medicine had not yet been removed.

Elizabeth's brother Harold made the trip from New York City to Geneva to be with his older sister, a most welcomed surprise and certainly much needed moral support. Others in the family were unable to do so but Harold represented the family and brought their many words of congratulations to this most impressive Blackwell honoree.

The trek to the College that January morning was a chilly one. For this occasion Elizabeth was outfitted in a black silk dress and cape, a lace collar and cuffs with her hair in a stylish braid. On Harold's arm they moved inconspicuously among those who were walking toward the ceremony. To Elizabeth the situation was intriguing, for at that moment she was anonymous and yet within the hour all would know who she was. Such, she thought, were the fickle elements of sudden celebrity.

All candidates for the degree were to assemble in the school of medicine. And although

Elizabeth had decided not be incorporated in the grand march from the school to the church she nevertheless had to report in order to register.

But when they reached the building and before entering, Elizabeth was greeted by a young man who presented her with a note. Upon opening it she grimaced.

"Who's it from?" Harold asked.

"Doctor Webster."

"And...?"

"And he wants me to be in the procession with the other candidates."

"And...?"

"And I have no intention of doing so."

"Why not?"

"Harold, it's enough that I'm receiving a degree in medicine but for me to gloat about it by exaggerating my presence would not be proper."

"I think you're being a little too sensitive, Elizabeth."

"Perhaps so, but I don't wish to exit this college with derogatory comments about my behavior being the only legacy I have."

With Harold taking hold of the large handles and pulling the door open, they moved inside where they joined the others awaiting the moment for the grand march. There were snippets of small talk, nervous talk, mostly about trivial matters. It was obvious emotions were running high. The waiting, it seemed, was insufferable.

"Elizabeth," came a voice from behind her.

She turned to see the same student who had previously given her the note. "Yes."

"Doctor Webster said to give you this."

Elizabeth frowned, shook her head and took the note. Upon reading the contents her shoulders dropped and she exhaled a long sigh. "I can't believe this. He's actually pleading. This is so embarrassing."

At the end of the hall a flourish of activity interrupted her thoughts. Members of the faculty began arriving bedecked in their traditional gowns with colored hoods draped brightly around their shoulders. Elizabeth took hold of Harold's arm. It was time to exit and leave for the church.

"We must go now," she said and felt his resistance. "Howard, no, I told you I am not going to walk in that procession. It just isn't proper."

"A shame," he quietly replied. "You should be there."

It was a silent walk to the large ornate church where Elizabeth would be immortalized, although she would not think of herself in those particular terms. Her mind rehearsed exactly what she would do. It was important, she determined, that she of all people do it absolutely correct, for obviously all eyes would be on her and the slightest misstep would subject her to disapproval.

Upon reaching the church's front steps Elizabeth hesitated.

Howard looked over. "Nervous?"

"Not really."

"Then what is it?"

"The irony of it all. In all honestly, Howard, this ceremony today isn't going to change anything. The hostility and injustices will continue to exist. The vile rudeness will still confront me and I will be barred from having any kind of practice."

"But fresh air is seeping in. It may not come rushing in right now but soon there will be a gust of new air."

A quick smile was given. "A gust?" she asked. "Surely you exaggerate."

"I don't believe so. But be that as it may be I believe it is time to go in."

By prior arrangements Elizabeth and Howard were to take a seat in the back row where they would wait for the procession to enter. Once the procession had cleared, the two would join the group and proceed to the front of the church. There her classmates would take their assigned seats in the first three pews, sans Elizabeth, and Elizabeth and Howard would sit in the first pew opposite them. All of this was by Elizabeth's design.

Turning to view the pageantry, Elizabeth saw a very proper Charles Lee strutting out front followed by the curators and faculty. Behind them marched the College's President Benjamin Hale with Bishop DeLancey. After that ensemble had passed Elizabeth could see her classmates enter, wide smiles upon their faces, many looking her way, a few bowing in her direction. When the class had cleared, Elizabeth and Harold stepped out into the aisle to fall in line at which time a favorite classmate of hers, George Field, always the gentleman, held out his arm for Elizabeth to take catching her by surprise. With just a brief pause she slipped her arm into his and Harold followed behind.

"Well, Lizzy," George whispered, "This is it."

"Yes it is, George. And I do appreciate this most gracious gesture of yours. Thank you very much."

"It's the way it should be, Lizzy. I'm sorry you weren't allowed to join us for the whole procession."

Elizabeth gave a quick smile wishing not to reveal the fact her absence was her idea, figuring someday Fields would most likely learn the whole truth.

As with all ceremonies of its kind, the graduation at Geneva College was laboriously structured. Traditions fused with rituals and bombastic pomp served no other purpose but to give those in administrative position an opportunity to be the center piece of glory. However, most of those assembled had come not to hear these men of title but to see the young woman get her diploma.

But within due time their patience was rewarded. A brief talk by President Hale was the last of the addresses and upon his final words the time had come to confer the degrees upon the graduates.

Donning a bright red velvet four-sided Tam O'Shanter, the President moved to a large leather high-back chair. To the side of the chair sat a wide round table on which rested the prized diplomas assembled in batches of four, secured by a wide blue ribbon. Seating himself he looked out upon the students and in a most portentous display issued the call for the graduates to come forth to receive their diplomas.

In groups of four, the young men ascended the steps, moved on to the stage and stood in front of the President. Remaining seated, Hale read the pronouncement bestowing the degree of medicine upon the graduates. Once done he removed his hat, reached for the group of four diplomas and handed them to the first student. They in turn bowed then quickly moved to the far side of the stage where they descended and returned to their seats. The procedure was repeated until all the male students had been given their diplomas. A single diploma remained on the table.

A hush immediately fell over the church and every eye trained on Elizabeth. It was the moment for which they had come, the moment in which they would witness history being made.

President Hale looked at Elizabeth. "Domina Blackwell," he called.

Hesitating momentarily, then in a slow, deliberate motion, Elizabeth rose from her seat and began the short walk to the stairs. She could feel the same tingling in her finger tips she had felt before whenever the moment was electrified by a significant occasion. It was necessary to inhale deeply several times to distill all signs of nervousness. Continuing to move with deliberate caution she ascended the steps and headed to where the President sat. Positioning herself in front of him she was suddenly caught completely by surprise as he leaned forward and stood. For several seconds the church grew still. Gradually a slight murmur began to waft through the crowd, for the President of the College had just broken a long-standing precedence as he rose to award a diploma.

Removing his hat he placed it on the table then proceeded to read the prescribed Latin decree. He reached down and retrieved the diploma. Her eyes fixed on the rolled-up thin piece of parchment secured by a small blue ribbon. In that precious document she now saw all that had transpired before: her agonies and humiliations, her struggles, the multiple rejections and insults no longer a miserable yoke to bear.

In a most ceremonial manner, President Hale handed the diploma to Elizabeth and without a word gave a low, graceful bow.

For a moment Elizabeth seemed flustered, as if not knowing what the proper protocol was. She turned to leave then looked back at the President. Already precedence twice had been breached when she impetuously added a third to the list. She spoke.

"I thank you Sir. With the assistance of the Most High, it will be my lifelong effort to bring honor on this diploma." As soon as she had expressed her thoughts she bowed, watched him bow again and then feeling most embarrassed hurried to the steps to move quickly off the stage.

Those assembled erupted in a thunderous applause. When Elizabeth reached the far edge of the pew where her classmates were seated, George Field stood and opened the small pew gate as those sitting there moved over to make room for her. Elizabeth could feel the emotions churning. Tears welled up and her whole body throbbed.

"Oh, George," she half sobbed, "thank you, thank you so very much for this."

"Step in...Doctor," he said his voice cracking.

At that moment Elizabeth wanted to embrace this gracious man. But to do so would have been quite scandalous and certainly at that most precious moment she was not about to jeopardized everything just so she could release a burst of emotion. Her look of deep appreciation told Field all that needed to be said and she made her way into the pew to take her seat with the other newly ordained physicians.

Once the charged atmosphere in the church had settled Doctor Charles Lee rose from his chair and strolled to the podium holding a rather thick stack of papers in his hand. Those attending the ceremony instinctively knew they would have to endure an apparently long talk by the Dean of Faculty.

Nearing the conclusion of his talk, Lee redirected the theme of his message and began extolling praise upon the first woman physician, declaring to those gathered that Elizabeth was an outstanding academic leader, ranked number one in her class, and that she had exhibited excellent scholarship and true ladylike deportment throughout her two terms at the school. Adding one last comment to his address and continuing to focus on Elizabeth, he told the gathering that Elizabeth had successfully passed every course of study offered, eliminating none, and had truly earned her degree in medicine; that Elizabeth was fully qualified to practice as a physician and that her degree was absolutely merited.

As before, the applause was deafening and Elizabeth felt chills sweeping down her arms and gripping her whole body. She wanted to cry, to cry hard and long with the joy in her heart struggling to be released. Yet she shut her eyes and slowly lowered her head and proceeded to blush for the fourth time that morning.

There would be various accounts written of the events that morning in Geneva. Several major newspapers had small clips reporting on the occasion without much embellishment on the historic significance of it all. As she exited the church on the arm of her brother, Elizabeth Blackwell had a look of contentment; of pure delight and satisfaction. She cared not at that moment what was to be written or reported or bandied about. Words of disrespect, of hostility; derogatory comments and rude slurs or what Victorian and moral codes she may have violated had no bearing on who she was as she held tightly to that small diploma with the thin blue ribbon.

"I wish Father were alive to see this," she told Howard.

"Oh?"

"Yes, he always had to admonish me to do my studies and complete my lessons. I wasn't much of a student when young. He would have enjoyed seeing what his persistence had accomplished."

Howard laughed. "That's hard to fathom, you not studying."

"But you know, Howard, not everything is learned in the classroom. And I'm not too sure I'm ready to absorb the new lessons awaiting me." She looked again at the diploma then held it up. "I'm talking about the firestorm this little piece of parchment is about to unleash. Neither the world of medicine nor I am ready to embrace this triumph." She shook her head. "Somewhere further on, history will have to judge if this was wise. But for now I'm ready to go home."

Chapter Fourteen

It was as if she had now become the enemy. Whereas before she was considered to be the devil's handmaiden, she was now seen as the devil incarnate.

The iconic clacking of the steel wheels on the tracks was quite intriguing to Elizabeth. She enjoyed letting the rhythmic sound tease her imagination, trying to develop a concept of word patterns. She could see from her brother's dowdy expression he had no interest in the novelty. But to her such was the uniqueness of rail transportation and Elizabeth was thoroughly enjoying every minute of the experience.

It was the day after graduation. The train had just left Albany heading toward New York City. It would be in that city that Elizabeth and Howard would part; he remaining there while Elizabeth would board another train and continue on to Philadelphia. She had determined that upon graduation she would return to Philadelphia to continue her studies, seeking opportunities for post-graduate work in practical applications, a requirement for certification.

Howard glanced over to examine Elizabeth. There was that same contemplative expression on her face he had seen before. He wondered if perchance she was revisiting her thoughts about the future, a future she had discussed with him before; the possibilities of her being admitted to a medical school in Philadelphia where she had been rejected only three years earlier. Elizabeth argued that now with her degree in medicine a whole new level of contention had opened making a vast difference in the circumstances surrounding her position. It was a rationale Howard found lacking in practicality and to a large degree felt his sister was having trouble believing it herself.

"Are you thinking about Philadelphia again," he said breaking the silence.

She shook her head. "No, not really. Just listening to the wheels."

He gave her an inquisitive look. "Wheels?"

"The wheels, Howard, the train's wheels. Can't you hear them? Why did you suppose I was thinking about Philadelphia?"

"Just that you seemed to be in deep thought."

Elizabeth laughed. "Train wheels will do that to you if you're not careful."

"But seriously," Howard questioned. "Have you heard anything?"

It was a sigh of frustration that gave her answer then she added, "Well, yes. I was invited to meet with several of the professors at the University hospital, which I intend to do, and perhaps sit in on some of their lectures. But nothing is fully established at this time as far as being engaged by the hospital or lining up any post graduate courses in practical medicine."

"In other words they're not committing themselves."

Elizabeth looked at her brother and closed her eyes.

"I see," Howard said. "And if they don't wish to admit you what about the other institutions?"

"No word back from Jefferson and I'm not familiar with the newer hospitals in the city."

"In other words..."

"Don't say it Howard. I know what it means."

It was an abrupt enough response to bring the conversation to an end. It had become obvious her newly acquired degree wasn't carrying all that much importance to it and was not making much of an impression on the medical community. But there were invitations to meet with the professors and the lectures, a step, perhaps, in the right direction. Still, in summary, that was the full extent of the professional courtesies.

"I've also been thinking lately," she went on to say, "that perhaps I won't have any choice but to travel to Europe if I wish to continue my studies. I've been told by several of my professors and doctors that my best advantages would be in Paris and I have been giving it serious thought."

"Paris? Indeed. And what assurance do you have there?

"I've been given several letters of introduction by Doctors Lee and Webster."

"But no real assurances?"

Her eyes snapped at her brother, the combination of anger and frustration showing at the continuation of the conversation. She wished to end it. There was no reason to drag out the agony. "If you wish to think that way," came the terse answer.

The subject was dropped. Obviously by the silence there was nothing more either of them wanted to discuss, certainly not Elizabeth. She had no interest in belaboring the points concerning Philadelphia or Paris. At times, as she was preparing to leave Geneva, she wondered why she was even bothering to go to Philadelphia. It would be simpler to just take up residency in Paris where she felt, based on what her professors had expressed, she would be admitted to a teaching hospital and be able to get the advance education she needed. But her finances were not all that sufficient. Studying in Philadelphia would be more economical plus Philadelphia had some of the finest medical schools in the country. And she would be close to her family. There were too many benefits for staying in the country if only she was able to break through the barriers that constrained her.

When they arrived in New York City it was a tearful goodbye for Elizabeth. She had truly enjoyed the four days spent with her younger brother and without knowing when it would be they would be together again it made the parting all the more traumatic. But eventually Howard had to stand back as Elizabeth boarded the train to Philadelphia leaving him alone there on the platform watching the train slowly disappear.

It was a late afternoon in May of 1849 when Elizabeth arrived by train at the port of Dover. A dark, heavy rain had followed her from London and it appeared it was not about to let up. Her wide parasol was of immense value.

Europe became the venue of choice after five short weeks in Philadelphia. As she had suspected but refused to accept, the medical community in the United Sates was not about to acknowledge a woman, degree or not. The pangs of rejections sprung anew and the rudeness appeared to be more severe than when seeking attendance in the schools of medicine. It was as if she had now become the enemy. Whereas before she was considered to be the devil's handmaiden, she was now seen as the devil incarnate.

There was no choice. Regardless of the prospects for success, Elizabeth Blackwell was persona non grata in her adopted country and Europe beckoned.

By virtue of a most generous offer by her cousin in England, she was afforded the voyage across the ocean, a trek not at all welcomed by Elizabeth. But surviving the experience once again she soon made her plans to travel to Paris where she would continue her studies. The city on the Seine was her last refuge of possibilities as a result of continued rejection. Similar to the attitude and position in The United States, the medical profession in England was also not willing to invest in the movement of women practicing medicine. They were cordial and polite, as the English were apt to be, but determined not to accept women into their profession. Paris therefore became the only remaining citadel of opportunity.

The docks at Dover were quite crowded. Those traveling to and from France filled the area with a bustling mass of people and Elizabeth found the congestion intriguing. The mixture of languages appeared not to confuse anyone, for they moved about as if knowing exactly where to go and what to do while Elizabeth found it necessary to read from the instructions that had been given to her by her cousin Samuel. She soon located the boat that would ferry her across the Channel to the port city of Calais a distance of some twenty eight miles.

Not looking forward to another trip over water, she convinced herself the Channel was not an ocean and the calm waters would not trouble her as the ocean voyage had. It proved to be true and in fact Elizabeth found the excursion to be somewhat enjoyable.

"Traveling alone?"

Elizabeth glanced to her side seeing a tall, distinguished looking woman. Her perfect English revealed her nationality and the warm, motherly smile served as a welcoming beacon for Elizabeth.

"Yes, my first trip to France," she told the woman.

"I'm Margaret Chambers, London."

"Elizabeth Blackwell, the United States."

"Oh, the colonies. How interesting. It is so nice meeting you, Miss Blackwell."

"Nice meeting you as well."

"And what brings you all this way, my dear?"

"Studies."

"Ah yes, the lure of France and the culture of the romantics. Going to Paris? They all do."

"Yes."

"And do you have someone greeting you when we reach Calais?"

'No," Elizabeth answered. "I'm venturing out on my own."

"Oh, my," Chambers said in a surprised tone. "You are a rather strong and brave woman."

Elizabeth laughed. "So I've been told."

"Well, Elizabeth, if you don't think my husband and I would be too forward we would be more than pleased to assist you in finding housing for tonight in Calais and with your train ride into Paris tomorrow morning. The city is our destination too and it would be no trouble helping you with your new adventure."

"That would be most kind of you, Mrs. Chambers. How very nice. Thank you. Yes, I would welcome that. It would be a big help."

"Fine. And I'll introduce you to my husband, Frederick, as soon as I can locate him. He is off roaming the boat, his habit whenever we make the crossing."

For Elizabeth, the presence of Margaret Chambers was most fortunate. Her assistance would be invaluable. It was also quite beneficial that Margaret Chambers did not recognize Elizabeth, for to have done so could have made their journey less comfortable. Elizabeth preferred to remain anonymous.

Rain followed them across the Channel. The port of Calais was dark by the time they arrived except for a few lanterns in various locations and the large lighthouse whose light added some illumination when it swung over the land. The lights assisted them in finding their way to the Customs House.

184

When she reached Paris the next day the city was not the handsome, gay and elegant center she had envisioned. And once she and her traveling companions cleared the Parisian Custom House where the officials searched their belongings for butter and cheese, they parted company and Elizabeth found herself standing on the sidewalk seeing nothing of the Paris she expected.

But the sights of Paris would change once she had settled into a small room she would lease until her sister Anna arrived in the city. And once settled she set about organizing her time for the various appointments established through her referrals. Her mission quickly took precedence and the matter of Paris' charm slowly faded.

After her third week in the French capitol she sought out the residence of a Monsieur Louis where she would present him with a letter of introduction. The exact position he held in the medical circles was unknown to her except that he was a highly influential and prominent citizen. She was never provided with his first name and felt at a disadvantage knowing little about the man. He was, in some way, a person of mystery. But of all her recommendations, Monsieur Louis was considered to be the most important of them all.

After some difficulty she found his home, leaving the letter and her calling card with the man's maid before returning to her room to await his answer. The next day, there was a knock on Elizabeth's door. Her landlady announced she had a visitor, which was a surprise to Elizabeth. Upon opening the door there stood a rather tall, slender gentleman who introduced himself as Monsieur Louis.

"Monsieur Louis," Elizabeth stammered, obviously a bit flustered by his presence. This important Parisian would come to her modest room himself? "Please, please come in," Elizabeth said leaving the door open once the gentleman had stepped inside. "Would you care to be seated?" she offered, her voice continuing to tremble.

"Docteur Blackwell, it is a pleasure meeting you," he said, his baritone voice and soft pronunciation seeming so delicate and refined. His mannerisms impressed Elizabeth who by now felt somewhat intimidated.

"And a deep pleasure meeting you, sir." she quickly added. "Thank you for coming here to visit with me. It is very generous of you."

Choosing the high-back chair by the window he gave quick glances around the room and sat. "This is your residence, n'est pas?" His eyes did a thorough sweep of the room.

"Yes, for the time being," she answered. "I will most likely move once my sister arrives or I secure an admission to a teaching hospital."

"Ah, yes, the teaching hospital...the reason why you contacted me, correct?"

"Yes. I was told that..."

"The letter...poorly written I must say, horrible French, alluded to the fact you are seeking practical experiences. Am I correct in assuming that?"

"Yes. It is my..."

"And I understand you have been rejected by all the institutions in America for this purpose, true?"

Elizabeth flinched at the style of his questioning. "Yes, much to my disappointment."

Nodding he stood and gazed out the window for a period of time. Without turning he observed, "Your surroundings have a very delightful garden in the courtyard here. Have you had the opportunity to enjoy it?"

"Yes, and I agree, very delightful."

"You enjoy the outdoors?"

"Yes," she answered wondering what the garden had to do with their discussion. "Nature has always fascinated and delighted me," she told him.

"Paris is known for her beauty. I assume you've had opportunities to observe our fair city?"

"Actually I've just arrived," she answered. "I've been busy attempting to see the directors of the hospitals."

"I see, yes, the hospitals, the purpose for you being here." he said, then began moving about the small room. He remained silent for several seconds giving the room further inspection. Finally he spoke. "Docteur Blackwell, in my opinion I believe you would do best by entering La Maternité."

"La Maternité?"

"La Maternité de Paris, the lying-in hospital for the destitute women of Paris. If there is anything to learn about medicine it would be there."

"But isn't that an obstetrics hospital and the school is for midwifery?"

"That is correct."

"But I am a doctor."

"Yes, but one who has just graduated without any practical skills and who needs more training in a hospital setting before she can set up her own practice. One who is being denied that opportunity everywhere because your credentials are not being recognized by most of those in the medical profession."

"In other words," she said feeling her anger grow, "As you see it this is my one and only opportunity?"

"Precisely. Yes. You see, Docteur, the institutions in Paris are not as liberal as you might have imagined. In Paris a woman in medicine is still a foreign concept. You may gain admission for observations at some facilities but not for actual working experiences. And I know of what I speak. But La Maternité will afford you the opportunity to be actively involved, not mere observation but true participation. It is an excellent opportunity. In a very short period of time you will obtain more valuable practical knowledge and experiences than could be obtained elsewhere."

"But my directions are toward surgery not midwifery."

He smiled and moved toward the door telling her as he was leaving, "You think about it, Docteur, and I'll leave instructions with you on how to obtain admission. Then if you decide to take advantage of this opportunity contact me and we can proceed further."

Laying a grouping of papers on a small end table he let himself out and before Elizabeth could discuss the matter further he was gone. Stepping away from the door she dropped into a chair and stared at the floor. His proposal was utterly absurd. To spend time practicing midwifery was regression and not advancing her education in any manner whatsoever. It seemed now the advice to focus on Paris was perhaps not the best she could have gotten. Certainly she was finding nothing to encourage her except the opportunity to work and study as a midwife not a physician. Absurdity: blatant and superfluous absurdity.

Elizabeth turned to stare out the window feeling again the resentment she had felt so many times before. At every crossroad she has met confrontation fueled by ignorance and antiquated protocols. Attempts to bring about change and move the field of medicine forward were being thwarted with a degree of animosity unbecoming the medical profession. The

189

situation produced only frustration not growth. She had no remedy. It appeared there would be no cure. Physician heal thyself indeed. Such absurdity.

Chapter Fifteen

June, 1849
Paris, France

No longer was there any doubt. The luxury of self-denial was shattered. She had the purulent ophthalmia and she was now in serious danger of losing her eyesight.

If ever there was a time for Elizabeth Blackwell to be frightened it was at that moment while crossing Boulevard Raspail with her sister Anna. "Move faster, Anna. I want to get out of here."

"Don't be silly, Elizabeth. There's nothing to be afraid of. I want to listen to what they're saying."

"No, I mean now! I don't like the mood of these people."

"It's just a simple little protest, Elizabeth. We have them all the time in America."

"This is not simple, Anna. These people have guns and they're angry and we're much too close. I don't like it."

Shifting her feet Anna sighed. "And I thought you were the brave one."

"More wise than brave," Elizabeth countered pulling on her sister's sleeve. "These demonstrations have been getting more violent lately and there's word that President Bonaparte is preparing to suppress these gatherings and if he does then the violence is going to get worse."

Elizabeth began dragging Anna away from the loud gathering. By the flickering light of the blazing torches angry faces could be seen staring in the direction of the two women. Elizabeth increased her pace. The ruckus from which they were retreating came upon them unexpectedly, encountered on their way back to the apartment after securing groceries.

The course of Elizabeth's lifestyle in Paris had changed in that early part of June. Anna had recently arrived in France to take up residence in Paris while working on translations of the works of the French socialist Fourier and the novels of Georges Sand. Traveling with a friend, she acquired an apartment on the Rue de Fleurus overlooking the Luxembourg Gardens. Elizabeth joined them several days later. And while Anna went about her work in the apartment, Elizabeth, with letters of introduction, continued attempting to secure acceptance into a hospital where she could do her practical studies.

One evening shortly after encountering the mob, Elizabeth glanced away from the magazine she had been reading and looked over at Anna who was writing in a journal. "You know, Anna," she said, "I had hoped that Paris would have been more open minded than what I'm finding."

"Oh, it is," Anna answered. "In fact at times this grand city is too liberal."

The assessment caused Elizabeth to laugh. "Not liberal enough as far as I'm concerned."

"Your problem is not with the people of Paris, my dear sister. It is with the doctors. You know that. Women just are not being accepted into the field of medicine. It's that simple."

Elizabeth stood and began to pace the room. Staring at the ceiling she complained, "I refuse to accept that my only opportunity in this whole city, in this whole world, is at a maternity hospital...as a plebe...as a plebe if you will...at a school for midwifery. That is so utterly contrary to the progress I've made and especially to my needs."

"But it *is* an opportunity," Anna reminded her.

"Oh yes, indeed, that it is," Elizabeth agreed; her sarcasm being too obvious. "Yes, regretfully, unimaginable, but, yes, it is definitely an opportunity."

"Then perhaps you should swallow your pride and accept the offer."

Elizabeth whirled around to stare angrily at her sister. "Swallow my pride?" she exclaimed. "I have no pride, Anna. I am not standing on pride. It is simply that La Maternité will not be an advancement in my education. I will be going backwards."

"But it will afford you some practical experience, exactly what you're seeking. Not to the extent you would receive in a full hospital, but nonetheless it would be experience. And right now you have absolutely no other choice, as it was with Blockley. This is reality, Elizabeth, a fact you need to look at very seriously."

It grew very silent in that living room. Elizabeth turned to look away, remaining angry at her sister, but it was, as always, because Anna was right. And yet Anna was not necessarily espousing anything Elizabeth hadn't already considered.

The surrender to reality came about on the last day of June when Elizabeth and Anna journeyed along the Seine in a carriage ride to La Maternité. Once Monsieur Louis had been contacted it took but two days to make all arrangements for her to be accepted. Now as they approached the building, Anna was taken aback by the immense stone structure.

"My word, Elizabeth, are you certain you have the correct address?"

"Yes, definitely. Why?"

"This can't possibly be your hospital. From all appearances it looks like a prison."

"Prison?" Elizabeth laughed. "That's absurd. It's the correct address all right"

The sight that stood before them did indeed resemble some ancient structure from the past. Built in the form of a formidable fortress it could very well have been a monastery or large convent, but certainly not a prison. Of some irony and unbeknownst to Elizabeth the outer appearance was truly reflecting the monastic life Elizabeth would experience once she ventured inside those looming walls.

After bidding Anna farewell in the small front foyer, the only area in which visitors were allowed, Elizabeth entered through a narrow door accompanied by her supervisor and came into a darkened chamber with cold stone walls that smelled of mold. Several dank hallways lead off in different directions giving Elizabeth an immediate impression of a cloistered institution.

"You'll be assigned a bed in the student dormitory," instructed Madame Charrier, the head of the young students as she escorted Elizabeth down the long corridor. "You'll be assigned certain hours to work in the delivery room and nursery, which will include days of twelve hour shifts. Some nights you will not sleep."

"But doesn't that reduce effectiveness?" Elizabeth asked, then instinctively realized she had posed the wrong question.

"Mademoiselle Blackwell, you will need to stop thinking as an American and begin adapting to the ways of the French. You are here to learn and not play." Turning to face Elizabeth, Madame Charrier continued, "Also, you will need to spend time with the others to improve your French. You have a reasonable grasp of the language but at times you are most difficult to understand."

Trying to stifle a slight grin Elizabeth felt it best to simply nod and speak as little French as possible when around Madame Charrier. But for certain her French would vastly improve being totally surrounded by the language with no English to be heard for the next three months.

"Tonight, once settled, you will join your group and your leader in the delivery room. We have eight women about to deliver. You and the others will assist and care for the babies until the necessary postnatal observational period has passed. You'll be working through the night."

"And the lectures," Elizabeth asked, "when do they commence?"

"The first of August. But don't trouble yourself with that for now. You have much to do and learn before you undertake those."

Elizabeth followed the old woman. There were no further instructions or discussions as they made their way up two flights of creaky wooden stairs to the dormitory. When they entered, Elizabeth viewed a gathering of young women, some perhaps as young as sixteen, all wide-eyed and eager to become midwives. The sight was quite disheartening for Elizabeth.

These young girls would not be medical companions, not even intellectual peers. She was, indeed, about to enter into an isolation of austere proportions.

If ever there was a portion of a person's soul that quivered each time the thought of another day in a place that was both feared and detested, Elizabeth felt it often those first few weeks. She was far out of her realm and the work to be performed was disappointingly rudimentary. Yet, as basic as it was, she was acquiring the practical experience of hospital work, although finding it mostly redundant. For all practical purposes she was more on the level of the resident physicians. Her medical knowledge was equal to theirs, but her knowledge came from books with very little real life experience. That was the separation, yet her status and achievement did not go unnoticed.

It was on a warm midweek afternoon following a lecture when one of the department physicians at the hospital, Doctor Marseille Dubois, approached Elizabeth. "Mademoiselle Blackwell," he said stopping her. "I wish to speak with you."

"Doctor?"

"I have become aware of your amazing background, your degree in medicine in the United States, and in exploring your background I have come to learn you are here because of your gender, that you cannot get practical training at other hospitals, correct?"

"Yes, you are correct," she said, reluctant to discuss the matter.

He stroked his beard while nodding. "Yes, yes, I see. But there are, of course, other possibilities for you here at La Maternité. If you were to consider remaining with us for two years you could achieve certification in obstetrics."

The suggestion caused Elizabeth to smile. "But I'm really not interested in obstetrics, Doctor. Surgery is my goal. As you pointed out, I'm undergoing training here as a midwife simply to gain some practical hospital experience."

"But the ways of midwifery will not advance you in your career. You do have free time to do other, more involved tasks while attending to your duties."

"Such as?"

"Surgery, serious patient conditions and treatments, activities of that nature."

"Are you suggesting that those opportunities would be offered to me?"

"I could see to it, yes."

"With the expectation of me gaining certification in obstetrics?"

The man flashed a puckish smile. "You may grow to enjoy it, yes."

Elizabeth hesitated before responding. Then allowing him his brief moment of anticipation she closed the door on the discussion. "Thank you, Doctor Dubois. But I'm afraid obstetrics is not my field of interest right now."

Disappointment showed on his face. "You need time to think, I can see that. Yes, time...that is what you need." Nodding he turned to leave. Then looking back he smiled and said, "Perhaps it is best if we leave all this up to destiny."

Elizabeth Blackwell did not believe in destiny; could not accept that all things were preordained. It was simply through careful planning and well executed actions that a person was propelled in the directions they pursued. Yet unknowingly Elizabeth was being stalked by destiny in La Maternité. With each step she took, with each action she performed, the undisciplined hand of fate was leading her to a conclusion far beyond what her careful plans included. There were no conditions that would have changed her actions or her decisions.

The moment of collision between Elizabeth and fate took place while performing one of her many duties in the area of the hospital where sick or injured infants received treatment. Quite often her assignments were of a singular nature sans any group involvement. And being alone made her easy prey.

Entering the ward at six forty-two that morning in the first week of October she began working alone in the nursery by a very dim lamplight. Attempting to turn up the flame she grew impatient with the lamp's apparent malfunction. The room remained in a semi-darkened state. The assignment she was given was to syringe the eyes of a small infant in order to clean away the pus and infection caused by purulent ophthalmia, an infection that caused severe injury to the eye, possibly blindness. The baby had contacted the disease from his mother who was suffering from gonorrhea. The reason for the baby's suffering both irritated and repulsed Elizabeth.

She moved to the small table sitting next to the crib in which the infant lay. The implements to be used had already been neatly laid out for her. Because of the dim light, she bent over closer to get a better view of the infected eyes. Retrieving the syringe, Elizabeth began to carefully squeeze the syringe with a solution of clearing water.

Then destiny stepped in.

At that precise moment an unexplained breeze swept through the nursery causing Elizabeth to shiver briefly. As she did, her hand inadvertently tightened on the bulb of the syringe causing the water to spurt out with a heavier dosage. The water splashed in every direction bouncing off the baby's infected eye, some of it splashing directly into Elizabeth's left eye. A cry of surprise spoke of her shock.

Jumping back she quickly grabbed a towel to wipe the water away from her eye fearing she may have endangered herself, a situation that could possibly prove detrimental if the water had actually splashed into the eye. Grabbing a bottle of clear water, Elizabeth desperately soaked a washcloth and began wiping the eye. Disposing of that cloth, she soaked another and wiped her entire face. Short dabs with a towel soon removed the water and Elizabeth stood in that darkened room staring out, craning to see her surroundings, attempting to notice any change in her eyesight.

Realizing it was too early to determine if any damage had been done, she hurriedly finished with her assignment and rushed off to one of the lavatories to look at her eye in the mirror. With her face practically touching the mirror, the left eye was meticulously examined. A slight redness could be seen but it was impossible to know the cause.

For several hours after the incident it appeared Elizabeth might have escaped any damage. However, the disease was known to develop rapidly and consequently later that day Elizabeth could feel a slight irritation in her eye. The redness that had formed was noticeable and raised a question in the mind of one of her fellow students working in the infant ward with Elizabeth.

"Your eye," She said. "What's wrong with it?"

"I don't know, Yvette. I might have caused some damage to it this morning while treating a new born infant."

"Does it burn?"

"No, but it feels as if a grain of sand has gotten in to it."

"Has one of the doctors taken a look at it?"

Elizabeth shook her head. "The doctors are entirely too busy to spend time looking into an eye that has a spec in it," she rationalized.

"Still you should have it examined."

"It's nothing," she insisted. Yet Elizabeth Blackwell, the doctor, was not fully convinced of her own self-diagnosis. The pain that had developed forced her to come to terms with the fact she very likely did injure the eye with the purulent ophthalmia infection. But Doctor Blackwell had come to recognize that most people generally drew quick conclusions with illnesses and therefore she decided not to do so but to give the eye time to manifest anything serious. That decision, she realized, was not a wise path to follow but out of denial she chose to ignore wisdom in favor of delusion.

That night it became all too apparent she had indeed contacted the infection from the baby, for the lids of her injured eye had begun to swell. By morning the eye was completely closed from the pus and she was beginning to lose vision in the right eye as well. No longer was there any doubt. The luxury of self-denial was shattered. She had the purulent ophthalmia and she was now in serious danger of losing her eyesight.

Dressing as quickly as possible she hurried to the student's infirmary hoping a doctor would be available. To her delight Doctor Hippolyte Blot, a young intern working on his certification, a person of whom she had grown fond was tending to another student and was able to take time to look extensively at the eye. His expression spoke of Elizabeth's plight.

"Immediate treatment is needed Elizabeth."

"Yes, I know. I'll put in for a leave to seek treatment at one of the hospitals."

"Your request will be denied, you know that. You need to be treated here." He attempted giving her a reassuring smile. "Don't worry. You'll be getting constant attention. We'll begin treatment immediately."

"But Hippolyte no one here can ignore their duties to provide me with constant care."

He shook his head in protest. "The patients here are not as serious as you. Leave here and prepare for bed rest. As soon as I speak with my supervisor I'll be back to begin treatment."

Surprised by his response she questioned him. "You're going to assume my case?"

"I'm qualified, yes, and can make the time better than the others."

"But you stated I would need constant care."

"Yes, Elizabeth, I will request that I attend to you regularly since I have begun the initial treatment." There was almost a slight teasing to his response. "Now please return to your bed to begin your rest and I will be with you shortly."

Within a half an hour Blot returned and began treating the eye. His touch was quite gentle. He never looked away, staring intently at

Elizabeth's face. Elizabeth had a comforting feeling of total confidence in Blot's handling of her case and was most pleased it was he who would be attending to her. The two had become good friends from the first time they had met. They had spent free time together discussing the practice of medicine and what the future held for the profession. Blot was obviously impressed with Elizabeth's status of being the one who broke the gender barrier. His admiration of this feat provided a strong bond between the two. Now he was to be her physician in attendance and the relationship would take on a different profile.

That evening, having been summoned, Anna came to visit hoping to boost her sister's spirits, but the sound of soft sobbing from Anna did nothing to bring hope to Elizabeth.

"Anna, please don't cry," Elizabeth pleaded. "It doesn't help matters."

"Oh, Elizabeth, of all people for this to happen to, why you?"

"Because I'm involved in the treatment of the sick, Anna. There's always danger for those who care for the infirmed. It's inherent with the work."

"Then let us pray the treatments you'll be getting will cure this infection."

Elizabeth rolled her head slowly back and forth. "The treatments are limited. But Doctor Blot is doing all he can and all we can do now is wait and see."

By the next morning both eyes were closed and Elizabeth knew Anna's prayers were cast in doubt. Special accommodations were created to assure the best of care was being given and Hippolyte Blot did, indeed, provide constant treatment. For three days he syringed the eyes every two hours, day and night, removing the films that had built up over the left eye, supervising the medicines being applied and reassuring Elizabeth all would be well.

"It seems we've been able to reduce the swelling somewhat," Blot told her on the fourth day of treatment. "How does the eye feel?"

"The heavy pressure does seem to be receding. And I also believe the fever is gone am I not correct?"

"Yes, normal temperature," he said. "I can also see the right eye is responding and there is a good chance you'll recover full sight in that eye."

"And the other?" Elizabeth asked with a noticeable hesitation to the question.

Hippolyte Blot's mouth drew up tight. "Too early to truly tell." He waited before continuing then spoke in a quiet tone. "I would be irresponsible, Elizabeth, if I tried to give you encouragement when the symptoms are not all that positive. Generally..."

"Generally," she interrupted, "the disease does its damage and leaves the victim blind."

"You are perhaps making too quick a judgment...doctor."

Elizabeth smiled at the recognition. "I'm familiar with the disease. And I am quite familiar with the general outcome when the infection has lasted this long."

"It's only been four days, hardly time enough to be making a prognosis."

Elizabeth waved her hand. "I can assure you, Hippolyte, blindness is imminent."

For three weeks the eyes remained closed confirming to Elizabeth her prediction that she would be blind in her left eye for the rest of her life. Fortunately, as Hippolyte Blot's had suspected, the right eye began clearing and the vision, although blurred and unfocused, had returned allowing her to determine objects and persons that surrounded her as she lay in her bed.

As the days of treatment and recuperation expanded into the waning months of autumn the relationship between Elizabeth and Hippolyte Blot grew stronger. For the most part Elizabeth found the involvement conflicting with her steadfast determination to avoid any close bonding which might create distractions that could interrupt her goals. At times she tried to place aside her feelings for him. Yet she looked forward to Blot's visits and when he did enter the room she found no conflict taking place. The quandary actually amused her and she kept all these matters closely guarded giving wonder to what could be.

When November came to an end, and her eyesight in the right eye began to improve, Elizabeth developed a resolve to continue in medicine regardless of the final outcome of her vision. "I will have to seek new ways," she told Anna during one of her visits. "I'm sure I can be useful in the medical field without the requirement of full eyesight."

"Aren't you giving up a little too soon?" Anna asked a bit of chiding in her words.

"No. I'm slowly regaining sight in my right eye and I will be leaving here shortly. I intend to continue my studies in practical medicine. I know now and accept the fact that I will never be able to practice surgery. But I'm a doctor, Anna, and through God's grace I intend staying one."

When the day came for Elizabeth's discharge she found Paris covered by a gray sky and the weather cold and damp, so typical for the end of November. Anna had come to assist her. Bandaged and weak, Elizabeth leaned heavily on Anna's arm as they made their way to the carriage stationed outside the hospital's front door. There, waiting to bid her fond adieu, stood Hippolyte Blot.

"I wish you the best of everything," he said, a touch of sorrow to his words.

Placing her hand on his arm she smiled. "Thank you my dear friend. I will miss you and never forget the loving care you provided me. I am starting to see now and it is all because of you."

The streak of a grin quickly gave way to a mournful look. "I'd like to correspond with you."

"Yes," she said, "that would be nice." Removing her hand to take Anna's arm she gave a quick smile. "Au revoir," she said spending time gazing at him. Then impetuously, she leaned in and kissed his cheek. Hesitating for several seconds she turned and made her way to the massive entrance door. She was gone. They never stayed in touch.

Viewing the cold stone walls for the last time with what limited vision she had Elizabeth boarded a carriage with Anna, sitting in an impassive mood as it began moving slowly away. Her six month stay at La Maternité had ended with some practical experience gained but with a much altered life plan forced upon her. She had to wonder, riding along, remaining silent and listening to the soft clopping of the horse's hooves, if her time at La Maternité was of true value. And while that question would continue to haunt her for many years, in her immediate analysis she determined La Maternité provided more than it took away. And for that she was grateful.

Chapter Sixteen

October, 1850
Paris, France

"Anna, it's not just a hospital it is the Saint Bartholomew, just one of the more prominent hospitals in London, perhaps in all of Europe, that's all."

The weather had taken on a moderate character showing more respect for those who enjoyed the outdoors. For Elizabeth the outdoors meant freedom, an escape from the apartment and away from the feeling of being trapped. At first, with her activities limited, the apartment had become a Bastille of frustration. Much to her chagrin her limited eyesight continued to be an added obstacle to completing the rest of her medical training. With hospitals still not giving consideration to a woman, let alone a woman with limited eyesight, the goal became absolutely unattainable.

With time her vision in the right eye improved significantly and once the weather began to cooperate, Elizabeth sought solace in the beautiful Luxembourg Gardens that stood but one block from the apartment. She could walk there, not having to depend upon Anna. It was difficult, but with her improved vision simple tasks could be done and Elizabeth considered the short walk to her favorite retreat a simple task.

One Wednesday morning she decided to visit the Gardens early instead of waiting for her regular noontime hour. For some reason the early morning brightness streaming through the apartment's windows had a mystical lure to it. All the elements and objects surrounding her gave the impression of being fresh and invigorating and new. The change in time would also allow her a chance to determine if fewer people would be in the Gardens at that hour thereby allowing her the serenity and full pleasure of nature she was seeking.

As Elizabeth made her way toward the Gardens the sun began spreading its rays on the street between the buildings that lined Rue de Fleurus. By the time she had reached the tree-filled park the sun had risen sufficiently to where it created the dappling display of light that gave the Gardens its unique personality plus providing for a more warming environment.

She found her usual bench and sat down to await the flock of pigeons that typically arrived whenever a human stopped to rest. Their soft cooing and constant begging amused Elizabeth yet she never brought bread crumbs to feed them. They, she thought, were entirely too rotund and needed no extra food from her.

While enjoying the relaxing moment, her mind turned to thoughts of the time she spent at the Priessanitz Institute in Grafenberg, Bavaria several months earlier. The application of hydrotherapy was the focus of its program designed to provide restorative treatments for a number of ailments including despair and depression of which Elizabeth had been suffering. She spent six weeks at the institute, had taken all the treatments and followed the strict regimen, but to her dismay the therapy was not beneficial. She had no recourse but to return to Paris, her spirits not mended and her eyesight not at all improved. Now resting there on the bench, observing the few visitors who strolled by, she couldn't help but wonder if the trip to Grafenberg was made more in desperation rather than conviction that the hydrotherapy treatments would truly be effective. "It doesn't matter," she whispered as if the pigeons would understand.

It was close to the noon hour when Elizabeth returned to the apartment. Anna was in the kitchen preparing a small lunch for the two of them.

"Elizabeth?" she called out upon hearing the front door close.

"Yes, Anna. I'm back."

"And how were the Gardens this morning?"

"Nice," Elizabeth answered walking into the kitchen.

Anna looked up. "Just...nice?"

"Nice, Anna...nothing spectacular, nothing grandiose, just nice."

"Ah. Well, I've prepared a little lunch for us."

Elizabeth shook her head. "I'm sorry you went to the trouble. I'm not very hungry."

A look of dissatisfaction showed on Anna's face. Her sister's temperament had not changed much despite having her vision improve. Still, Elizabeth remained in a brooding mood.

"You should eat something," Anna insisted.

"I'm sorry Anna, I'm just not hungry."

"That's fine. Oh, by the way," Anna said, putting her plate on the small kitchen table. "You received a post today."

"A post? For me? Who's it from?"

"Our cousin in South Staffordshire."

"Kenyon?"

"Yes, Kenyon."

"Um, that's interesting," Elizabeth said puckering her mouth. "Wonder what's on his mind?"

212

Anna laughed. "Well, my dear sister, I do believe you'll have to open the post to find that out."

"Brilliant," Elizabeth replied giving Anna a mocking look. "Where is it?"

"On the console table in the foyer."

Elizabeth made her way through the parlor to the front entrance to retrieve the letter. Running her finger under the flap she lifted out the sheet of paper, unfolded it and with a slight effort she could make out the contents. Halfway through her head jerked up and she gave a quick squeal. "Anna, Anna," she called, rushing back to the kitchen.

"What? What is it Elizabeth?"

"Listen to this," she said waving the letter in front of Anna's face. "Kenyon tells me that he had learned from Samuel that I wanted to study at a hospital in London. Quite fortunately it turns out he knows the dean of Saint Bartholomew's Hospital. It seems that after a strong plea on my behalf the dean has agreed to submit a petition to the treasurer who in turn will submit it to the Medical Council of the hospital." She stopped and stared at the letter.

"Yes, go on," Anna said.

Elizabeth looked up and sported a large grin. "Go on? What do you mean go on? That's it. Don't you understand what that means?"

"Kenyon has gone pleading on your behalf to get you into a hospital in London."

"Anna, it's not just a hospital it is *the* Saint Bartholomew, just one of the most prominent hospitals in London, perhaps in all of Europe, that's all."

"And?"

"And what?"

"Have you been accepted?"

Elizabeth's sigh spoke of her frustration with Anna's lack of understanding. "This is just the first step, Anna. It has to go to the Medical Council and then if they agree it goes before the hospital's House Committee and then they have to act on it. So it will be a while before I hear anything. Isn't that exciting news?"

Anna smiled. "Of course it is, Elizabeth. I know how much that would mean to you. You would finally get the opportunity you've been seeking ever since you graduated from Geneva."

"Eighteen months, Anna, for eighteen long months I've been trying to gain admission to a hospital as a recognized student doctor so I could do my residency and it appears I am about to achieve that goal. Oh, God bless cousin Kenyon, a genius, a mastermind, a true friend and..."

"And a family member," Anna added. "Never let it be said that the Blackwells don't stick together."

Anna watched as Elizabeth continued reading the letter. There was a sudden change in her sister's person. Gone was the morose expression replaced by the smiles that once graced Elizabeth's face. But not only that, Anna

214

also noticed a renewed excitement the letter had brought about. Elizabeth's hands were trembling.

It took one month for a decision to be made by the House Committee at St. Bartholomew Hospital. Their acceptance of Elizabeth as a student doctor, an intern, with all the same privileges afforded the male resident interns, came in a simple letter to her Paris apartment. The correspondence also included her voucher for admission to the hospital school and a cordial note of welcome from the Dean, Doctor James Paget.

And while it took a month for the decision, it took Elizabeth just three days to make all the arrangements to leave France and return to London to begin what she hoped would be her final stop on the path to becoming a full practicing physician.

"Do you have your trunk packed," Anna asked watching Elizabeth scurrying about the apartment.

"Yes, of course, of course...packed and labeled and ready for pickup."

"Pickup? It's going with us to the train depot is it not?"

Elizabeth stopped, stood erect and blinked. "Oh my, yes, you're absolutely correct. What was I thinking? Yes, it is going with us."

Anna shook her head. "Elizabeth, calm down, will you? Your train for Calais doesn't

215

leave until four o'clock. We have another half hour before we need to leave for the station."

"Now, you've arranged for the carriage haven't you?"

"Yes, yes…everything is arranged.

"We don't wish to be late, you know."

Anna threw up her hands in frustration. "You're being impossible," she said and stormed away.

Elizabeth stood nervously looking out the window waiting for the carriage. A half hour wait was entirely too long. But then the wait was either in the apartment or at the station, it didn't matter, for the train would leave at precisely the designated time no matter how impatient Elizabeth would become.

As prescribed, the train did leave on time as did the ferry at Calais and the train from Dover to London. All elements were exactly as they should have been and by early morning Elizabeth stood in the London Bridge Station preparing to begin anew a fresh new love affair with her beloved London.

After spending a restless night in a noisy hotel near the station she was able to secure lodging at the Thavies Inn, a quiet grouping of houses isolated off Holburn lane. Of some delight to her, the entrance into the small homelike apartments was most unusual, by way of an underground tunnel. But of greater delight was the fact that she was but a mere five minute walk to the hospital. Not only was the complex she had rented a fortunate happenstance, but it turned out to be quite convenient as well.

Wasting no time, she made arrangements to begin her training at the hospital and upon introducing herself to Dean Paget she was invited to his traditional class breakfast for new students, which was held in his home located on the hospital grounds. As it turned out, the exquisite repast took place the next day.

As Elizabeth eagerly walked to the breakfast function the next morning, she couldn't help but hum a soft tune to accompany her lively steps and feeling no obstacles would now alter her path to fulfillment. Elizabeth Blackwell had become transformed and neither injustice nor ignorance would interfere with her mission, which at that moment appeared indestructible.

The Dean's home sat nestled among large trees in close proximity to the hospital. Elizabeth moved along the wide sidewalk to the home having no trouble finding it. Within minutes she stood at the front door preparing to enter into a vastly different environment.

Upon greeting her, Doctor Paget showed an eagerness to bring Elizabeth into the gathering as though he was about to introduce a celebrity, a spotlight Elizabeth had always attempted to avoid. Yet the Dean now had his prize in hand and he was not about to be deterred. She soon joined a group of young men whose conversations ceased the minute Doctor Paget ushered her into the parlor.

"Gentlemen," he said in a loud, auspicious voice. "Allow me to introduce from the United States, Doctor," and he deliberately paused for emphasis, "Elizabeth Blackwell."

The silence remained and then one by one they began applauding, for Elizabeth's reputation had long preceded her and she stood not only in a position of recognition but in admiration as well.

Elizabeth smiled, a nervous smile, as she realized she was in a similar surrounding to that of Geneva. Besides being well known by these students, Elizabeth Blackwell also remained a curiosity piece, and, interestingly, her classmates at Saint Bartholomew's were accepting her exactly as the young men had back at Geneva. Male medical students of the day, she surmised, were most likely identical in mind everywhere, especially when it came to sharing time and space and lessons with the only female medical doctor in the world.

To Elizabeth's delight Saint Bartholomew became the perfect haven for intellectual pursuit and an opportunity to develop a practical application in medicine. From the intricate surgeries being performed, some of which she assisted, to the long, detailed treatments of the vast array of diseases, to the magnificent lectures, Elizabeth began to gain the valuable training and knowledge so critically needed to attain eventual certification. She was especially diligent in transferring her notes into carefully organized folios to which she would refer often during her time spent at the Hospital.

But her life wasn't totally confined to study. After settling in London she began to make new acquaintances; women who shared Elizabeth's zeal for reform. She enjoyed the gatherings and outings, listening to the ideas and concerns expressed by those who saw the suppression of women's rights as a moral blight on their country.

Shortly after the new year was underway, when Elizabeth was attending an afternoon tea with some of her new acquaintances, the matter of her future arose unexpectedly. Until that point Elizabeth had not given the subject much thought, being that she had just begun her studies at the hospital.

As she stood by a small table on which a variety of petit fours were neatly displayed she felt a tap on her shoulder. Mrs. Deloris Jameson, the hostess pointed as she spoke. "Elizabeth," she said "Look who's back from Germany. It's Florence."

Elizabeth turned to see one of the new friends with whom she had established an acquaintance. "Florence," she exclaimed a wide smile broadened across her face. "My dear Florence. It is so wonderful having you back. I've missed you."

Florence Nightingale threw open her arms to embrace Elizabeth. "Elizabeth, you haven't changed a bit," she teased smiling at her

219

assertion. After all she had only been away four months

"Of course not," Elizabeth teased back. "We never change, always young, always vibrant and..."

"Always as charming as ever," Nightingale finished. It caused both to share in a hearty laugh.

"I was thinking of you the other day, "Elizabeth said.

"You were? What prompted that?"

"Garbage in the streets."

Nightingale grimaced. "Oh, that again. I shutter just thinking about how this city, well, any city for that matter, allows such contaminated conditions to prevail. I'm sorry to say, Elizabeth, but this situation of terrible sanitation is prevalent everywhere. It's a growing menace and I'm afraid if nothing is done major outbreaks of horrid disease will grow to pandemic levels."

The comment surprised Elizabeth. "You believe it's that prevalent?"

"Look around you, Elizabeth. Here in London unsanitary conditions can be found everywhere, even in the more affluent areas of the city. The streets and gutters are filthy, garbage is strewn everywhere, sewage in the poorer parts of the city gathers in all the low lying areas. Yet this matter, unfortunately, remains a political problem and is ignored by our leaders because it would be too costly to fix. Thus the problem continues in antipathy."

"I see you've been crusading again."

Nightingale smirked. "You know me. I can't stop. I have this compulsion to right every wrong."

"Well, if it's of any comfort to you, Florence, I share your conviction. You're absolutely right. The unsanitary conditions that are left to exist do indeed present a great health risk for all peoples."

"I appreciate your support, Elizabeth and I know how you feel," Nightingale said then gave a long sighed. "Are we two the only ones who recognize the problem?"

"Well, I certainly see there may be many opportunities to change conditions when I enter my own private practice."

"That would certainly be a beneficial approach to the problem. By the way when do you believe you'll be entering your practice?" Nightingale asked.

Elizabeth lifted her shoulders in a questioning gesture. "It all depends on the progress of my work at the hospital. That should be in April. But if not I still need sufficient training to get my certificate to enter practice and be licensed."

"By the Society of Apothecaries here?"

Again Elizabeth shrugged. "Well, yes, if I intend to practice in England."

Nightingale cocked her head. "Are you saying you might not take up a practice here in England?"

Elizabeth gave a quick shake of her head. "I don't know, Florence, I'm truly not sure what my future will bring. I'm quite undecided. I must first complete my training and then I'll be in a better position to decide my fate."

Elizabeth's ambiguity apparently disturbed Nightingale especially in the matter of possibly not remaining in England, for her face turned sullen and her eyes cast downward as in a pang of rejection. "I see," she said softly.

Elizabeth could feel the disappointment of her friend. The matter of her future was not something she had truly planned on discussing at that time, especially with Florence, for it was, indeed, quite unsettled. Her internship should be concluded by the end of April. She would then be eligible for certification if she so desired. But beyond the completion of her work at Saint Bartholomew's she had no definite plans.

The subject was dropped and the two women continued their discussion with Nightingale describing her experiences in Germany. When the tea concluded and the two parted, Elizabeth returned to her room at Thavies Inn with a heavy feeling of regret. It had not been her intention to engage in a disappointing discussion with Nightingale, for it caused a most uncomfortable situation. Elizabeth knew that soon she would have to decide on her future role in medicine, but at that moment all she wanted to do was focus on her training and the future would be something to be dealt with later.

As April concluded, the matter of her future could no longer be avoided. She had completed her training at the Hospital thus leaving her eligible to enter private practice and begin her chosen mission of treating poor women and children. However, the question of where this could or would occur quickly became a pressing question. Finally in analyzing all aspects of such a dramatic leap forward she eventually drew the only conclusion she had. Although she would have preferred to have established her practice in the land of her birth, that as it turned out was not necessarily where it could begin. It became too apparent that if such a practice were to be undertaken it was going to have to be in America.

In all reality, the major reason for bypassing England for America was financial. While in Europe she had scant funds and what little she had was earned by her writings and from what was generously provided by Anna. She had no capital to invest in a private practice nor did she have any large circle of close family members from whom she might seek support. In addition, with her sister Emily now beginning her studies in medicine at the Medical College of Cleveland, Elizabeth realized the attitude toward women studying medicine was changing in

America, more so than in Europe. Yet, in the final analysis and with all factors taken into consideration, the issue of money still dominated her decision to return to America.

In July Anna came from Paris to spend a couple of days with Elizabeth before she sailed to America.

"Have you heard from Emily?" Anna asked wondering about their younger sister's plans.

"Received a letter a few days back on my inquiry."

"And, what did she think of the idea of joining you in your practice?"

Elizabeth folded one of the towels she was preparing to pack and shrugged. "I'm not too sure. I believe she would warm to the possibility once she has her degree. But then she too will have to gain practical experience and I'm thinking she most likely will seek those opportunities here in Europe. America may be thawing to the idea of women in medicine but the opportunities are still very limited if not closed."

"A strange paradox."

"To say the least."

"Couldn't she train under you?"

"No. No, not really. She would have to be licensed to practice medicine in a private office. Hospitals are the only institutions where practical training can be obtained.

"And how many years would that be?"

It was a question Elizabeth had to analyze and she spoke aloud in doing so. "So let's see. She will be entering college this fall, that will be two years, graduating in eighteen fifty-three, then two years or maybe less studying here in Europe takes us up to fifty-five and so I imagine she will be of a mind to start her practice at that point and I will have my practice well established by then with room for another doctor."

"Assuming you start a practice."

Elizabeth looked up and frowned. "Oh ye of little faith," she teased. "Of course I will have my own practice."

"And you expect no objections or efforts to prevent that by the medical profession?"

"Anna, I can establish my practice whether the doctors like it or not. They can't stop me."

"Oh, they will try, dear sister. You know they will try."

"Try, yes. Succeed, no."

Anna watched her sister go about methodically packing the trunk. She would be missed. Anna had grown accustomed to being with Elizabeth even after Elizabeth moved to London. The decision to return to America Anna could understand; could see how the effects of minimum resources would force the issue. The matter of resistance by the medical community still rested uncomfortably with Anna. She did not have the overt optimism her sister had always maintained and saw the reality of the situation. Yet, despite what appeared to be insurmountable odds, Elizabeth had attained successes that were unimaginable just four years prior and there stood no reason why it would not continue.

"When do you plan to leave?" Anna asked.

"Next week. I will travel to Dudley to spend the day with Howard and Cousin Samuel and then from Dudley continue on by rail to Liverpool where I will sail. Quite honestly, Anna, I am not looking forward to journeying once again over that cruel ocean."

"But you have the summer seas this time, Elizabeth, and the trip should be with less ship movement."

Elizabeth puffed out her cheeks in mock sickness. "If there is any movement but straight ahead and smooth, even the slightest of motion, I will be affected."

"Then stay here."

The room grew silent and Elizabeth laughed. "If only it were possible, Anna. But I must attempt to try in America, for all things there lend themselves to my reaching my goals. Our family is there and we have many friends interested in my pursuit. Once successful I can always return."

The conversation seemed to end at that point. All that was to be discussed had been said and Elizabeth continued on with her packing as Anna headed for the kitchen to prepare their meal. Anna needed to put the thought of her sister leaving behind her, for it would render Anna one less close family member in a foreign land. It was true that Anna had her younger brother Harold and various cousins living in England. But there was not that special bond which she enjoyed with Elizabeth.

Thus, toward the end of July in 1851, having spent tearful moments of parting with friends and family members, Elizabeth set her nerves and stomach to endue yet another voyage across the dreaded ocean to undertake new ventures and most assuredly to an uncertain future in her medical aspirations.

Chapter Seventeen

Collins leaned forward. "Then Doctor Blackwell, let's get busy putting your wonderful idea into reality. I will arrange a meeting with our Quaker leaders and we will begin to establish a Foundation for your infirmary."

In the summer of 1854, three hundred and twenty thousand people lived in New York City. Deaths from smallpox had risen, crime had jumped up sharply and newly elected Mayor Jacob Aaron Westervelt had just redesigned the uniforms for the one thousand men of the police force. Of great importance the city was presenting the Exhibition of the Industry of All Nations, a major event that was to draw thousands of visitors to the newly constructed Crystal Palace. President Franklin Pierce was to give the dedication address in July. All eyes were on that illustrious city.

Yet no one paid any attention to a young woman placing a small hand-printed sign in the window of a small room in a forgotten section of the city near Tompkins Square. No one noticed or cared except the poor who lived there in the squalor of the slums. It was a beginning, a rather modest beginning. Yet it had taken several years of struggle to progress even that far.

In the summer of 1851, with very little money in her possession, Elizabeth stepped off the boat onto the wharfs of New York City. All that she owned was packed in her small trunk. She stood there in the sweltering heat with absolutely no idea of where to begin.

"Need help, lady?"

The voice startled Elizabeth causing her to turn quickly to see who had spoken. There stood a rather haggard old man; his clothes tattered by wear. But he displayed a charming, pleasant smile, one Elizabeth suspected as not to be trusted, a common reaction formed in New York. Then he spoke again and changed her mind.

"I'm a cabby ma'am. Do you need a cab?"

She smiled relieved to have found someone to assist her. "Yes," she said. "I need to go to a rooming house in University Place."

"Yes, ma'am, know the area well."

Taking her trunk by the handle he began dragging it across the rough boards of the wharf to where he had his horse tied. Neither one spoke. It was a solemn procession to the waiting carriage and a rather uninspiring welcome back to her adopted country. Securing a room in New York was the only arrangement she had made prior to sailing from Europe. The remainder of her venture was to be determined once settled in.

It seemed quite logical to Elizabeth that she would find a position in the women's department at a large city dispensary. Upon requesting an application for a physician's position at the front desk she was amused by the reaction she received.

"You mean nurse," he said.

"No physician."

"I'm sorry madam," he said hesitantly, "but you are a woman."

"Yes, and a physician."

"But..." he paused, shook his head and reached into a file containing employment applications. "This will be thrown away, you realize."

"No," Elizabeth replied, "I do not realize that. It is a legitimate application."

"Yes, of course it is," he said smiling. "When completed, place it in the slot in this door next to me and return in one week to learn of its disposition."

Taking the application, Elizabeth moved to a writing desk to fill in the form. Looking up she saw several hospital personnel standing at the front desk staring at her. All were laughing. On seeing Elizabeth eying them they immediately turned their heads and dispersed.

Surely the ridicule of her application would have spread throughout the dispensary before the day was concluded.

Later, upon returning to inquire of the application, she was told in a very polite manner to wait, as the head of the women's department wished to meet with her.

When the director appeared he greeted Elizabeth warmly. "Doctor Blackwell," he said shocking Elizabeth that he should pay recognition to her status. "It is a pleasure meeting you. I am Doctor Warring."

"Doctor," she said. "Thank you for meeting with me."

Taking her arm he guided her to a quiet corner. "Your application for a position caused quite a stir."

"Yes, I can imagine."

"You realize, of course, that it was immediately rejected by the board of governing doctors." His statement was made in such a matter-of-fact manner that Elizabeth felt as though they never got past the first line with her name on it.

"Because I am a woman."

His head tilted. "That and who you are. For what it is worth I was the only one who did not vote to reject your application. But then," he said smiling, "I am considered to be somewhat of a lone wolf here at the dispensary. I do respect your position."

"Thank you Doctor Warring for your support."

"If I may," he said, "I would like to make a suggestion."

"Please do."

"I believe you must realize you are totally unaccepted in the medical profession of New York City."

"I have felt their wrath, yes."

"And you must also realize there will be no positions open to you in a medical facility."

"I had hoped things might have changed," she answered.

"They haven't," he said. "Therefore I might suggest you give strong consideration to opening your own dispensary. That will be your best opportunity to practice medicine in this city."

Elizabeth stared at the man. "That is rather unfortunate isn't it?"

"Realistic, I'm, afraid." It became the last comment on the matter.

Upon leaving the dispensary Elizabeth gave consideration to what Warring had to propose. Indeed, it appeared her only alternative was to open a dispensary on her own. Yet the matter of how to achieve such a feat remained the troubling question.

The answer came about through innocent circumstances. Encouraged to expand her interest in the field of physical education for girls, Elizabeth decided she could present lectures on the topic to not only provide important information but to earn a small stipend as well.

Established in a Sunday school room in the basement of a church, she attracted a limited gathering of ladies interested in the subject. Among those attending were some members of the Society of Friends, Quaker ladies. A cordial friendship with the women developed and eventually Elizabeth was invited to become the personal physician of some of the Quaker families in New York.

It wasn't until two years later that Elizabeth thought back to the suggestion made by Warring of opening her own dispensary. It came about in a discussion with a Quaker friend she had met at one of her lectures. Cornelia Hussey had always been intrigued with the work Elizabeth did for the poor women and children in the slums. She was impressed with Elizabeth's dedication.

"You need to centralize your work, Elizabeth," Hussey said

"Centralize?"

"Yes, that dispensary you keep talking about. In serving the poor in their homes you lose valuable time. If you had a central location...that dispensary you have mentioned, then they could come to you and you'd have the time to serve many more."

"Well, yes, I have given some thought to that. But it takes money, Cornelia, to open such a place."

There was a slight laugh given by Cornelia. "Elizabeth you don't need to worry about money. That's what you have friends for. I've been talking to some people and we've been trying to figure out how we can help you with your work. We decided that we could help best by getting that dispensary of yours opened and running.

"Do you mean you and your friends would...could help finance the opening of a dispensary?" she asked.

"Yes, that is exactly what I am saying."

It took Elizabeth some time before she could reply. Then she stammered in expressing her gratitude. "Thank you...thank you so much...thank you."

Elizabeth watched Clara Donahue leave the examining room. It seemed this habitual visitor wanted to vent out her displeasure with her husband and family rather than be examined for a bad cough. It was difficult listening to the woman's lungs due to her incessant chattering. But despite several frustrating moments when Donahue was asked to refrain from speaking, the examination finally concluded with a potion given to treat the malady and a request to return in a week.

The minute the front door was opened Clara Donahue stood face to face with Elizabeth's younger sister, Emily. For several seconds there developed an impasse until Emily stood aside allowing Donahue to leave.

"I'm back," Emily called when entering the waiting room.

"Finished so soon?"

"Yes, I have enough material for my needs so I thought I'd stop by here to see if you needed any help." The young medical student had spent the day at the library doing research for her thesis. She was staying at the house with Elizabeth.

"Ah, excellent, I can always use your help. I'm pleased you came early."

Emily gave a quick glance around the room. Three patients filled the small space. "Looks like a reasonable afternoon," she said.

"Normal caseload," Elizabeth said lowering her voice.

"All nonpaying I assume."

Elizabeth shrugged. "I don't ask. If they can pay they will. But generally not."

Emily looked at the list of patients to be seen. There was nothing too serious; conditions she could handle herself. But she was only there to assist. Being that she was only a medical student at Western Reserve University in Cleveland she could not attend to anyone medically. However her help was of value to both sisters.

"I received a letter from Mother yesterday," Emily said.

"Oh, what did she have to say?"

"She's concerned for your safety."

"My safety? What on earth for?"

"The mean-spirited and vulgar letters and comments you got when you first started your practice."

"They were harmless," Elizabeth insisted. "I paid them no mind."

"Is all of that over with now?"

"Well," Elizabeth answered pausing. "Not really. Just today I received another rather nasty post; crude and quite insulting. I still don't understand what those in high positions find so objectionable about a woman practicing medicine."

Emily drew back and gave a short laugh. "Don't understand? Elizabeth, those letters told you why they objected to you being in medicine."

"But those are just idle insults, no reasoning; no logic behind them. Calling me a woman of questionable morals are simply flagrant attempts at intimidation."

"So it's continuing then? And are you hearing any more lies from the physicians about you being incompetent and untrained and practicing medicine illegally? You know, it's a shame that people listen to those men and believe them."

"No, I haven't heard any further comments. But it doesn't matter if people believe those lies, the poor don't, Emily, and that's who we're serving, which," she said looking around the room, "I believe we best get back to doing."

Emily hesitated. "You remember don't you, Elizabeth, that I must leave tomorrow to return to Cleveland. I'll be graduating in January."

"Yes, yes, I do remember and I do so much want to attend your graduation."

"Oh, you'll have to make an extra effort. I won't have much time after graduation since I'll be sailing for England for my training soon afterwards."

"I will certainly try, Emily. But if for some reason I'm unable to attend I will definitely see you before you sail for England." Elizabeth reached over and took a hand towel off a rack and began drying her hands. "You know, Emily," she said turning to look at her sister, "as I see more and more women patients I realize that someday soon I will need to make some changes."

Emily's eyes squinted. "Meaning...what? You'll need help? Are you thinking that perhaps I should come here after graduation and train with you on the job?"

"No, no, of course not. You can't do that. You wouldn't be licensed. No, what I'm saying is that I foresee the day when I will need to enlarge this little operation of mine into something bigger and by then you will have finished your training and may want to join me in this growing venture."

Emily drew back and turned to look away.

"You have time to think about it," Elizabeth added quickly.

"No, I don't have to think about it, Elizabeth. Of course I want to be a part of your vision. It's just that..." she turned around to look at Elizabeth.

"Yes, just what?"

"It's just that I'm afraid you may be pushing yourself too hard. There may never be an opportunity for a new..."

"Don't worry, Emily. I certainly have no plans of wearing myself out. I'm a practical person. I'm no fool. All of what I have worked for would be wasted if I became incapacitated and could no longer pursue my passion. You don't have to worry. I'll be here strong and able when you've finished your training."

The subject was not discussed any further that day or when Emily said her goodbyes the next morning. The matter of the enlarged facility had been forgotten.

In the autumn of 1855 Elizabeth, now at the age of thirty-four, found herself moving quickly along leaf covered sidewalks searching for a horse-car for the short ride across town to the home of Mr. Stacy Collins, one of her early financial supporters. After vacillating, as she was often prone to do, she finally realized she needed to discuss the concept of an infirmary if she was to continue adequately serving the poor women and children in the poverty areas of New York.

Upon arriving at his home she waited before ascending the steps. She was not especially good at asking for money. Advice she could seek with no problem. But when it came to the art of soliciting sums of money, and in this case a rather large sum of money, she felt incapable and reluctant, envisioning herself in the role of a street beggar.

However, Stacy Collins held no such viewpoint of Elizabeth. He held her in high esteem and his deep sense of humanity made him one of her staunchest advocates.

"I like what you've written Elizabeth," he told her after she had spent a good twenty minutes reviewing her plans with him. "You certainly have done a commendable study of the problem. I especially find your patients' comments rather intriguing, a worthy insight into their hearts as well as their sufferings."

"I appreciate that, Mister Collins," she told him. "Hearing you say that is most encouraging."

Collins leaned back in his chair and smiled. "But you didn't just wish to visit with me to review this idea of yours did you?"

Feeling her face flush she returned his smile and squeezed her hands together. "You don't know how difficult this is for me, Mister Collins."

"Oh but I do Elizabeth. But why? I'm no blind man who can't see the pleading look in your eyes. And I'm also not an ogre. I know you came here to state your case and seek my advice on how to fund this worthwhile project. But I have always believed in your efforts so why wouldn't I be interested now?"

"And I am most appreciative of your support and that of the others. It's just that..."

'It's just that you don't feel it proper to ask again, Correct?"

Elizabeth looked at him and found his teasing smile reassuring. "Correct."

"Elizabeth, you should know better. Your friends among the Quaker community have gathered around you not only to encourage your brave mission and aspirations but we have also had you serve as our own personal physician. Why the very first baby you delivered was our granddaughter and we still seek your services when needed. You're like a member of our family. You should feel no reluctance to include us in your concept of service to others. As you know that in itself is part of our traditional testimonies. Surely you wouldn't think we would turn you down."

"To be quite honest, Mr. Collins, I don't believe in taking any person for granted. But you are absolutely correct. I have come asking once again and you and the other Friends are the only ones to whom I can turn."

"Splendid," he said with a slight chuckle to his words. "So, now that you've been able to acknowledge your mission let us set about discussing the many different ways you, your sister and that other young lady joining you can obtain the needed funds; a plan for not only gifts from the Friends but through other projects that raise funds for worthy causes such as yours."

"Such as?" she asked

"Well, a very popular format I've seen and have even attended is a bazaar. It is very popular these days and attracts quite a bit of attention. And with the lectures you're now giving you could charge an admission fee. And I surmise there would be many other methods that could generate funds."

"But Emily, Maria and I cannot run these activities while attending to patients."

"Oh no, you...we...would gather together many others to carry out these functions on behalf of the infirmary."

Elizabeth stared into the eyes of the man sitting across from her and saw the enthusiasm that matched the commitment of his words. "Yes, yes," she said a quiver in her voice. "Of course, I can see how all of this can be brought together for the support we'll need."

Collins leaned forward. "Then Doctor Blackwell, let's get busy putting your wonderful idea into reality. I will arrange a meeting with our Quaker leaders and we will begin to establish a Foundation for your infirmary."

Elizabeth could only sit motionless, stunned by the pace of the discussion and equally shocked by the quickness of the conclusions being reached. In her mind she had just barely asked for financial help when Stacy Collins was advancing a multitude of theories on how to obtain that support. She wanted to cry out her deep appreciation but found herself without voice. The emotions that swelled in her throat allowed her lips to move but she was voiceless. Unexpectedly tears began streaming down her cheeks causing her to quickly place her hands over her face to hide the embarrassing moment. Finally she spoke. "Oh, Mister Collins, I am so grateful for your willingness to assist me in this, so eternally indebted to you and the other Friends.

"I know Elizabeth," he said standing. "I know."

Elizabeth left the home of Stacy Collins that chilly morning having advanced further into the dream of a full service infirmary. Yet it was, as it began, still a dream. On the ride back to her house she attempted to tabulate the many details that such an ambition was going to entail and the course of action she and the others would need to chart. There would be, of course, great jubilation among Emily and their newest partner, Maria Zackrzewska, who shared Elizabeth's goal of creating the infirmary.

By the start of winter that year not only had initial funding been secured but a cadre of supportive physicians had also been found and from that grouping a study committee was created adding both substance and credibility to the infirmary concept.

Yet all was not perfect. Weakening the momentum and eroding much of Elizabeth's enthusiasm was the continued strong opposition against her, perpetrated by the bulk of the medical profession in New York City. As she was to learn, the tyrannical powers of this redoubtable body of men was yet to be felt. Any advancements made by this corrupt woman, this felon of custom and tradition, was not to be without its consequences. The infirmary would have to be developed while fighting hostility from an obtuse and mean-spirited group of the city's most prominent and powerful physicians. The more Elizabeth succeeded the larger and more damaging the war became. And in such a battle the poor, as always, were to be the potential victims.

Chapter Eighteen

January, 1856
New York, New York

Although fierce opposition to everything about her was not a new experience for Elizabeth, a different kind of antagonism was now forming and it gave her and others cause for concern.

Tugging the heavy coat tighter around her body to ward off the icy wind Elizabeth stared into the stodgy old face in total disbelief. "You're not serious are you? You're refusing to rent me space for my hospital because I'm a woman?"

"You're a she-devil," he shot back, his face contorted in anger. "You want to do nothing but cause me trouble. I want nothing to do with you."

"But this is for a hospital for the poor. Don't you understand that? This isn't about me but the poor out there," Elizabeth answered

245

waving her hand toward several people slogging along the snowy sidewalk. "Is that causing trouble?"

"You'll bring the police," he yelled. "You're not a real doctor. If someone dies in my building because of you I get into trouble. I want nothing to do with you. Get away...NOW!" The resounding echo of the door slamming in her face sent Elizabeth staggering back, her eyes ablaze in anger.

Remaining at the door Elizabeth's hands clenched into tight fists. She wanted so much to pound on that door and give a verbal lashing the likes of which would have singed the old man's face. Yet the strong Quaker upbringing of her youth prevented her from seeking such revenge. Instead she joined her sister on the sidewalk where she proceeded to mumble the tongue-lashing as they moved away from what was now becoming her nemesis: landlords.

It had been a little more than five months since Elizabeth had her conversation with Stacy Collins. The funding was now well established and Elizabeth was setting out to explore potential sites in which to house her new infirmary. However, regardless of where she searched the results were always the same: landlords refusing to rent their space; each one with a different excuse, but all laced with the frightened insinuations that great harm would befall them if they cooperated with the Blackwell sisters. They insisted Elizabeth and Emily were imposters and if a death occurred there would be no death certificate issued because the two women were not true doctors placing the landlords in great peril. The emphasis was always on the fact the sisters were pretenders and charlatans. That was a constant. Many of the building owners also argued that by treating the poor, unsavory elements would show up to the property making adjacent properties lose value causing them problems with their neighbors. And without any men present, great harm could come to the women and they, the landlords, would be blamed.

Of no coincidence, the same charges were also levied by the medical profession. It was obvious that a very effective propaganda campaign had been formulated and was being waged against Elizabeth. It was the core of the city's physicians who vociferously condemned Elizabeth and yet chose to hide the fact she had received full certification from the Board of Medical Examiners for the State of New York thereby certifying that Elizabeth was, indeed, a true and legitimate doctor of medicine. It was a convenient omission and it served their purpose well.

Walking down Houston Street toward Lafayette, Emily could see the anger and frustration reflected on Elizabeth's face. "There are many more, Elizabeth, many more property owners who aren't like this one. We'll find them."

But Elizabeth didn't hear what Emily was saying. She had slipped into thoughts far from where they walked. As they continued down the sidewalk her head shook slowly. Then abruptly she stopped, turned and looked at Emily.

"We've been doing this all wrong, Emily," she said. "Why are we here searching for space when we have many friends in this city who know property owners; our friends of high standing and impeccable reputation? I'm sure they can apply their friendly persuasion to convince one of these owners to lease us space for our infirmary."

"But Elizabeth we've asked for so much from them already."

"Yes, I know, I know, and I would hesitate approaching them again if it were not for this strong opposition we've encountered. The closed doors are just too daunting to deal with. We've got to turn to them again and pray they're successful."

"Why can't we just continue our services out of the house?"

"Impossible, Emily. It's entirely too small. We need a larger place where we can treat the overload we have, and do in-patient services, where you can do your surgeries and Maria and I can see patients in wards. We need room, lots of room."

"Perhaps you're being too ambitious," Emily offered.

Elizabeth stopped walking to turn and face her sister. "Ambitious? Well then if you believe we are being too ambitious you explain that to those poor women and children who come to the dispensary these days who can't be treated because we don't want to be too ambitious. Tell them we're going to shove them aside because we can't handle the case load; that they have to wait. You tell them that, Emily because I am not going to. Yes, I am ambitious and I intend to remain as such."

For Emily it was an unjustified rebuke. It was her obligation, Emily felt, to shave down the over zealous drive of her older sister if for no other reason than to conserve the energy consuming Elizabeth. Her drive to create an infirmary had become an obsession beyond control, upsetting her to the point where she was not sleeping well, eating poorly, rushing patient care and losing her patience with both Emily and Maria.

"There's no need for that," Emily said. "I'm trying to be the voice of reason."

Elizabeth chose to ignore her sister's admonition and proceeded to continue toward the house. Emily shrugged and fell in line with Elizabeth and the two continued on in silence. Emily's thoughts were churning in a multitude of circles. With a chastising shake of her head she followed knowing that at this point in her sister's life Elizabeth was feeling unfulfilled. Of all the ludicrous ideas, Emily argued. Elizabeth

Blackwell feeling unfulfilled. That kind of thinking, she concluded, was going to kill them both.

In late March a meeting was held with a newly formed advisory committee for the purpose of strategizing procurement of a suitable building for the new infirmary. One of the participants was Cornelia Hussey. Cornelia's interest in Elizabeth's pursuits had continued to grow ever since she aided in establishing the first dispensary. Now she sat with the others to assure Elizabeth's concept of a much-needed infirmary would definitely come to fruition.

"I've been in discussion with a friend of mine," she told the group that evening. "And he believes he might have a property owner who is not easily persuaded by the medical profession; not likely to believe the tales being told of you Elizabeth."

"Excellent, excellent, that is excellent news, Cornelia. When do you believe he'll be speaking with this man?"

"He didn't say. Right now he's in Philadelphia on business and will be away for a month or so."

Elizabeth's shoulders dropped. It meant another delay, prolonging the possibility of securing a facility. That troubled her. Delays had become a venomous serpent for Elizabeth. Drawing in a long breath to calm her spirits Elizabeth looked up and feigned a smile. "Then we will wait for his return," she said attempting to put a positive tint to her remark. "And where might this building be?"

"64 Bleecker Street, off of Lafayette."

Elizabeth's eyes closed attempting to imagine the location. "Up from Houston?"

"Yes, a spacious building, Elizabeth. It's perfect."

"Can we afford it?"

Cornelia Hussey smiled. "Not to worry, Elizabeth, We'll see to it that we can."

"Oh no, Cornelia, all of you have put so much money in to this already. You can't do more."

"But we truly want to do more, Elizabeth. This is such a worthwhile project and so needed. We can't think of any better way of serving those who are less fortunate than to have this infirmary opened and operating."

Her mood changed. No longer did the delay matter and Elizabeth tightened her mouth to keep from crying with joy. Grabbing a quick deep breath she said, "Thank you so much, Cornelia." She looked around the room. "All of you thank you so very, very much."

But the progress on securing the building did not move as quickly as the committee had envisioned. Despite the willingness of the building owner to lease the space to the committee, who now served as the official governing body of the newly incorporated infirmary, complications arose in seeking a

251

zoning change that would take it from residential to a business and medical status. Several members of the committee speculated that perhaps politics played a major part in the several months' delay.

Although fierce opposition to everything about her was not a new experience for Elizabeth, a different kind of antagonism was now forming and it gave her and others cause for concern. The attacks had become more fierce, and personal denigration appeared to be the tactic of choice from some quarters of the medical community. Although there were those in that community who broke rank and took an interest in Elizabeth's quest to establish an infirmary, they nevertheless felt obligated to advise her against making this bold move.

It appeared that the more brutal attacks came from the affluent physicians, those who saw the possibility of their female clientele choosing to be treated by a fellow female. The potential of loss of income increased the flames of their assaults against Elizabeth and therefore made the challenge of establishing her infirmary all that more difficult. Regardless of the argument, the fact was those physicians were not treating the class of people Elizabeth's infirmary would attract. There was absolutely no monetary threat. Yet they pushed forward with their campaign of discrediting Elizabeth.

The ugliness of it all manifested itself one evening during an address given by Elizabeth, an activity she had begun to do on a regular basis as part of the committee's efforts to raise funds. Unknown to her, in the audience, was an attendee hired by a group of the more vociferous physicians whose sole purpose was to interrupt Elizabeth's presentation and engage her in an argument challenging the propriety of women being physicians. The young man had been well rehearsed in the opposing points harbored by the physicians.

Elizabeth was well into her address on the laws and life of the physical education of girls when the initial volley was launched.

The perpetrator was seated in the third row almost directly in line with her. He was tall, an advantage, and he spoke in a loud, condescending voice. "And by what authority do you make these statements?" He called out as he stood.

The audience, as well as Elizabeth, was stunned by this rude interruption. The young man was about to repeat his charge when the audience clamored for him to sit down. But Elizabeth raised her hands and explained to the crowd that it was perfectly all right, she didn't mind the challenge and that she would gladly address the young man's question.

It took several seconds for the audience to quiet down. But being paid handsomely to disrupt and harass, the agitator remained standing and began calling out his question once again when Elizabeth, realizing what was happening, raised her voice in an effort to drown him out. "By the authority of God." It was the first thought to come to her mind in seeking a rebuttal that would hopefully stun her antagonist. She had no idea why she said such a thing, for surely that would bring about a newer attack. She was correct.

A hush descended on the room and the young man stood silent, but for only seconds. "Not only do you misrepresent but you blaspheme as well. How dare you refer to God!

"I do not know what your God says to you," Elizabeth responded in a loud voice, "but my God says to love thy neighbor, to take care of the poor and downtrodden, to give aid to the sick and suffering. And..."

"You cannot hide behind sacred scripture. You are an imposter, posing to be a doctor when all of us in this room know full well there is no place in the medical profession for a woman."

Elizabeth began feeling her anger starting to bubble to the surface and she struggled to contain it, not allowing this episode to escalate into a shouting match. Still she felt it was absolutely necessary to defend herself. "And the Board of Medical Examiners for this state is thereby wrong?'

"The board would not condone a female doctor. You are an imposter...a charlatan who is trying to deceive these people in order to take their money. You are a criminal."

"But have you reviewed the medical board's files? If you had you would see my name inscribed on their records as a legitimate, certified physician licensed to practice medicine in this state."

"Ha," he shouted. "Another lie. Of course you can say that because we do not have access to any such file. It is easy to lie when the proof is unavailable."

The audience was now becoming annoyed with the exchange and several voices called out for the young man to be quite. Ignoring their demands he focused on his instructions to cause a disruption, bringing discredit to Elizabeth Blackwell before a crowd in any manner conceivable. Many had reached a point of agitation and several people began throwing their programs at the man. Two attendees in front of the protester stood, turned and shouted for him to leave if he didn't like what was being presented. Flying programs pelted some audience members and from shouts to rough shoving to fists being thrown, people became engaged in a surprising melee without any direct cause being truly understood.

Elizabeth called for calm but the clamor drowned out any plea for order and she felt it necessary to hurry off stage. The promoter of the event had left the wings in an attempt to break up the clamor. Many of the patrons were leaving and Elizabeth found herself shaking.

"That little display was nothing," she heard and turned to see the young agitator standing but five feet away. "Keep up your pretense Miss Blackwell and you'll regret having launched this dangerous crusade."

"Are you threatening me?"

"I'm simply passing along wise advice. If you perceive it to be a threat then that is your prerogative and not my intent."

Their paths never did cross again and there were no more disruptions at her lectures. At first she was hesitant to continue giving talks, but the income derived from them was quite substantial therefore it was practically mandatory that she continue.

But the blatant display of ignorance was far from over.

Chapter Nineteen

December 1856
New York, New York

By her way of thinking the cutting of the ribbon was not so much for the opening of the new infirmary as it was for cutting the bond that kept women for thousands of years from practicing medicine.

It always seemed to Elizabeth Blackwell that winter was the most fertile time for the brain and provided an excellent environment for intellectual pursuit. There was something invigorating about those cold, grey and dank months that somehow stimulated the mind. Now, while sitting on the long divan in the parlor of Cornelia Hussey's attractive home, that impression seemed to be manifesting itself once again. She was there that morning to confer with the Infirmary's board of trustees regarding the refurbishing of the home on Bleecker Street.

Once the property had been officially leased and inspected by the trustees they set about recruiting volunteer craftsmen to assist in the task of converting an ordinary building into a hospital. Elizabeth knew what she wanted but was not well versed in the requirements needed for transferring those ideas into reality. That was the purpose for the morning's conference, to learn more of the means of achieving that goal.

"Elizabeth." It was Cornelia. "Good Morning to you. I was told you were here."

"Good Morning, Cornelia," Elizabeth responded rising from the divan.

"You're the first to arrive. Here, let me take your coat. I've just made coffee would you care for some?"

"Oh, yes, please. That sounds perfect on a bitter morning like this one."

"Bitter, indeed," Cornelia said hanging Elizabeth's coat in the front closet. "But I'm afraid the bitterness isn't due to the weather."

"Oh? What do you mean?"

"I received word from our landlord that last night someone threw rocks thorough the front windows of our building."

"Windows broken?"

"Yes, a bit of senseless vandalism I suppose."

They reached the kitchen and Elizabeth sat at the small breakfast table. "Or intimidation or a warning," she said looking up at Cornelia.

Cornelia stopped pouring coffee and gave Elizabeth a quizzical look. "You don't mean someone deliberately did that to scare us off?"

"That's precisely what I mean. Our city's medical community has not stopped their harassment and now with us starting our infirmary I'm afraid the pressure to make us relent will increase."

"Well, certainly the physicians on our board would find that kind of behavior abhorrent."

"But they can't stop it. The vast majority of physicians in New York, or for that matter worldwide, strongly retain the notion that there is no place for women in medicine."

"But property destruction is criminal. Surely they wouldn't resort to that."

"It is only criminal for the one or ones who threw the rocks."

The room grew silent as Elizabeth took a sip of her coffee and Cornelia moved to a counter to arrange some cookies on a plate. Their thoughts lasted but a few seconds, interrupted by the sound of the front door bell.

"The others are arriving," Cornelia said. "Bess will get it."

"Do the board members know of the rock throwing incident?" Elizabeth asked.

"No."

"Then let's not inform them. I need this meeting to be kept on a positive level."

"Yes, I agree" Cornelia said. "No need to add distractions."

There were six members of the board and advisory committee who were able to attend. That number was sufficient to review some of the floor plans and schematics compiled by the craftsmen.

"These drawings are crude," Doctor Valentine Mott pointed out to the gathering. "The men have little time for this, as they are kept rather busy these days so we get their attention during their spare time.'

"Their limited time," Elizabeth queried, "also applies to the actual work, right?"

"I'm afraid so, Elizabeth."

"What, then, are we talking about as far as time is concerned?"

"From what I see here I would think five or six months."

"Oh, much sooner than I expected," Elizabeth said.

Mott laughed. "Well, there's not all that much remodeling to be done. You and your sister have done an excellent job of utilizing existing space to meet your needs, Elizabeth."

"I'm wondering, Elizabeth," one of the members, a Doctor Willard Parker, inquired, "if the surgical suite is going to be large enough? I see by these plans you requested this room here," he said pointing to a space in the corner of the building, "to be enlarged by only five more feet."

"I believe it will be, Doctor. We won't be having the usual surgical team that the main hospitals have. It will most likely be Emily and me. You also have to remember, Doctor, we won't be doing major surgeries but minor work when needed."

He examined the papers more closely and then shook his head. "I see that they left the windows in."

Elizabeth glanced at Cornelia. "Yes, to help with the lighting. But perhaps better placement of the lamps could be arranged," she added knowing that would not work. Natural light was so much better than the oil lamps no matter how many there were. Plus, the excess smell of the burning oil mixing with the ether was potentially too dangerous. Opened windows would help remove the ether fumes as well. "What else is there to review?" she asked leaning in to look at the plans hoping the matter of the windows would quickly fade.

The design of the wards and the examining rooms became a topic of concern. When asked what the capacity might be for the wards Elizabeth answered without hesitation, "Constantly full." Those physicians sitting around the table gave each other doubting glances, for it would be humanly impossible for three doctors to tend to two wards full of patients. Yet Elizabeth Blackwell knew that the

261

poor women and children in the slums of New York who needed to be hospitalized far outnumbered the 20 beds she envisioned for the hospital.

After the meeting ended Elizabeth prepared to leave citing a full patient load back at the dispensary.

"Emily and Marie have their hands full," she told Cornelia as she donned her heavy coat. "And as word spreads we see the need for a larger space and an increase in service."

"How are the plans going for the use of the infirmary as an adjunct to the medical schooling of other women?"

"We have the State medical board's approval to provide that opportunity. As soon as we open the doors we can begin offering practical training for those women getting their medical degree."

"And you're limiting it just to women?"

Elizabeth stopped buttoning her coat and looked at Cornelia, a wide smile crossing her face. "Yes," she said in a strong determinate voice. Nothing else needed saying. It was, so it appeared to Cornelia, Elizabeth's way of running the saber completely through the bulk of the New York City medical society and doing it with delight.

"You'd best be going," Cornelia said. "The weather's taking a turn and trying to secure a cab at this time of day is going to be difficult."

Elizabeth nodded. "Fortunately you are not that far from the main avenue,"

Yet it took Elizabeth close to twenty minutes before a carriage came. By then, as Cornelia had predicted, the weather had taken a turn for the worse and snow began falling. Fortunately the wind was mild thus not making the drop in temperature a major inconvenience.

Once inside the cab, Elizabeth gave thought to the recent addition to her life. It was during the last month that she had decided to abandon the solitary existence which she had been living. While that form of segregation was effective during the earlier drive to achieve a degree in medicine and obtain certification as a physician it no longer served the same purpose. Now Elizabeth found the seclusion distractive. Subsequently she decided to adopt a child to provide the companionship she had come to see as a necessary addition to her life.

Katherine "Kitty" Barry was a seven-year-old orphan whom Elizabeth met at the emigrant depot on Randall Island. It was the inclusion of this beautiful child in the life of Elizabeth Blackwell that gave new meaning to Elizabeth's efforts and crusades. Kitty provided a new-found enjoyment in Elizabeth's pursuits. Now Elizabeth viewed many things through the simplistic eyes of a child, eliminating the clutter that often destroyed clear thinking. Kitty Barry became an important part of Elizabeth's life.

When Elizabeth arrived at the dispensary she found Emily alone tending to the patients. Maria Zackrzewska had been called out to a home to treat a woman who had fallen and broken bones. There were four patients waiting, three in the chairs and a young woman who chose to sit on the floor by the door. When Elizabeth entered the house Emily was bidding farewell to a woman and child she had been treating.

"Oh, Elizabeth, I'm so happy you're here. It's been quite hectic today and I'm afraid we will be working into the night."

"Maybe not," Elizabeth said removing her coat. "The weather is getting worse. The wind and the cold may deter our patients from coming here. Is Kitty home from her studies?"

"Yes, she's upstairs reading her books," Emily said drying her hands, "Arrived home about an hour ago. How did the meeting go?"

"Excellent. The members feel we will most likely have the house remodeled within five months."

Stowing her coat in the closet Elizabeth turned to see who the patients might be, if she recognized any of them. As Elizabeth moved, Emily grabbed her arm. "Elizabeth," she whispered, "see that woman there on the floor."

"Yes, what about her?"

"I've just now noticed how terrible she looks. She needs immediate care."

Elizabeth glanced over and saw the young woman huddled tight, arms wrapped around her legs. Her complexion had taken on an odd-looking ashen tone. Moving quickly to attend to her she noticed the woman moan while slipping further to the floor. The bulging profile could clearly be seen. There was no doubt.

Elizabeth called out. "Emily, hurry, help me get this patient into the treatment room. She's having a baby and I believe she's starting to deliver."

Placing one arm around the woman's back and the other hand on her arm Elizabeth began to lift.

"No, no, no," the woman cried, her body going limp.

Signaling with a wave of her hand Elizabeth told Emily. "Get these people out of here for privacy. She's having her baby now...in this room. We can't move her. Get some water...bring towels right now...and a blanket for the baby.

Emily began moving the three women into the treatment room, two of them being curious turned to peer at what they might see. "Please wait in here," she said trying to turn their faces while closing the door. Hurrying to the supply cabinet she grabbed several towels and practically threw them at Elizabeth, who by now had the woman on her back, knees elevated and apart.

Emily found a large deep pan in the kitchen and began pumping water into it urging on the water as she pumped. "Come on now...come on," followed by a complaint. "Old junk," she grumbled. "Takes too long...entirely too long." Then just as Emily was about to lose her patience the water gurgled and gushed out in spurts. Quickly shoving the pan under the rushing water the pan began to rapidly fill.

With water splashing on the old wooden floor Emily rushed to where Elizabeth knelt but before she could reach Elizabeth she stopped to watch as Elizabeth lifted a tiny pink body up by the legs and heard the baby cry. The pan was set down and Emily dipped one of the towels in the water to begin cleaning the newly born infant.

"Auk," Elizabeth groaned. "My surgical scissors. Emily, in the cabinet is a sterile pair. Could you get it please?"

Pushing herself off from the floor Emily moved quickly to the cabinet and upon returning noticed the complexion of the mother more ashen than before. "This woman needs to be in a hospital, Elizabeth."

"Can't. She has no money," Elizabeth commented. "And the Almshouse on the island is too far away and too long of a trip.

"But...but we can't just send her home."

Elizabeth glanced up at Emily and nodded.

"Then...does she remain here until we can find her family who can take her home to rest?"

"No, no" came a trembling whisper from the woman. "No rest...no time for rest...got to care for others."

Elizabeth and Emily exchanged glances. "Your husband can look after the others," Elizabeth suggested.

"No husband. Five children at home. They have no one to help them."

The room went silent. Several of the women who had been in the treatment room began leaving while attempting to glance over the hunched body of Elizabeth as she attended to the mother and baby.

Elizabeth looked up. "Emily, try to find where this woman lives and then get those children and bring them here. They can spend the night here as we watch over their mother."

"I know this woman." It was the voice of one of the other patients. "I can bring the children here."

Again the room stilled until Elizabeth eyed the woman and spoke to her. "And your condition? Why did you come to see me?"

Obviously it was a matter the woman wished not to discuss in front of the others. Her face reddened and she leaned down to whisper in Elizabeth's ear

Assured the woman did not have a disease that could have been spread to the children Elizabeth nodded. "Emily will go with you. Thank you for your help. Is it far?"

"Two blocks away, two doors down from me." She looked again at the mother. "Is she going to die?"

"No, but she needs rest and your help is appreciated. I will be able to give you something for your condition upon your return. I suggest the two of you leave now as the weather is getting worse."

Pulling herself up from a kneeling position Elizabeth moved to the kitchen to wash up and boil some water to sterilize her scissors. While getting more water she called out to Emily. "Take some blankets with you to bundle up the children in case they don't have warm wraps."

"What about food?" Emily asked running an arm through the sleeve of her coat.

"We'll make do with what we have." She paused and shook her head. "Oh, why couldn't we have had the infirmary now?" It was a rhetorical question and Elizabeth mumbled an answer unheard by Emily as Elizabeth went about finishing the tasks she had begun.

It was the impatience of Elizabeth that caused Emily to extend her concerns for her sister's health and for the tension it was causing. The two had discussed the situation before but that only acerbated the tension. Elizabeth argued that someone had to stay on top of the project or it would never get done. Emily felt Elizabeth's anxieties were causing her to be irritable, not helping her health. Maria Zackrzewska elected to stay out of the squabble, that it was a sibling matter. But even Maria could feel the tension and subliminally it was affecting her as well.

By the middle of April of 1857, despite Elizabeth's anxieties, progress on conversion of a regular residence into the likes of a hospital had been made. The surgical wing kept its windows and a slight enlargement of the wards added two more beds to each room. The treatment rooms were increased to three when Elizabeth and Emily decided to reduce the space of their offices. There was no sacrifice for Maria since her space wasn't all that roomy to begin with.

At two thirty on a sunny, mild Wednesday afternoon Elizabeth burst through the front door of the dispensary her face ablaze in ecstatic joy. The exuberance startled the six women gathered in the front room. A baby began to cry. The clamor brought Emily and Maria into the waiting room

"It's finished," Elizabeth called out adding to the clamor. "The infirmary is finished," she continued as she made the rounds of the room hugging anyone who was in her path, patients and doctors alike. "We can start moving now. Cornelia is securing us a wagon to help with the move. Isn't that exciting," she said starting a second round of hugs.

"Does that mean the dispensary is going to be closed?" one of those waiting to be treated asked.

Elizabeth stopped in her enthusiastic outbursts and stared at the woman. Inadvertently she had just unsettled the patients by exclaiming the good news of a new facility. To them eliminating the dispensary in this small house on Fifteenth Street meant the elimination of their medical services. Closing down equated to closing out and Elizabeth knew her good news would soon, through the swift rumor mill of the underneath city, translate into bad news for the poor women in New York.

"No, no," Elizabeth explained. "You will still get the same medical attention. Nothing has changed, just the location that's all and with more services."

"Where?"

"Over on Bleecker Street,…64 Bleecker."

She could see the woman calculating the new distance to be traveled. "Bleecker," she said in a monotone indifference. "Um, nearly thirteen blocks from here."

"But it will be a hospital, free to you; you won't be turned away like at the other bigger hospitals. This will be your hospital."

The patients eyed each other. Elizabeth could see they were thinking, almost hearing their words. Distance, the problem was distance. What was convenient was now inconvenient. What was comfortable was now uncomfortable. Complications. They saw complications. And all the while as Elizabeth attempted to reassure them that nothing was changing the group's communal thought, overriding Elizabeth's voice, was that everything had suddenly changed. Their spirits dropped as Elizabeth's was rising.

On May 12, 1857, the sky honored Elizabeth Blackwell by remaining clear and therefore allowing the sun to shine in its brilliance and warmth on the small section of New York City on Bleecker Street. The New York Infirmary for Indigent Women and Children was to be dedicated in a small but impressive ceremony. Out of the three hundred and twenty thousand inhabitants of the city, only a small pittance knew of the historic event occurring in lower Manhattan. Some of those who gathered came from out of town just for the occasion. It was a most auspicious moment yet it went practically unnoticed. Of course it was an extremely important day in the life of Elizabeth Blackwell, an occasion her sister welcomed with great embrace, for the long journey had come into fruition. Gone were the anxieties and tensions and most of all the pressure from fear of failure. Elizabeth Blackwell had succeeded and the small world of supporters and loved ones rejoiced.

Elizabeth believed in tradition for such occasions. Among several, she insisted there be a ribbon cutting ceremony. And while she wished for this tradition to be a major part of the overall observance she could not find a ribbon that would adequately suit the occasion. It had to be red and wide and long. When asked why the color red she surprised those who had asked by saying it represented the flow of life in a body, the blood. Some of her friends found that representation to be a bit crude but she stood by her decision feeling her choice was most appropriate.

The cutting ceremony itself was staged to be dramatic. Elizabeth did indeed want to make the symbolism a dominant factor in the minds of those attending. By her way of thinking the cutting of the ribbon was not so much for the opening of the new infirmary as it was for cutting the bond that kept women for thousands of years from practicing medicine. She intended to incorporate that aspect in her brief talk. With Kitty holding one end of the ribbon and Emily the other Elizabeth slowly moved the large pair of scissors across the wide ribbon keeping all components of the celebration as dramatic as possible. The effort was a bit too obvious and elicited several chuckles as she performed her moment of triumph.

Afterwards she was engaged in a discussion with Emily who stated she was a bit embarrassed by Elizabeth's dramatics. "It really wasn't needed," Emily said as they began cleaning off the refreshment table.

"These little sandwiches Mrs. Powell made," Elizabeth responded, "were simply outstanding, didn't you think so?"

"You're choosing to ignore me once again. I don't think the long drawn-out cutting was necessary."

Putting the last bite of one of the sandwiches in her mouth, Elizabeth gave a slight chortle and continued heading toward the small kitchenette adding, "To you it was dramatic. To me it was ceremonial." Setting the plate on the counter she turned to continue her rebuttal. "This, Emily, was a very historic moment. I may sound pompous but what we have accomplished will go down in history as a very significant turn in the annals of medicine."

"I agree, Elizabeth, it was most historic. But two minutes to cut a four inch wide ribbon? Mister Booth couldn't have done a better melodramatic routine."

"Mr. Booth did not open a major facility either."

Emily came to where Elizabeth and Kitty stood wrapping the leftover sandwiches to be placed in their newly purchased ice box, a luxury some thought extravagant for this charity hospital. But Elizabeth argued that it could help keep some medicine potions longer if they were kept cool and thus the purchase was made. Now, the celebration's leftovers were also to be preserved because of the box.

"Supper for tonight?" Emily asked.

"I don't know if I will have an appetite for supper. I just kept nibbling as I spoke with our friends."

"I'm still hungry," Kitty told her mother.

The young child's constant appetite was always a source of amusement for Elizabeth. "Then maybe we will save some of this for tonight's dinner. Would that be all right?"

"Yes ma'am. I'm glad it wasn't all eaten. There were a lot of people there."

"We did have a good showing didn't we?" Emily noted.

"It was wonderful," said Elizabeth. "And I'm so happy that our dear friend Reverend Henry Beecher was able to come in for the celebration. I'm so sorry Harriet couldn't make it."

"Reverend Beecher's blessing was quite inspiring even though it was a tad bit long."

"Men of the cloth have a propensity to do that, Emily, and that is the price one pays for having God's blessing brought upon so worthy a cause as this one."

"But now all that is over my dear sister and tomorrow we begin a new era of service to the poor."

"Plus opening it for practical training to those women graduating from medical school."

With the food stowed safely away in the ice box and the dishes stacked in the sink for future washing, the two sisters declared their day concluded. They had retained Elizabeth's dwellings on Fifteenth Street as their residence thus allowing for every inch of space at the new infirmary to be utilized. And it was to that residence they directed themselves, tired yet enthused; strained but satisfied and certainly filled with pride.

"Tis a nice evening," Elizabeth said as they locked the front door. "Would you be amenable to walking home instead of taking a horse car?"

Emily frowned. "Maybe tomorrow. My legs are crying for a rest. After all, Elizabeth, today was quite strenuous."

"Ah, yes it was, but ever so rewarding." She sighed. "So very rewarding."

Chapter Twenty

April 12, 1861
New York, New York

"President Lincoln has called for more medical assistance," she added.
"He is turning to institutions such as ours to help and I believe we need to develop a strategy for our role in the war effort.

For some peculiar reason it was an extremely frenzied day for The New York Infirmary for Women and Children. The patient load had gotten out of hand. Appointments were delayed and the staff was feeling the pressure of the chaos. What was not needed at that moment was the event of the day; the tragedy that changed history forever.

At first it was thought the wind had blown the front door open. Swinging wide with such fury it slammed against the wall causing three of the six women sitting in the waiting room to jolt out of their seats. The young boy, the neighborhood newspaper boy, scrambled inside, his face overly distraught. "They fired on Fort Sumter," he screamed. "We're at war...there's going to be a war."

Upon hearing the commotion Elizabeth rushed from the treatment room down the corridor almost colliding with the young boy. Grabbing him by the shirt she admonished him. "Stop shouting. This is a hospital. What's all this fuss about?"

"War, Doctor Blackwell, war." His high-pitched voice retaining his excitement; arms thrashed about as he talked; words flowed out as if a waterfall. "They started shooting cannons at Fort Sumter...they started the war."

Whereas a few minutes earlier the room was as active as a bee hive now there was absolute silence. The young boy drew the angry stares of those assembled in the room. Elizabeth could see the pall of apprehension forming on their faces. A large woman, Amelia Jefferson, sitting at the end of the row of chairs rose and began crying. She walked in circles while wringing her hands and began lamenting that her men were going to be killed; her husband and boys, all off to war, they would be killed.

Fearing the possibility of a panic erupting in her waiting room Elizabeth spoke as calmly as her jangled nerves would allow. "We don't know all the details, Mrs. Jefferson," she said. "We don't know what the President will do to counter this attack. We may just be engaged in a few minor battles."

"War is war, Doctor Blackwell," Jefferson cried out. "They're going to kill all our men."

It was difficult bringing any reason to the woman. Worse yet her fatalistic view was beginning to excite the others quickly causing staff in the other sections of the hospital to pour into the waiting room inquiring of the turmoil

"War," the young boy shouted as Elizabeth grabbed him by the collar of his ragged shirt and pushed him out the front door closing it before he could issue any further inflammatory words.

"They fired on Fort Sumter," she said, again calmly. "And right now that is all we know." She then moved to where the patients were sitting. "And that is all we know," she repeated in a stern voice. "No need to imagine anything else right now. You all need to calm down and we'll get to you for your treatments as soon as we can."

It was not news the nation wanted to hear. It meant civil war. The consequences of such a conflict would change the course of not only many lives but operations such as that of the New York Infirmary.

"The whole nation is rallying around the war effort," she told her management staff several weeks after the firing on Fort Sumter. "Unfortunately this conflict has escalated into a major engagement." She looked around the room evaluating the faces of those gathered. "President Lincoln has called for more medical assistance," she added. "He is turning to institutions such as ours to help and I believe we need to develop a strategy for our role in the war effort. Therefore I want to hold a meeting with just our staff next Thursday "

On Monday of that week Emily stopped Elizabeth in the hallway waving a newspaper. "Have you seen this," she said a touch of anger to her voice.

"No, what."

"Our closed meeting is being advertised here in the New York Times as a public meeting. This is unbelievable."

Elizabeth snatched the paper from Emily's hands and searched for the article. "How in the world could this have happened?" Elizabeth asked shaking the paper.

"Obviously someone let the Times know; maybe thinking it was an open meeting."

"No one from our staff would do that."

"Then perhaps a patient overheard us talking."

Elizabeth folded the paper and handed it back to Emily. "It's too late to get the newspaper to retract the story."

On Thursday the infirmary's modest waiting room was crowded with women curious about the nurses program, so much so that those seeking treatment had to wait in one of the treatment rooms.

Emily was given the task of organizing and running the meeting. "First of all," she began, "welcome to all of you. We were not exactly expecting such a large turnout, but we are pleased to have you with us to work on this important need. Being that our original plan was to have a staff discussion regarding the Infirmary's role in the war effort, we decided to go ahead and involve this group and seek your collective ideas to help steer our course of action."

The room was silent. Several of those attending looked around as if wondering who might speak first. Finally a woman near the back of the room raised her hand and was called upon.

"What kind of medical help is the army asking for?"

"Trained personnel to serve in the field," Emily answered. "In our case it would be nurses."

"You would train them?"

"Well, we're not sure. It's doubtful we have the capacity to do so, but it may be we have a secondary role of some kind."

The woman continued with a further question. "Then do you want us here this morning to help plan what that exact role may be?"

Emily nodded. "Yes, help us find some answers."

It was a challenge that the women attending the meeting were not prepared to hear. They had come to the infirmary to learn how they could volunteer to be a nurse for the war. Instead they were now being asked to assist the Infirmary in making a decision on how best it could serve the needs of the government for the war.

It was an hour-long meeting and afterwards in Elizabeth's office Emily and Elizabeth discussed the session.

"It was good having the women give us their thoughts," Emily said.

"Interesting that they came to the same conclusion you and I had."

"Yes," Emily said, "that the task of training the nurses is a tremendous effort, especially with the number of nurses the army will require."

"Too large for our small staff to train. I am drawn to what several of them suggested that we hold a larger meeting at which we could then recruit and screen women for nurses training. That I think we can do and it could probably end up being our role."

"It would be my guess that the army would welcome an offer such as that," Emily said

"Make a note, Emily," Elizabeth said, "to get the army's endorsement on this and then ask what their needs are before we go any further with this idea. And on the subject of the meeting didn't someone in the group suggest a place to hold it?"

Emily looked at her note pad. "Yes. One of the women thought it was possible we could use the Cooper Institute."

"Yes, I remember her saying that. Hopefully we can do that rather soon."

"We can check on that tomorrow."

"And with this venture we will need the Time's help in spreading the word."

"When we hear back from the army we can then request a representative from their medical division to be at the meeting to give the details of what they're expecting from the nurses. Which reminds me," Emily said reaching over to retrieve a letter that had been resting on Elizabeth's desk. "What about this?"

"What about it?" Elizabeth countered.

"Are you going to accept the position of superintendent of army nurses?"

"It hasn't officially been offered, Emily. I told you the Army is giving stronger consideration to Dorothea Dix for the post."

"But the position should be in the hands of a medical professional such as you not an activist."

Elizabeth shrugged as she retrieved the letter from Emily's hand. Folding it she said, "Those are decisions that will be made by the army. I have a strong feeling the job will be given to Miss Dix"

"When will you hear?"

"Perhaps in a couple of weeks. I believe the President is being advised of this. In the meantime, Emily, we cannot be concerned with that abstract matter. We need to help in the war effort the best way we can."

"What did you hear about Bellevue's possibilities?"

"I spoke with their director yesterday morning and he was thinking of a training program that would take about one month to adequately prepare the women for service. We could possibly tie our efforts in with that program if the army approves our offer."

Emily folded her notes and shook her head. "If you think we're busy now, wait until we start this new program of screening eligible nurses."

Elizabeth had not ventured onto any battlefield during the 4 years of the Civil War. However, despite that fact, the horrors of the war were sadly known to her and the others at the infirmary through accounts given by the field nurses upon their return. Even with the most vivid descriptions relayed to the group it was impossible to fathom the atrocities experienced by the women. To Elizabeth war was an abomination and the work of medicine in attempting to save the lives of the war's victims posed a paradoxical situation. As some of the nurses regretfully phrased it, death would have been a kinder alternative. But they were sent to save lives and in doing so they unwittingly imposed a penalty on those whose lives they had saved.

It was a long period of stagnation for the small infirmary. Not that it wasn't kept busy, for it was, but the meeting of new needs had to be set aside until the conflict was settled.

By late 1865, after the Civil War had come to its bloody conclusion, the infirmary's board of trustees and the physician's advisory committee, both of whom Elizabeth had assembled with the help of her long-standing supporters, had assumed more of the governing responsibilities of the infirmary. Emily had taken over all the administrative duties and Elizabeth had focused her attention more on the matter of sanitation and hygiene.

It was also in that year the state legislature conferred college powers upon the infirmary to establish a school of medicine for women. Within a year the college was well established and began providing studies for young women interested in pursuing a degree in medicine.

It was sometime afterwards that Elizabeth brought to the surface a possibility she had been harboring for close to a year. It came up while Elizabeth and Kitty were having dinner with Emily. Emily finely broke a silence that had gone on far too long

"Your mind is elsewhere."

Elizabeth's eyes moved slowly to Emily. "The college's new location, it's troubling me."

"Oh, how so?"

"We're having a problem securing the building next to the infirmary."

"But I thought that was all settled."

"It was until the owner of the property required more money. He and the board of trustees are in negotiation. It means a delay."

"Then keep it at in the lecture room at the New York University where we've had it all this time.

"Impossible. We need our own space. We are truly handicapped having it at the University."

"But the college is running well. Our student body has grown. What do a few more weeks or months matter before you can begin converting over that building?"

"I want to avoid delays, Emily."

"But why the rush?"

Again Elizabeth's attention seemed to wander. Finally she addressed Emily's question. "I received another post from my friends in London."

"Oh, I see...that again."

"Yes, that again. They're progressing well but wish for me to return to give their cause for equality of women in medicine a more enthusiastic boost."

"And what have you told them?"

"I've told them about our new medical college for women and how it is a great adjunct to the infirmary."

286

"In other words you've chosen to ignore their request to return to England."

"I am not ignoring their request," Elizabeth said fiddling with her food. "I'm just not ready. The college is important to me and I want to be sure it is well established before I venture off on to something new."

"And once it is then what? Do you leave?"

Elizabeth cocked her head as if in a debate, a debate that did not exist, yet she wished to give the illusion of engaging in one just the same. "It is going on twenty years now Emily, since I graduated from Geneva," she finally said. "I've come to the conclusion my work here in the United States is pretty much concluded. The infirmary is operating perfectly thanks to your very capable guidance and the college is well established. I believe I am more needed overseas than here."

Emily chose not to respond. It wasn't what she wanted to hear. Yet the possibility of her sister returning to England had been discussed numerous times. Speaking slowly she said, "Yes, you will be going back. You will be gone from here."

Nothing more was said Elizabeth gently nodded and turned her eyes away not bothering to finish her dinner.

Chapter Twenty-One

1873
Rome, Italy

*"I have not seen the supposed new Albert Segal.
And until I do see a new Albert Segal it would be
most imprudent of me to place all that I own into
your hands."*

Rome, November, 1873
My Dear Emily,
*I write to you from the Eternal City of
Rome to where I retreated for serious health
reasons. I have been diagnosed with biliary colic,
as you had suspected. It has rendered me
absolutely useless and quite fatigued. As you
know I have been experiencing this debilitating
condition off and on for the past three years and
it has disrupted my work with my friends here in
Europe on the causes I hold so dear. But now I
am forced to sit and rest and to find a better
climate for which Rome was suggested. And while*

I do seem to do much better in the Italian climate I nevertheless don't quite understand the reason for sending me off to Rome. This is not some quiet countryside retreat and at times I find the bustle of city life a bit disturbing. It may just be that my temperament has suffered because of my discomfort. But nonetheless I do find Rome a lovely city where an abundance of history awaits the curious visitor practically at the very end of every fingertip.

I am most eager to return to London, for my work there is quite involved. The finishing points in completing our London School of Medicine for Women were near conclusion when I was forced to seek a remedy for this illness of mine. Hopefully I will be able to return soon to finish the work and open the school. Doctors Garret-Anderson and Jex-Blake have been keeping me informed as to the progress of that project. My anxiety for returning is somewhat related to my concern for Sophia's judgment in matters regarding the London school. Elizabeth Garret-Anderson is more level headed and yet she is not always able to direct Sophia in the proper direction. Attempting to resolve problems long distance is most difficult.

But for now I relax and heal in the golden sunshine of this city and pray for a quick recovery. Please take care of yourself and I shall stay in touch.

Your loving sister,
Elizabeth

Elizabeth rested the pen aside the letter and moved her eyes out the window adjacent to the writing desk. The apartment she rented, for how long she didn't know, had to have a view of the city, a rather commanding view so she had stipulated. But what she observed at that moment were pigeons, three of them, plump and tall, resting on the wide window sill, their bobbing heads blocking the sight of the Vatican's St. Peter's dome. It was an occurrence she had come to ignore by simply rising out of the chair and peering over the heads of the insubordinate pigeons.

"A letter, Doctor," came the voice of Kitty Barry making her way languidly into the room. From the very beginning, when she was adopted, Kitty had developed the habit of addressing Elizabeth as "doctor," an acknowledgement neither Elizabeth nor Kitty felt obtrusive. She waved the envelope as if the ink needed to be dried.

"From whom?"

"Albert," she said, her answer given in a slight tone of indifference. It was an attempt to feign a disinterest in this young man, finding him out of favor at the moment.

Albert Segal had recently come into the lives of both Kitty and Elizabeth having become acquainted with them during an outdoor party hosted by one of Elizabeth's friends. Since that time many visits and outings had been enjoyed by the trio. His interest in the women had a curious nature to it seeing that Segal was closer to Kitty's age than Elizabeth. He was twenty-six, Kitty twenty-nine. And yet Segal appeared to shower Elizabeth, now fifty-three years of age, with more attention than Kitty. Kitty had come to develop a romantic interest in this dashing gentleman from Virginia and it seemed reciprocal. Elizabeth, however, found Segal to be in need of reform, for the young man had a penchant for the reckless spending of his father's fortune as well as drinking entirely too much alcohol. But in the eyes of Kitty Barry, Segal was giving her mother more attention than her and that brought about a slight case of jealousy.

"I suppose you wish to hear the contents?" Elizabeth asked.

"No," was the answer. "It is addressed to you."

"I'll let you know if he sends you any greetings."

"I doubt that he will. It's probably just more of those discussions you two have been having about Albert's spending of his father's money."

"It is not his spending habits I'm attempting to reform, Kitty, although Lord knows that certainly can be improved. It is wasting his life with alcohol that I'm concerned about."

Kitty shrugged. "I prefer him the way he is."

292

Elizabeth watched as Kitty disappeared from the room wondering what had brought about her daughter's sullen mood. Retrieving the letter opener from the desk's top middle drawer Elizabeth opened the envelope and pulled out a small note.

"He's coming to Rome," Elizabeth called out to Kitty. "He says he doesn't know exactly when."

"Good," Kitty replied unemotionally as she continued her trek to the kitchen where she would begin to prepare dinner for the evening. After all, the letter was sent to Elizabeth, and Kitty had not received a similar notice of his pending trip to Rome. Why then should she become elated at the prospect of his arrival?

"He says he wishes to spend time with you," Elizabeth called out.

A cutting knife was slammed down on the counter. "Then why in all that is holy didn't he write me and say that," Kitty practically screamed.

The apartment became silent. Several seconds later Elizabeth appeared at the kitchen door. "Because there was no need to write two letters, Kitty my dear. Besides, the letter was basically his answer to the questions I had asked. He is apparently digressing again and I'm afraid he has become disinterested in changing his ways."

"Maybe he's not the pure, saintly man you think he ought to be. I am sure he wouldn't

293

appreciate knowing the way in which you refer to him."

Kitty continued to prepare their meal, seething somewhat by the fact Albert Segal, her considered intended, had not apprised her personally of his visit. It was most upsetting.

Albert did show up six months later and made his appearance, as he had promised. Not knowing who was rapping on the door Kitty answered it. She stood face to face with the man she thought she loved.

"Good morning my dear Kitty," he said and reached out to take her hand. "Oh my, but you look more ravishing than I remember."

"Good morning Albert," Kitty said, but the tone was a bit casual, unlike the last time they had talked. And he noticed that.

"Something wrong?"

"No, why do you ask?" she said withdrawing her hand.

"May I come in or are we doomed to converse in this manner for the full length of my stay in Rome?"

"Please come in," she said and turned to look down the hall. "Doctor," she called out in a loud voice, "your patient...I'm sorry, Albert is here."

Albert Segal cocked his head and peered curiously at Kitty. "Patient?"

"Doctors have patients, do they not?"

"And you see me as a patient of your mother?"

"Are you not?"

"I'm afraid, Kitty Barry, you have totally confused me with not only your tone of voice but your comments as well."

"Fine," she said moving away looking not at him but at Elizabeth who was approaching the pair. "So now we are even. Therefore let the confusion reign."

"Albert," Elizabeth said. "How are you?

"Elizabeth," he said, "so good to see you."

"I suppose you two wish to be alone," Kitty fumed exiting the room.

"What is bothering her?" Albert asked.

"I dare not venture a guess. Sometimes that child completely baffles me. Her moods can change instantly. Obviously this is one of those times." Elizabeth walked with him to a divan in the front parlor.

"Well," he said waiting for Elizabeth to sit before taking a place next to her. "We will let Kitty have her huff while we discuss something important."

"Important?"

"Yes, very much so. I have great news. I have earned a seat on the New York Stock Exchange."

"Oh, Albert, that is wonderful news. And the new floor trading method appeals to you rather than the old seat arrangement?"

"Much better for the likes of me."

"I suppose your father put up the cash to purchase the seat?"

With a slight embarrassing laugh Albert answered, "Yes, Father felt I should do something with my life and after enrolling in courses to learn the market processes he agreed to secure me a seat."

"Then you obviously have proven to him you are no longer a spendthrift."

"Spendthrift is such a harsh word my dear Elizabeth."

"But it did fit the Albert Segal I remember."

"And have tried to reform."

"And your drinking? Have you moderated that as well?"

"I understand a trader on the floor of the exchange must be sober at all times. But I didn't come here to discuss my reformation."

"Oh? Then you came only to see Kitty and me, correct," She said reflecting a teasing smile.

"Indeed, I came especially to see you...with a proposition." He stopped, shifted his position and smiled. "I believe that one who invests her money must have strong confidence and trust in her trader to not only protect her investment but to make it grow."

"I see. An honorable and too obvious an observation." She paused, giving thought to what he had just said. It occurred to her Albert Segal's visit had an ulterior motive and he didn't come just to call on them. "In other words, Albert, what you are leading up to is you wish to handle my investments on the floor of the exchange, am I right?"

The coy look revealed Elizabeth's supposition to be correct. "Very astute," he said. "You are precisely correct. I know you have treasured your wise investment over the years and have been protective of your worth. But you have displayed an ultra safe approach to growing your investments and I believe that is because of a total lack of understanding of how the market works."

"I am not a gambler, Albert," Elizabeth told him beginning to grow somewhat apprehensive of the direction of the conversation.

"But I am not advocating approaching the market as a gambler."

"Then, dear Albert, what are you advocating?"

He turned to look directly into her eyes. "Because we have developed a rather close relationship, Elizabeth, I felt of all people, you would be most comfortable with having me assume full control over your portfolio of investments and having me develop a growth program that will greatly enhance your net worth."

"Full control? Are you advocating that I turn all my investment over to you whereby you will make all trading decision on my behalf?"

"You sound apprehensive."

"Albert, my dear friend, if you recall I have been counseling you for these past many months on your wild propensity to spend money in a reckless fashion. Your father has even written me asking that I not be kind in counseling you but that I get you on the right path. And each time I discussed the matter with you your rejoinder was to go to the nearest pub. I was attempting to correct a young man who showed total lack of responsibility. And now you are asking me to place my entire financial portfolio into your hands?"

"You make it sound quite horrid, Elizabeth. I have reformed."

The moment had grown tense for Elizabeth. Whereas past times with Albert Segal were enjoyable she now found herself wanting to distance herself from him. She still had good feelings for the young man but the sudden injection of her financial security into the relationship greatly disturbed her and she began to look upon Albert Segal in a different manner.

"This is so rather sudden, Albert," she said. "Obviously you realize I cannot make an intelligent decision at this time. I will need to give your proposal serious thought and careful analysis."

"But there is not much you have to analyze. You certainly have faith and confidence in my ability. I believe you had determined that long ago."

"It's not your ability I have to evaluate, Albert. It is your person."

"My past behavior, correct?"

298

"Albert, I am not condemning you for any indiscretion you may have shown in the past. But when we parted last you had not revealed any signs of improvement. I have not seen the supposed new Albert Segal. And until I do see a new Albert Segal it would be most imprudent of me to place all that I own into your hands."

"I see." All features on his face revealed the hurt and disappointment brought about by Elizabeth's rejection. Slowly he stood and moved to stare out the window. "I assumed we had a different kind of relationship, Elizabeth. I suppose I over estimated that relationship. Assumptions, so I've been reminded many times, are for fools." He turned to look at her. "And who can trust a fool with their money?"

"Albert this is not rejecting you. These are simply the facts. Your handling of my affairs is not a dead issue. I must simply take time to give it very serious thought."

Segal stood motionless staring at Elizabeth. His mouth quivered slightly as if he wanted to speak but hesitated for fear he might say something to be regretted. Without any further words he turned to move toward the front door. He then stopped, turned and said, "I never expected this to happen."

"But you do not understand the wisdom of my decision. You're rejecting it."

"As you have rejected me."

Frustrated by the tenor of the conversation and of Segal's behavior, Elizabeth moved off the divan and walked passed Segal to the door. Opening it she nodded her head and told him, "You best go now, Albert. You need to be alone to gather your thoughts. But if you wish to return someday to visit with Kitty and me, the subject of investments will not be included."

A quick smile formed on Segal's face as he looked at Elizabeth. "I see," he said. "Please give my regards to Kitty." He then moved quickly through the doorway and was soon gone from sight.

"What was that all about?" It was Kitty who had been standing in the hall observing Segal's departure.

"I believe Albert Segal has just paid us his last visit Kitty."

Kitty squinted turning her head in question. "Why do you say that?"

"He has been rejected and I don't think the young man knows exactly how to handle rejection."

Kitty Barry lowered her head, paused several seconds and without saying anything further turned and left the room. Neither Kitty nor Elizabeth ever saw Albert Segal again.

Chapter Twenty-Two

1876
Bordighera, Imperia, Italy

"If you publish this book, Elizabeth," Quigley said rather dimly, "I can guarantee you that your name would be a forbidden word in England."

As she leaned in to finish the outline for the next day's lecture her hand twitched and the pen dropped to the floor. Specks of ink stained the wooden planks beneath the tall desk at which she sat writing. Pushing her arm tightly against her abdomen in an effort to quell the pain, Elizabeth slowly doubled over, emitting a soft moan as she fell to the floor. Resting on her knees, her hands flat against the planks, she attempted to call Kitty but was unable to do so. She began to vomit.

The Biliary colic had returned. At first she gave it little attention since the pain was mild and she thought it merely a touch of gas. But at that moment, as she fought not to collapse, Elizabeth knew the blockage of the duct that moved the bile from the gallbladder had returned. It could no longer be ignored.

After returning to London from Rome she cautiously lived each day wondering if this chronic disturbance would reoccur making it impossible for her to pursue her newly cherished endeavors. Some years before, her time spent practicing medicine had begun to lessen as the ardent role of crusader attracted Elizabeth's attention.

Included within that new pursuit was the element of educator, an involvement that gave Elizabeth a whole new sense of belonging; being able to pass along the knowledge she had gained. It was while in Rome that Elizabeth received an important post from Doctor Elizabeth Garrett-Anderson, England's first woman doctor and a former student at the New York School of Medicine for Women. Having formed a long-standing relationship with Elizabeth, Garrett-Anderson wondered if Elizabeth would be interested in the position of Chair of Gynecology at the newly established medical school for women in London, an institution Elizabeth Blackwell had helped create. Delighted at the challenge Elizabeth readily accepted.

But now, two years later, she found herself on the floor of the office in her home in Dorset Square unable to call for help suffering excruciating pain. She knew the condition was not going to dissipate.

"Kitty." Her voice could hardly be heard. Changing her position she called again. "Kitty." The second effort produced results.

"Doctor?"

"Come here…I need your help."

Kitty rushed to the room where she found her mother sitting on the floor, her face contorted in pain.

"Doctor," she cried hurrying to Elizabeth's side. "It's the pain again, isn't it?"

Elizabeth struggled to nod, having no desire to speak. Quickly placing both her arms under Elizabeth's arms Kitty moved Elizabeth to a divan. There Elizabeth was able to lie on her back to relieve the pain.

"I'll go get Doctor Ethan," Kitty said.

Managing to raise a hand Elizabeth waved off the suggestion. "No," she barely uttered.

"But you need to consult with someone. Doctor Ethan is the one you always turn to."

Elizabeth did not agree. After all, Elizabeth Blackwell was a physician. She had been through this before and had received advice from other physicians. She instinctively knew what needed to be done.

Initially the remedy was unacceptable. She came to realize it meant she would have to leave London again, possibly forever. It meant abandoning her chair of the Gynecology department. It meant forgoing any further engagement in the movement for reform and women's rights.

"But you have no choice," Kitty told her several days later while they were discussing her options.

"I realize that, Kitty. And I am trying to find other possible means wherein I can continue my work."

In subsequent days, Doctor Elizabeth Blackwell had no other choice but to move from her beloved London to a climate more conducive to curing her illness.

In the fall of 1876 Elizabeth Blackwell and Kitty Barry once again packed their belongings and set off to Nice, France eventually settling in Bordighera, Italy.

Bordighera was a popular retreat for the English and Elizabeth was delighted to discover many fellow Londoners in the town.

One morning on the veranda of Elizabeth's apartment an acquaintance, Helen Quigley, inquired about Elizabeth's latest endeavor.

"I've been thinking of writing a book."

"Oh, on what subject?"

"Sex education for children."

Helen Quigley didn't respond. Instead she took a long sip from her cup of tea. Finally she spoke. "You do know you are treading on very dangerous grounds, don't you Elizabeth?"

"Dangerous? What is so dangerous in teaching children...and adults, about their own bodies and its functions?"

"It is a subject civilized people don't discuss, especially with children."

Elizabeth shook her head. "But that's the problem, Helen. Because nobody talks about it children grow up ignorant of the subject and each generation then suffers the consequences."

It was obvious Helen Quigley was not about to convince Elizabeth Blackwell of the improprieties of her proposed book. But to preserve their friendship, Helen shifted away from the subject and commented on sites she had visited in Bordighera. The diversion disappointed Elizabeth, for she felt it necessary to support her intentions to write what Helen considered to be a scandalous book. The morning ended earlier than Elizabeth had planned.

It took Elizabeth five months to write her book and for Kitty to review it for corrections. But Elizabeth felt a need to convince Helen Quigley of its value. Thus one afternoon while having tea Elizabeth offered Helen the manuscript to read. Reluctant at first, Helen eventually agreed. But when she returned the manuscript it was not the kind of review Elizabeth was expecting. "If you publish this book, Elizabeth," Quigley said rather dimly, "I can guarantee you that your name would be a forbidden word in England."

It took Elizabeth several seconds to collect herself. "What are you saying, Helen?"

Quigley laid the manuscript down on a small end table and put her hand on it. She began tapping her fingers on the top sheet. "I'm surprised you have to ask why, Elizabeth. You have written your comments and observations as well as giving your opinions in very graphic terms. This will never be accepted."

"But you cannot write advice to parents on how to treat the subject of sex with their children without giving adequate descriptions of the topics. To skirt the issues would render the book useless."

"What I'm saying, Elizabeth, is that the book is already useless because it will never be published or sold or made available to the public. No one will be reading this."

Neither spoke. Their eyes turned away from each other. The book had become a wedge between the two women.

Yet Elizabeth was determined to get the book published and neither Quigley nor Kitty could dissuade her from seeking out publishers in London. In all, she contacted twelve publishers, twelve important ones.

Disappointingly, when the replies came Elizabeth felt a sharp pain in her soul, for the comments in the rejections were rather scathing.

The subject of sex in a public forum was absolutely taboo, but to discuss sex so vividly with children, or at least suggest that parents discuss the matter of sex with their children, raised the ire of the publishers. Indeed, as Helen Quigley had predicted, Elizabeth's name, although unpublished, was becoming a forbidden word in London.

Despite the rejections, the book was published, done independently by Elizabeth. She found a small book store willing to carry it and several copies were eventually sold.

Then one day Elizabeth received a post from a Miss Ellice Hopkins and in high excitement she shared the letter with Kitty.

"I received this letter from a Miss Ellice Hopkins," she said, "who has bought my book and considered it to be most useful in the work she is doing. She states she has connections with the publishing group Hatchard and Company in the person of an acting member of the firm, a Mister Hudson. After reviewing the book he has agreed to have Hatchard and Company publish it. Isn't that exciting? The book, Kitty, is going to be published by a large publishing company in London. It will now be widely circulated and the education of the public will begin."

"That is exciting, Doctor. I'm very happy for you. I know how important this is for you."

Yet not all was well in the inner walls of Hatchard and Company. Elizabeth's book made it through the typesetting process and proof copies had been run. The next phase would have been the printing of the book. But that was as far as the process went.

Dear Doctor Blackwell,

It is with deep regret that I write to you to inform you that Hatchard and Company will not be able to continue with the handling of your book, "Counsel to Parents on the Moral Education of Their Children." While Hatchard and Company has never broken faith with an author I am afraid we must do so now. The senior member of the firm, Bishop Hatchard's widow, has seen a printer's proof of the book and was so enraged she tossed it in the fire and declared the publication of the book be stopped immediately. It is fortunate that we had only entered into the final stages before running the book on the presses. I am sorry for this inconvenience.

Sincerely Yours,
H.T. Hudson

For several seconds Elizabeth stood staring in disbelief at the letter. Four days would pass before she regained her composure and wrote a letter to Miss Ellice Hopkins.

My Dear Miss Hopkins,

Again I express to you my deep appreciation to you for interceding on my behalf with Mister Hudson to publish my book "Counsel to Parents on the Moral Education of Their

Children." Regretfully the widowed wife of Bishop Hatchard has seen fit to cancel that arrangement. Therefore I am afraid your diligent efforts have been in vain and the book, much to my regret, will not be published thus denying the pubic valuable information and encouragement for early childhood education on the fact of human sexuality. Needless to say I am disheartened by the entire matter.

Sincerely Yours,
Elizabeth Blackwell, M.D.

She sat staring at what she had written digesting the contents determining that it did not reveal the anger she felt toward the publishing firm. Satisfied with the letter, she posted it that afternoon.

"Kitty," Elizabeth called out days later, "Would you please check to see if the postman has delivered anything yet."

"We receive nothing until later in the afternoon, Doctor."

"Perhaps he has come early today."

"Perhaps," Kitty responded, "you are showing your anxieties once again."

"Perhaps, my dear daughter, you are showing you insolence once again."

Kitty appeared in the doorway of the parlor where Elizabeth sat. "Is there any reason why Miss Hopkins should be writing you?

"I believe she will. I believe she will express her dismay at the book being discarded."

"Then you will have to wait until this afternoon."

Elizabeth had to wait for over a month before she heard from Ellice Hopkins.

My dear Doctor Blackwell,

I believe I have some encouraging news for you regarding your book "Counsel to Parents on the Moral Education of Their Children." A small gathering of elderly clergymen were encouraged to review your book and upon doing so drew a conclusion that the book, as written, read more as a medical journal rather than a type of classroom publication. Therefore with that viewpoint in mind and considering the subject matter to be health and moral related, these gentlemen felt that a change in the title of the book indicating it was a medical publication, could then be published and circulated to the general public. The proposed new title is: "The Moral Education of the Young, Considered under Medical and Social Aspects." I assured Mister Hudson that you would have no objections with the proposed new title and therefore he is proceeding with the printing of the book and it should be ready for distribution within a month or so.

I hope this arrangement is satisfactory with you and this letter finds you in improved health.

Sincerely Yours,
Ellice Hopkins

Elizabeth closed her eyes. Her mind churned with a multitude of thoughts from great joy to incredulity. If was as if these clergymen had simply waved a magic wand over the manuscript, and without changing any of the text had converted the contents from a sex education manual for parents with small children to a medical journal with moral implications. By simply changing the title, the book became acceptable. A subtle, inconspicuous change gave credence and purpose to a publication that under the old title was condemned as lewd and sinful. She gave thought to the amazing art of rationalization that can be done by the human mind.

"Is it good news?" Kitty asked stirring Elizabeth out of her muse.

"Yes. The book is to be published. The magic wand did it."

A look of confusion covered Kitty's face. "Magic wand?"

"Indeed," Elizabeth said smiling, her hand waving the letter about as if it were a wand. "The sorcerers have seen the wisdom of the day and have bestowed upon the world the benefit of their magic. Now you see it, now you don't."

Kitty shook her head. "It's got to be the medicine you're taking."

Chapter Twenty-Three

1907
Kilmun, Argyllshire, Scotland

"Your mother, Miss Barry, is eighty six years old.
She was a bit frail before the fall. Now she has
damaged her frail body and mind and the
systems will be functioning in a different manner,
in a different accord."

Of course, it could not be confirmed by those who
lived there, but apparently the warm climate and
fresh sea air in Bordighera, Italy had curative
powers beyond any medicinal remedies yet
conceived. At least that was the conclusion Kitty
Barry drew from her two year observation of
Elizabeth while they lived in the small village by
the beautiful Mediterranean. Elizabeth, on the
other hand, attributed her cure of the
devastating colic to be a combination of medical
treatments and a strong will on her part to rid
herself of this horrible condition. Granted,

however, the climate did aid in a restorative cure.

Regardless of the reason, Elizabeth's health had been restored and in 1878 she and Kitty made their way back to London where she continued in her position of Chair of Gynecology at the London School of Medicine for Women. After a brief residency in London, and because the position with the school did not demand a constant presence, Elizabeth decided she would prefer living where she could once again enjoy the magical lure of the sea. Convinced it was therapeutic in nature she and Kitty set out to investigate various villages and hamlet along the southern coast of England. In due time a home was selected and Elizabeth purchased the Rock House, a small home off Exmouth Place in Hastings, Sussex. The home provided a sweeping view of the English Channel and on those grey, misty days when the sounds of the large ships' fog horns wailed out across the waters Elizabeth enthusiastically embraced her newly discovered romance with the sea.

Her work with the school became the longest tenure of any for Elizabeth. Fortunately her duties were not all that demanding and the pace was a leisurely one conducive to giving her time to participate in the many causes she had embraced. She enjoyed what she was doing and yet as the years advanced Elizabeth's energy level began to wane. She found it necessary to reduce here activities and to seek more moments of rest.

It was at the turn of the twentieth century when Elizabeth, now seventy nine, became aware of the Clyde coast in Scotland. The area was a favorite summer vacation for many a Londoner. The quaint settings of the villages, especially those along the Holy Loch inlet, and the beautiful summer weather offered the visitor an opportunity to become lost in both its antiquity and charm. To Elizabeth the appeal was entrancing. She eventually decided that she and Kitty would spend the next summer in Kirn.

Then one day while having tea at a small sidewalk café with Kitty, Elizabeth overheard a couple at the next table talking about a village called Kilmun that sat across the Loch. The elderly man and wife apparently made the rounds of the hamlets in that area. The discussion regarding Kilmun piqued Elizabeth's curiosity and she couldn't stop herself from inquiring of the couple about the town.

"Why, yes," the wife said, "we truly love the place. It has a lot of history and marvelous shops. The food is excellent and the seafront is most inviting. There is a very nice hotel there as well."

"A hotel? Good. And what is it called?" Elizabeth asked, for that would suit her purpose perfectly if she decided she wanted to visit a different location for their summer vacations.

"Very simple," the woman said. "It is called the Kilmun Hotel."

Elisabeth laughed. "Couldn't get more basic than that."

"And you would enjoy the small church too; Saint Munn I believe is the name. There is a very interesting cemetery adjacent to the church that allegedly contains the remains of some very important people. I, of course, didn't recognize any."

"And I suppose the cost of vacationing there is equal to here?"

"It is, and, as you know, the local people are most accommodating, very friendly and enjoyable to be with."

The afternoon was slowly growing late when Elizabeth and Kitty began their stroll to the home they had been renting.

"Thinking about Kilmun?" Kitty asked.

There was no immediate answer. Then Elizabeth turned and spoke. "I am thinking, Kitty, that perhaps next summer we give Kilmun a try. The town does sound intriguing doesn't it?"

"I would agree. Your newly made acquaintances had nothing but high praise for the village. It sounded like a very positive recommendation to me."

By 1905 Kilmun had become a regular retreat for the two women and Elizabeth had become somewhat the resident celebrity even though she only spent the summers there. On each ensuing visit, Elizabeth became more and more impressed with the town. That summer, she decided she should let her feelings be known. Upon registering for their hotel room, Kitty spied Elizabeth taking longer than usual to sign her name in the register.

"Did I see you jotting something next to your name?" Kitty asked.

"Yes. I felt they should know of a patron's satisfaction."

"And what did you write?"

"I told them this was our fourth visit to this hotel and each time the air of Kilmun seemed more invigorating, and our host and hostess kinder."

"I'm sure they will appreciate that sentiment."

"I would have written more but I believe they needed the space for their other patrons to register."

The comment caused Kitty to laugh as they followed the porter to their room.

However, the visits to Kilmun would come to an unexpected and unfortunate halt two years later in 1907. After breakfast one morning while Kitty waited in the lobby of the Kilmun Hotel Elizabeth decided to return to their room to fetch a light shawl. On returning to the lobby Elizabeth had taken but two steps down the hotel's stairway when somehow she tripped causing her to plunge headlong down the full flight of stairs. Her head took the brunt of the

317

fall much to the horror of those who had witnessed the accident.

One of those was Kitty.

"Doctor," she screamed rushing to Elizabeth's side. Dropping to her knees Kitty placed two fingers on the carotid artery as hotel staff members gathered.

"Is she…"

"She's alive," Kitty answered briskly. "We need a doctor."

The clamor had now attracted a crowd of curious onlookers and yet no one moved to summon a physician. The lack of response angered Kitty as she pleaded for help again.

"Doctor MacLean is on his way," one of the porters told her.

It took close to fifteen minutes before the physician arrived. During that time Kitty checked to see if Elizabeth had sustained any serious injuries, and placed a blanket over her as a precaution against shock. Besides a single bruise on the forehead, there appeared to be no cuts or apparent fractures. But the bruise was substantial and Kitty feared it could possibly indicate serious brain damage.

"Miss Barry."

Kitty looked up and saw the porter standing with a tall gentleman holding a physician's bag.

"This is Doctor MacLean," he told her.

"Miss Barry," MacLean said giving a quick greeting while moving down to examine

Elizabeth. Viewing the bruise he gently touched the areas surrounding it and looked up. "This is not a good sign. We best get her to the hospital for complete examination.

"How soon can that be?" Kitty asked.

"I'll have the hotel summon an ambulance now. It should be here in about ten minutes." Opening his bag he retrieved a stethoscope and placing the chest piece on Elizabeth's chest began his examination. "The heartbeat is strong. Her breathing is a bit labored."

Elizabeth attempted to speak and MacLean held up his hand. "Don't speak, Doctor Blackwell. We have an ambulance on the way. We're transporting you to the hospital. You've had a very bad strike to your head."

"Doctor," Kitty said to Elizabeth, "you're going to be all right. We'll take good care of you. You're going to be all right"

Three days after entering the hospital, Doctor MacLean sat with Kitty discussing her mother's future.

"There has been some damage to the brain," he said. "The simple test we have applied shows some lack of certain functions."

"Meaning?"

"It means, Miss Barry, your mother will be having trouble making decisions that affect her everyday life among other dysfunctions. This will be complicated by a limitation of her physical capabilities as well."

Attempting to comprehend what was being said, Kitty remained silent. Looking at MacLean she asked, "My mother is going to be an invalid? Is that what you're saying, Doctor MacLean?"

"Not exactly, Miss Barry. I'm saying your mother is not going to be quite like she used to be, but on a limited basis."

"Then will she be able to continue her work?"

"I'm afraid not. She will neither be strong nor mentally alert enough to carry out her duties. In all likelihood she will recognize that fact on her own."

"And have you discussed this with her?"

"No, at this time she is not capable of comprehending what I say. However, I do believe she has been able to do a cursory form of diagnosis on herself and most likely recognizes the damage she has sustained."

Shifting her eyes away from the doctor to the wide window of the conference room Kitty asked, "Is this going to shorten my mother's life?"

"Possibly. Your mother, Miss Barry, is eighty six years old. She was a bit frail before the fall. Now she has damaged her frail body and mind and the systems will be functioning in a different manner, in a different accord."

Kitty stood and walked to the window. The day was quite sunny. She let her eyes wander through the flower garden that stretched the full length of the side yard of the hospital.

Her thoughts drifted to the possibilities she now faced with Elizabeth once they settled back in Hastings.

"I'm sorry, Miss Barry," the doctor was saying as her attention returned to the conversation. "But these are the realities of life."

"Any timeline," she asked.

"No." And no more advice was offered.

After spending twenty days in the hospital Elizabeth was transported back to her home in Hastings. The trip, a distance of five hundred miles, a three day trip by horse carriage, was arduous and discomforting for Elizabeth. After Several Weeks Kitty assumed full responsibility for the care of Elizabeth.

One morning several months later while at breakfast, Elizabeth brought up the matter of her future. "I realize I won't be returning to the school," she said fidgeting with the clotted cream.

The comment surprised Kitty, for the topic had not yet been discussed. Now suddenly it had been raised with a rather blunt comment. "Doctor Humphries would agree with you."

"Who?"

"Your physician here in Hastings."

"Oh. Well then, has he discussed my future with you?"

"He simply said you would not be able to continue on with the school and that your retirement would be required. Have you said anything further to Doctor Garrett-Anderson?"

"Elizabeth and I have not spoken since my fall."

"But she did come visit with you at the hospital."

The room became silent as Elizabeth stared at Kitty, her face reflecting confusion. "Elizabeth came to the hospital to see me?"

"Yes, three days before you were released. Don't...you...

"Doctor Elizabeth Garrett-Anderson?"

"Yes, Doctor, she spent close to an hour with you and you two talked about your position at the school and your possible replacement."

Again there was silence as Elizabeth closed her eyes and her hands rose to cover her face.

"You don't remember, do you?"

Dropping her hands Elizabeth cast her eyes down to the plate before her. "No, just as I don't remember too much at the hospital. And that, as I am sure the doctors had discussed with you, is going to be some of my behavior because of the injury to my head."

"Yes, they have discussed that aspect with me."

Nodding Elizabeth picked up a scone and broke off a small portion to apply a light dab of the clotted cream. "All those years at the school, Kitty. Now it is ended." Lifting the scone she continued. "Then I shall confine myself to the writing desk and finish the many manuscripts I have left undone."

"Such as?"

"The matters of morality in society. I have three manuscripts I began several years ago that need to be finished and sent off to my publisher."

"Maybe a sequel to your autobiography?"

"Oh, that," Elizabeth said in a disgusting tone. "That was such a failure, Kitty. Why would I pursue a sequel when the book only sold five hundred copies and received bad reviews in the press?"

"But are you sure you have the endurance for all that writing?"

"It's not a requirement you know. I write at my leisure. But it does fulfill a mission of mine and as long as I have the strength and ability I will do so."

But Kitty knew it was quite possible the manuscripts would not be finished. It was more likely that Elizabeth Blackwell would be resting more than writing.

The writing was sporadic. When the weather was nice the two would sit on the terrace to talk and enjoy the view of the Channel. Some time back Elizabeth had purchased a large rocking chair and it served her well. Conversation with Kitty in between long naps had become the norm. Elizabeth had taken up the luxury of reminiscing. And while she periodically confused some of the facts and details Kitty never corrected her mother.

"Did I ever tell you that I was installed as the first woman on the Medical Register of the United Kingdom?"

"I remember it well, Doctor. We actually had a small celebration."

"Oh did we?" Elizabeth asked smiling. "How nice. That was quite the honor, wasn't it?"

"Indeed it was. It not only established your credentials but it provided you license to practice medicine in the United Kingdom."

Elizabeth leaned her head against the tall back of the rocking chair and began to sway gently in a graceful motion. "A lovely day today."

Smiling, Kitty took hold of Elizabeth's hand. "It is, a very nice day. You're not chilled are you?"

"Oh no," Elizabeth answered then pulled the shawl tighter around her. "A bit breezy wouldn't you say. Tends to chill the body a wee bit."

Moving out of her chair Kitty told Elizabeth, "I'll prepare some tea for us. Would you like that?"

"Tea? Is it that time?"

"Not really but it might help take off the chill a bit."

"Yes, that would be fine," Elizabeth answered. "But there isn't a chill. It is such a beautiful day."

With hurried steps Kitty moved indoors to head for the kitchen. Unheard by Elizabeth was Kitty's soft sobbing, something she found herself doing more often as her mother's mind continued to deteriorate. The doctor's predictions were beginning to appear and it troubled Kitty to sit helplessly by unable to bring the mind of this brilliant woman back to the degree it once was.

"And no sugar," Elizabeth called out. Yet all her life she had taken a small teaspoon of sugar with her tea. Kitty would add it. Elizabeth would not know the difference. And the day remained beautiful much to Elizabeth's delight.

Being that it sat on the English Channel, Hastings' weather was most unfriendly at times. Clouds and rain along with various degrees of wind often compelled the residents to simply stay indoors rather than venture out and challenge the elements.

Such was the case in early May of 1910 when it seemed as though winter was especially long. Sleet was the rule of the day and walking on the sloping sidewalks in Hastings provided not only a challenge but a danger as well.

Kitty found it practically impossible as she tried to maneuver the slight slope on Exmouth Place. Her destination was the small neighborhood apothecary to refill a prescription for Elizabeth. The pain was secondary to the ever-present mental lapses and cognitive impairment. Her condition had slowly deteriorated over the three years since her accident. Still Elizabeth Blackwell did not look upon herself as an invalid. Distractions appeared to be her strategy for overcoming the obvious. She and her writing desk became very close companions and Elizabeth spent hours there doing what she loved best. But as Kitty observed, her writing was barely legible, the sentences were rambling and disjointed. The writings were useless. Yet it occupied Elizabeth's time and allowed her to delve back into the past.

As the days of May moved forward the weather improved and Elizabeth and Kitty were able to once again sit in the sunshine on their terrace. But Elizabeth displayed moments of lethargy causing Kitty to insist her mother get more bed rest.

During the last week of May the weather turned cool and the terrace outings were temporarily suspended. But the afternoon tea time was never interrupted no matter where the location.

"I have more cookies, Doctor, if you care for some."

Nodding, Elizabeth smiled. "Yes, nice and warm."

Rising from the table Kitty lifted the plate and began to move to the counter to place more of the newly-baked cookies on the dish. Stepping away she turned to look back at the table and caught a glimpse of Elizabeth holding her head with her hands. Her shoulders had slumped forward. Then with a soft moan Elizabeth fell face first on the table, her body going limp as she slid out of her chair.

The plate crashed to the floor. "Doctor," Kitty screamed, "Doctor."

Kitty found it difficult to breathe as anxiety raced through her body. She knew the symptoms and suspected a stroke. "I'm contacting Doctor Humphries," she told Elizabeth thinking it was possible Elizabeth knew what was happening around her. "He should be here shortly," she continued, praying that he was in his office that day.

Two months earlier Kitty had invested in the latest sensation, the telephone. It had been introduced into London before the turn of the century but was not available to all areas. Recently it had made its way into Hastings and Kitty felt it was absolutely necessary to subscribe to the system because of her mother's medical condition. She spun the crank to summon the operator.

"Operator," Kitty practically shouted into the large mouthpiece. "Please give me Doctor Humphries ...this is an emergency."

"I can't understand you, please repeat your request."

Breathing in deeply attempting to calm herself, Kitty spoke as deliberately as she could. "I have an emergency...I need to talk with Doctor Humphries."

"One moment please."

The wait was torturous. Kitty kept glancing over to Elizabeth. No movement had taken place. Her mother's body remained lifeless.

"Hello."

"Doctor Humphries?"

"Yes."

"This is Kitty Barry. I believe Doctor Blackwell has had a stroke."

"Is she conscious?"

Taking in another deep breath she said, "No...faint breath and pulse, eyes open, ashen face, no movement. Please hurry."

"I'll be right there Miss Barry.

Within ten minutes Doctor Humphries arrived. Peering at the prone body of Elizabeth, Humphries concurred with Kitty's assessment. "I agree with your judgment, Miss Barry," Humphries said feeling Elizabeth pulse and examining the eyes. "It has all the markings of a stroke. We will need to get her to her bed. If you'll assist me we can move her carefully across the room."

"Can you treat it?"

"I cannot even say, Miss Barry, that your mother has suffered a stroke. The appearances are there but it is difficult to be absolutely sure."

"Can we move her to the..." But Kitty never finished her question, for she was interrupted by Humphries placing his hand on her arm.

Quickly moving next to Elizabeth he drew a stethoscope from his bag, bent over and began examining Elizabeth. In anxious anticipation Kitty stood close to observe. But within seconds her hope diminished, for Humphries was taking much too long in his examination and Kitty felt a stabbing pain of fear rivet her entire body. It had now become too apparent. Kitty knew. He was searching for a heartbeat.

"She's dead isn't she?" Kitty asked crying. Picking up Elizabeth's hand she held it tight. "We've lost her haven't we?"

The chest piece was slowly lifted from Elizabeth and Humphries turned to look at Kitty. A single nod gave her his answer and the immensity of death's grip on the soul of an individual now crushed Kitty Barry into the depths of despair. Holding Elizabeth's hand even tighter Kitty bent over, her head falling on Elizabeth's chest as the sobbing increased. The only mother she had ever known, the woman she loved greatly for the past forty-six years was now removed from this earth, forever removed from Kitty's life. Elizabeth Blackwell only existed now in the pages of history.

Kitty received the death certificate two days later. She stared at the date of death: May 31, 1910. The emptiness of life now surrounded her and life became meaningless.

"As you know, Miss Barry, your mother made her funeral arrangements several years ago," Kitty was told by the mortuary director.

"Yes, I was aware of that. And after conducting some inquiries I believe the funeral can proceed as planned. She has one living family member in America who is too feeble to travel and therefore there is no need to prolong the service. I have notified the Rector at St. Clements's here in Hastings and he has set the service for June fourth. Her many friends in London and Paris who wish to be present for the services have also been notified.

"Should I then advise the Rector at Saint Munn's church of these plans? "

"Yes, Please."

Elizabeth's choice for her burial was a most tranquil location. Saint Munn's Parish Church in Kilmun is located at the base of a gentle sloping knoll situated approximately ten meters from the shoreline of the Holy Loch. The grave sites rise up to the summit of the knoll. Elizabeth requested a burial site close to the church.

"Doctor never indicated what she wished to have inscribed on her headstone," Kitty told the mortician. "It wasn't important to her. What is said about her after her death matters not."

"Then perhaps you can provide me with an appropriate inscription and a headstone design fairly soon."

"This much I know or have envisioned. A large stone cross, a white cross, I believe would be appropriate," Kitty said.

"Large?" How large?"

"Large. I'll leave it up to your imagination but something outstanding, something that can be seen from any vantage point in the cemetery."

The funeral director smiled, an eyebrow rose. "There are, I'm sure, limitations imposed by the parish. I will confer with the Rector at Saint Munn and will then discuss the design with you."

Writing down the instructions, the funeral director looked up, his head slightly cocked. "I'm curious, Miss Barry," he said. "Why did your mother choose the cemetery at Kilmun?"

"It was decided during one of our summer vacations. It was late morning after we had finished a walk on a serene forest path when she said she wished to be interred at the cemetery of Saint Munn. I can remember her expression as she told me she perceived that cemetery to be heaven-like."

The funeral service was held at Saint Clements. Many of Elizabeth's friends from earlier times had predeceased her in death. But several ladies from medical institutions and organizations who had known Elizabeth in her later years of service came to pay their respects.

The next day the burial was held in Kilmun at Saint Munn. Elizabeth had been cremated and therefore no wake or viewing was held. Most of those attending the services in Hastings had journeyed to Kilmun for the burial. There was a simple service at the burial site. A number of wreaths from England were sent, one with laurel leaves bearing the names of a number of lady practitioners had an inscription that read, "A pioneer— from some of those who are trying to follow in her footsteps." The church ladies held a small repast afterwards and by three o'clock the last of the mourners had departed leaving Kitty alone.

Leaving the church hall, Kitty pulled a light jacket tightly around her as she went to the gravesite to meditate in private.

The inscriptions she had provided were read again. In creating the texts it was her thought to provide two. One would contain the pertinent details of Elizabeth's life. But the second one, Kitty thought, would be from a speech given by Elizabeth in her later life that reflected the inner soul of Elizabeth Blackwell, a simple but eloquent reminder of how Elizabeth saw her life of medicine.

Kitty stared at the inscriptions.

In loving memory of Elizabeth Blackwell, M.D. – born at Bristol, 3rd February, 1821, died at Hastings, 31st May, 1910. The first woman of modern times to graduate in medicine (1849) and the first to be placed on the British Medical Register (1859)

It is only when we have learned to recognize that God's law for the human body is sacred as - nay, is one with - God's law for the human soul, that we shall begin to understand the religion of the heart."

The breeze whisked around the tall stone white cross and gave Kitty a slight brush of cold air. She pulled her arms closer to her body as she moved away to the waiting carriage. She didn't look back; her eyes cast down, her steps slow and reluctant. Off in the distance a boat's horn blew and several gulls fluttered across the shoreline of the Loch; simple, normal patterns of life in this small village in western Scotland. The struggles and pains and hardships buried there beneath that large white cross were gone now. All was tranquil in the cemetery in Kilmun.

Epilogue

At the time of Elizabeth Blackwell's death, sixty one years after receiving her degree in medicine, 7,400 women in the United States had become licensed physicians and surgeons. No field of medicine was without a woman physician, and women worldwide were entering medical schools and practicing medicine in both private care as well as staffing hospitals.

In 1949, on the 100th anniversary of her graduation from Geneva College, her alma mater (now known as Hobart and William Smith Colleges) named a new student dormitory in her memory. And in 1958, the College established the Elizabeth Blackwell Award for outstanding service to humankind. As an additional tribute to this famous alum, an 800-pound larger-than-life bronze sculpture of Elizabeth was dedicated in 1994 resting near one of the most-traveled walkways on the college's campus. At the dedication ceremony, President Richard H. Hersh said he found it, "immensely satisfying and entirely appropriate that the first and only representation of a human figure on this campus is that of Elizabeth Blackwell. That says so much about who we are and what we value."

In 1974 the United States Postal Service issued the Elizabeth Blackwell, M.D. commemorative postage stamp, and in May, 2007, the New York Downtown Hospital (now called the New York-Presbyterian/Lower Manhattan Hospital) and the City of New York recognized the founding of the New York Infirmary by Dr. Blackwell with a special celebration of its 150th anniversary. The corner of Gold and Beekman Streets was officially declared "Dr. Elizabeth Blackwell Place" in honor of her contributions to the fields of medicine, education, and equal rights. A permanent plaque in her honor is also located at that corner to commemorate both the occasion and the woman.

Perhaps one of the more significant hallmarks of Elizabeth Blackwell's legacy occurred on September 11, 2001 when the intriguing intertwining of the past with the present manifested itself across the world in a powerful event never to be forgotten. On that day two hijacked airliners slammed into the Twin Towers of the World Trade Center in lower

Manhattan and a new kind of horror gripped New York City. Situated but a few blocks away, the New York Downtown Hospital, a hospital founded 154 years earlier by Elizabeth Blackwell as the New York Infirmary for Indigent Women and Children, suddenly became the nearest and fastest first responder. Hundreds of the injured had been raced from that billowing miasmatic site to the hospital's emergency doors. It was the only acute care hospital for the people who worked and lived in that section of the city. The frenzied condition turned into a cataclysmic nightmare. The hospital was operating under extreme conditions. The power had gone dead kicking in the emergency generators and limiting electrical usage. Plus the lost of gas and water and the communication systems brought the hospital into an interminable situation stretching its human resources to unbelievable proportions. Yet despite this incredible situation Downtown Hospital triumphed just as Elizabeth Blackwell had done.

Unfortunately, the name of Elizabeth Blackwell is not known today by the vast majority of the general public. Ask anyone who Elizabeth Blackwell is and they have no idea. She lives primarily in obscurity.

About the Author

Robert Nordmeyer, a native of southern Illinois, has lived most of his adult life in Tucson Arizona. His career included work in broadcasting and administrative positions with nonprofit organizations. Retiring in 1998, Robert turned his attention to writing.

In addition to various op-ed pieces for the Arizona Daily Star, Robert has written a how-to book, *Guide to Organizing and Successfully Operating a Nonprofit Organization*, a collection of religious-based biographies, *Shepherds in the Desert*, and a magazine short story, *Poppa Day*.

His first novel, *Magnolias Don't Cray*, a study of interracial friendship in the racially charged atmosphere of 1965 Louisiana, was published as an e-book in 2014.

CPSIA information can be obtained
at www.ICGtesting.com
Printed in the USA
LVOW04s0959230716

497309LV00009B/60/P